Eli G. Foster

The Civil War by Campaigns

Eli G. Foster

The Civil War by Campaigns

ISBN/EAN: 9783337220969

Printed in Europe, USA, Canada, Australia, Japan

Cover: Foto ©Andreas Hilbeck / pixelio.de

More available books at **www.hansebooks.com**

THE

CIVIL WAR BY CAMPAIGNS

By ELI G. FOSTER

AUTHOR OF "REFERENCE MANUAL AND OUTLINES OF U. S. HISTORY,"
AND "FOSTER'S HISTORICAL CHART"

CRANE & COMPANY, PUBLISHERS
TOPEKA, KANSAS
1899

TABLE OF CONTENTS.

LIST OF MAPS.

4   CONTENTS.

INTRODUCTION.

Many good histories of the Civil War have been written. Nearly all of them devote much space to the details of battles and campaigns,—a most excellent thing for those who wish to devote their time to a comprehensive study of the war. The following chapters have been prepared for those who wish a more condensed account of the important events.

The facts have been diligently collected from leading standard works, and are presented in a new form. Instead of treating the subject chronologically, as works generally do, the author has written entirely by campaigns. The movements of one army have been fully treated before the discussion of another has commenced. It is hoped that this method of treatment will be found both interesting and profitable. Indeed, this method of presentation of the subject to young men and young women in the school-room has resulted in awakening increased interest in the study of the great war, and has been the means of preventing many confusions that would otherwise occur; and it has made the time spent in the study of the war more fruitful in result.

The military campaign maps tracing the movements of the armies are entirely original, and have been prepared expressly for this volume. A careful study of the maps "Grant's Campaign in the West," "Campaigns of Buell and Bragg," "Sherman's March to the Sea," and the "Army of the Potomac," will aid greatly in giving a clear and definite idea of the great theaters of the Civil War. The maps locating the battles and sieges have been copied from larger works. All fanciful pictures have been avoided; only maps intended to simplify the study of battles, campaigns, and the great movements of the armies, have been inserted.

But little attention has been paid to the movements of the various corps of the armies upon the field of battle. Too great detail has been purposely avoided. Those who desire this phase of the war are referred to the comprehensive works.

Many interesting minor events have been barely mentioned, some omitted entirely. The war was full of dramatic incidents. Books might be written, and in fact have been written, upon them. My aim is to present here only the main facts of the war, with now and again an incident appended to enliven and embellish the study of the movements of these ponderous armies in their Titanic struggles.

It is hoped that the omission of technical terms and the use of the campaign methods of treatment, illustrated by the military campaign maps, will be the means of so simplifying the subject that even the casual student may gain a clear idea of the various campaigns of the war in the minimum of time.

But little attention is generally paid by the average person to the study of the sources of revenue, without which governments cannot exist. The chapter on the financial measures to provide revenue for the war is inserted to supply at least an outline on the subject, and should elicit a more careful study of the financial question.

If the book finds its way into the hands of those who have not the time to read nor the means to procure the numerous excellent comprehensive works on the Civil War, and aids in promoting a better understanding of this great epoch in the history of our Nation, the mission of the author in writing the work will be fully attained.

                                           ELI G. FOSTER.

TOPEKA, KANSAS.

THE CIVIL WAR BY CAMPAIGNS.

CHAPTER I.

THE CAUSES OF THE CIVIL WAR.

Slavery and States' Rights were the two causes of the Civil War in the United States. They came before the people in a variety of forms, which, in spite of repeated compromises, only widened the sentiments between the North and South. The Missouri Compromise was the first of a series of enactments and struggles between the two sections on the subject of Slavery. The election of Abraham Lincoln on a platform opposed to the extension of slavery was the last of the series, which grew more bitter and antagonistic until it culminated in the firing upon Fort Sumter, April 12, 1861.

The Nullification Act of South Carolina, in 1832, was the first serious manifestation of the doctrine of States' Rights, which ended, finally, in the secession ordinances of the Southern States and precipitated the great American conflict.

STATE RIGHTS.—Different views were held by statesmen from the very beginning of our national history as to the nature of the bond which held the States together. It was maintained by one class of statesmen that the Union was a league or confederation, which might be dissolved at the will of any of the

States. Under this theory a failure on the part of the General Government to protect the rights, expressed or assumed, of any of the States, entirely released these States from obligations to the Union, and restored them to their former position of separate sovereign States.

Another class of statesmen held that the Federal Union constituted a nation, with a strong central government, and that no State could secede from the Union without the consent of all the others. These were the different constructions placed upon the Constitution, from which no serious conflict arose until certain material questions came before the people for solution. Chief among these were those which related to *tariff* and *slavery*. The South, which was engaged entirely in agricultural industries, demanded free trade. The North, which derived much of its wealth from manufacturing industries, called for protection. When the Tariff Act of 1832 became a law, it caused intense opposition among the people of the South, and led South Carolina to declare the act null and void, and to threaten to secede from the Union if the Federal Government should endeavor to enforce the law. The prompt and vigorous action of President Andrew Jackson in sending troops to the rebellious State, restored order; and Clay's compromise measure the following year pacified the leaders for a time. They however did not abandon the principle of secession, but only shifted it from the tariff issue, in which they had scored a victory, to the much compromised and yet uncompromising issue of slavery extension.

DIFFERENCES BETWEEN THE NORTH AND THE SOUTH.— The people who settled these two sections were entirely different in thought, habit, and customs. They sprung from different classes, though all were of English origin. The North was settled by the Puritans, who fled from the oppression and religious persecution of England in search of freedom and a purer system of faith and worship. The early settlers of the South were the Cavaliers, who were loyal to both the State and the religion of their king. The Puritans belonged to the middle class,—the yeomanry, the pride and support of England,—and came to establish homes for themselves. The Cavaliers belonged largely to the aristocracy and nobility, and came in search of wealth. The representatives of these two classes of society impressed themselves upon the development of the respective sections in which they settled, and moulded the customs and institutions for a more varied class of settlers who followed them. The character of the settlers in the North, as well as the nature of the soil and climate, tended toward the cultivation of small estates. But the early settlers of the South brought with them from England the idea of large estates, which climate and the introduction of African slavery aided to perpetuate. The one section was strongly imbued with the love of liberty and a desire for equal opportunities for all. Free schools were established, manufacturing sprung up, and cities multiplied. The other section became agricultural, and educational advantages were confined to the wealthy. This contrast in the character of the people, the difference in the industries of the two sections, and the different conditions of climate and soil, making slave labor more profitable in the South than in the North, show how easily one section could become slaveholding States and another free States.

GROWTH OF SLAVERY.— Slavery was introduced in the colonies in 1619, at Jamestown, Virginia. The importation of slaves was continued, and at the close of the Revolutionary War the slaves in the States numbered 600,000, while there were about 50,000 free persons of color distributed through the colonies. Europe in her greed for gain had woven slavery in her colonial policy that her home revenues might be greater. There was not a colony without slaves, though they were more common in the South than in the North. In vain had the Virginia House of Burgesses protested against the " inhumanity of the slave trade." The colony of South Carolina passed an act in 1760 prohibiting the importation of slaves, but the British government refused to sanction it. Other colonies had endeavored to place restrictions upon the trade, but without success.

The invention of the cotton-gin by Eli Whitney (1793) greatly stimulated the demand for negroes and increased the importation of slaves. Before the invention of the cotton-gin, the process of separating the seed from the cotton was slow, tedious, and expensive. By the use of this machine, one person could accomplish the work of several hundred hands. The cultivation of cotton was greatly extended, which made a demand for slave labor in the South, where cotton was grown, and increased the value of slaves. The number of slaves increased rapidly even though restrictions were placed upon slave traffic, and for-

eign importation prohibited by law in 1808. When the Civil
War began, the number of slaves in the United States was about
4,000,000. Southern opinion, which in the early colonial day
considered slavery an evil, gradually changed. Many had come
to regard it as a great moral, social and political good,—an institution ordained by Providence for civilizing and educating
the black race.

MOVEMENTS TOWARD FREEDOM OF THE SLAVES.—At the opening of the Civil War there were more slaves in the United States
than in all other countries combined. These were all confined to
the States south of Pennsylvania and of the Ohio river. All
the Northern States had freed their slaves, either before the
adoption of the Constitution or soon after it. Vermont took the
lead, in 1777; Pennsylvania followed, in 1780; and eventually
all other Northern States followed in abolishing slavery or providing measures to effect its gradual abolition. The last to abol-
ish it was New Jersey, in 1804.

Though America is the "land of the free," slavery clung to
its soil with greater tenacity than it did to that of European
countries. Great Britain gave freedom to the slaves in her colonies in 1838. Immediate emancipation of the slaves of the
colonies of the French Government was decreed in 1848. Other
European powers followed the example of Great Britain. Many
of the South-American republics provided for the abolition of
slavery—Mexico as early as 1829.

Washington in his will provided for the emancipation of his
own slaves. John Adams believed that slavery should be " ex-

tirpated from the United States." Jefferson, himself a slave-holder, declared, when speaking of this institution, "I tremble for my country when I remember that God is just." Patrick Henry, Franklin, Hamilton and Madison opposed the principle of slavery.

Most of the wisest and best men of the time, both North and South, looked forward with confidence and hope to the speedy abolition of an institution so averse to the principles of Christianity and so dangerous to the interests of society and the state.

THE NORTHWEST TERRITORY, ORGANIZED 1787.—In 1787 the country including the present States of Ohio, Indiana, Illinois, Michigan and Wisconsin was organized into a Territory, which was called the Northwest Territory. Freedom was guaranteed to this region by the insertion of this famous clause: "Neither slavery nor involuntary servitude shall exist in this Territory, otherwise than in punishment of crimes." This anti-slavery clause was submitted three years before, by Jefferson, for the government not only of the Northwest Territory, but also for that south of the Ohio river. The slavery provision was rejected for the territory south of the Ohio river; and later, four slave States—Kentucky, Tennessee, Alabama, and Mississippi—were formed out of it; while the territory to the north of the Ohio was permanently attached to the principles of freedom.

MISSOURI COMPROMISE OF 1820.—In 1803 the boundaries of the United States were extended to include that vast region west of the Mississippi river to the Rocky Mountains, known as the

Louisiana Territory. Of the various States afterward formed out of this region, Missouri was the first to apply for admission to the Union. The main question concerning the admission of this State was whether it should be free or slave.

Before the abolition of slavery in the North and the admission of the free States north of the Ohio, slavery had not become a sectional affair. Many in the South during the Revolutionary period believed in the gradual emancipation of the slaves. But sentiment had undergone a change; their chief concern became the perpetuation of the institution. Sectional lines were being definitely drawn on slavery as an issue. A new epoch in the history of slavery was instituted when Missouri applied for admission to the Union as a State, in 1819. The South endeavored to extend slavery to new territory, while the North opposed it. The discussion was long and acrimonious. It was the real beginning of the great political struggle out of which came the Civil War.

The famous Missouri Compromise provided:

1. That Missouri should be admitted to the Union as a slave State.

2. That slavery or involuntary servitude, except as a punishment of crime, should be prohibited in the remaining part of the Louisiana Purchase lying north of latitude 36 degrees 30 minutes, which formed the southern boundary of Missouri.

3. No provision was made relative to the admission of the Territories south of this line; but as slavery already existed there, they were tacitly surrendered to the slave-power.

Maine was admitted as a free State, on the principle that one free and one slave State should be admitted at the same time. The compromise from which so much was expected settled nothing. The Southern people continued to feel and to act as if they had been *hindered* in the exercise of their rights.

MEXICAN WAR, 1845-48.—Mexico declared itself independent of Spain in 1821, and established a republic. In 1829 the President of Mexico proclaimed the abolition of slavery within the limits of his territory. Texas refused to comply. The slave-power of the United States sent money, supplies and arms to Texas, and aided in stirring up a revolution with the express purpose of annexing more slave States to the Union. Sam Houston, former Governor of Tennessee, headed the revolution, and in 1836 Texas became a Republic, independent of Mexico. The next year she applied for admission to the Union, but opposition in the House and Senate, exposing the duplicity with which the Jackson administration had acted toward Mexico, for the time silenced the agitators for annexation. It was not long, however, until another effort was made to extend the slave territory. A joint resolution annexing Texas received the President's signature, March 1, 1845. It also pledged the faith of the United States to permit new States to be formed of this territory, not exceeding four. Texas thus became a full-fledged State in the Union, and President Polk sent troops to occupy the territory between the rivers Nueces and Rio Grande, which Mexico claimed as her soil. In the war which followed, the territory now comprising the States and Territories of California, Nevada, Utah, Arizona, New Mexico, and a portion of Colorado and Wyoming, was ceded to the United States.

THE COMPROMISE OF 1850 (THE OMNIBUS BILL).—In 1850 California applied for admission to the Union as a free State. This created a stir among the slaveholding States. The angry menace to harmony and unity again appeared. The primary object in annexing Texas and conducting the Mexican War was the acquisition of slave territory. The Wilmot Proviso, excluding slavery from all territory acquired as a result of the war, after bitter discussion was voted down. With the admission of Arkansas in 1836 as a slave State, came the admission of Michigan as a free State. With the admission of Iowa as a free State, the equipoise of slavery was maintained by providing in the same bill for the admission of Florida as a slave State, though its population was not near the number required for the admission of States. The admission of free Wisconsin balanced that of slave Texas. The admission of California as a free State would disturb the equilibrium between the free and slave States, and give to the North the most substantial benefits of the Mexican War and defeat the object for which it had been waged. A great political struggle ensued. Threats of secession were rife. Fiery and impassioned eloquence filled the air, in the midst of which, Clay came forward with his compromise bill.

The bill was stripped of provision after provision, until, when passed, it provided for the territorial government of Utah, and nothing more. The rejected provisions were afterward taken up one by one as a special order of business, and passed with but little change from the original bill. The Omnibus Bill was re-created. The following were its provisions:

1. California should be admitted as a free State.

2. New States not exceeding four might be formed out of Texas. The people of each State were to decide for themselves whether such State should be free or slave.

3. Texas should be paid $10,000,000 for her claim on New Mexico.

4. Utah and New Mexico should be organized as Territories without mention of slavery.

5. Slave trade should be prohibited in the District of Columbia.

6. Slaves escaping from their masters into free States should be arrested and returned to them.

The last clause is called the "Fugitive Slave Law," the passage of which caused intense opposition in the North. Personal liberty laws were passed by Northern States, prohibiting state officers from giving aid in the arrest and return of any slave. Counsel was provided for the arrested negroes, and the practical operation of the fugitive slave act annulled.

The passage of the Omnibus Bill was the death-knell of the Whig party; and instead of pacifying the feelings of the contending elements, it contained in its provisions the seeds for new and greater conflicts.

THE KANSAS-NEBRASKA BILL, 1854.—In 1854 Stephen A. Douglas introduced a bill which provided for the organization of two Territories, known as Kansas and Nebraska. The people of these Territories were to decide for themselves whether the States should come into the Union free or slave. It virtually repealed the Missouri Compromise, which guaranteed freedom to this section, and a territory nearly as large as the thirteen original States was opened to slavery. Of the two Territories, Kansas was the more southerly, therefore the more favorably situated for the planting of the institution of slavery.

Kansas thus became the battle-ground for the contending elements of freedom and slavery. Great preparations were made both North and South for the settlement of the State. Pro-slavery societies, known as Blue Lodges and Social Bands, were formed from the South. Pro-slavery immigrants poured into the new Territory from Missouri. The Emigrant Aid Society was formed by Eli Thayer, of Worcester, Mass. By means of it and similar societies, a stream of anti-slavery emigrants was sent to Kansas. At the elections, a great many Missourians crossed the border, intimidated election officers, and cast thousands of illegal votes for the pro-slavery candidates, who thus received a large majority of all votes cast. The anti-slavery settlers, who had cast a majority of legal votes, repudiated the election, and chose their own officers. With two rival Legislatures, and with the opposing parties of freedom and slavery bitterly contending for supremacy, matters soon drifted into civil war in the new Territory. The burning of houses, sacking of towns, and the taking of life continued for several years. This bloody drama awakened the conscience of many persons to the real intent and purposes of the slave-power. Although the pro-slavery party had

—2

the moral and material support of the President and cabinet, the State was finally won to the cause of freedom, and was admitted to the Union in 1861.

DRED SCOTT DECISION, 1857.—Dred Scott was a negro slave, who was taken by his master, Dr. Emerson, from the State of Missouri to the free State of Illinois; thence he was taken to Fort Snelling, near the present site of St. Paul. From the latter place, in which he married with his master's consent, he was taken back to Missouri in 1838, where with his wife and children he was sold to John F. A. Sanford. Dred Scott sued for the liberty of himself and family; alleging that his residence in a free State and in a Territory from which slavery was excluded by the Missouri Compromise, established his freedom. An action for trespass, brought in a St. Louis court, was decided in Scott's favor, which was reversed by the Supreme Court of the State. The case was then taken to the Federal court. Able counsel represented both sides. The case ceased to be of a personal interest only, and assumed national importance as a contest for constitutional principles between the slavery and anti-slavery parties. Both the Circuit and the Supreme Court of the United States decided against the freedom of Scott. In the final decision, the court affirmed that "no negro, slave or free, who was of slave ancestry, was entitled to sue in the courts of the United States."

After denying its own jurisdiction of the case, the court passed upon the merits, and proceeded to discuss the constitutionality of the points which were of interest to the opposing parties. It declared the Missouri Compromise was unconstitutional; that slave-owners could carry their slaves into any of the Territories, and that the people of those Territories could not lawfully hinder them; that a negro was not a citizen, and by terms of the Constitution could not become a citizen of the United States. A mandate was issued directing the suit to be dismissed for want of jurisdiction. Dred Scott soon obtained, by grace of his master, that freedom which the courts denied him.

By this decision of the Supreme Court, which is considered the most infamous of all its decisions, slaves could be taken anywhere, and slavery made national. Instead, however, of extending the institution, as was the intention of the judges (a majority of whom were from slave States), it united the people of the North in a more determined opposition to the extension of slavery.

ANTI-SLAVERY PUBLICATIONS.—The opinions on the slavery question separated the people of the North and South. The effort on the part of the South to extend the institution was the source of the most bitter friction between the two sections. A majority of the people of the North at the time of the Missouri Compromise had not thought of abolishing slavery in the Southern States; in fact, this was not their intention at the beginning of the Civil War. There were some inspired souls in the North, however, who at an early date devoted their talents to the abolition of slavery. Some of the most prominent deserve mention. The press and the platform were used with great effect to arouse the public conscience to a realization of the great national wrong.

The "Liberator," a weekly journal published by William Lloyd Garrison, then a youth of twenty-six, appeared in Boston in 1831. The spirit of the paper is indicated by his words in the first issue:

"I will be as harsh as truth, and as uncompromising as justice. On this subject, I do not wish to speak or think or write with moderation. No! No! I am in earnest—I will not equivocate—I will not excuse—I will not retreat a single inch—and I will be heard!"

He was dragged through the streets of Boston with a rope around his body; he was threatened with death if he did not desist; but he still continued to publish his paper and to organize abolition societies, until the great wrong he assailed was eradicated.

Frederick Douglass, a runaway slave from Maryland, edited the "North Star" at Rochester, New York.

Rev. Elijah P. Lovejoy attempted to establish a religious and anti-slavery paper, first at St. Louis, Mo., and then at Alton, Ill., 1835–37. Three times in one year a pro-slavery mob destroyed his press. While engaged in setting it up a fourth time, a pro-slavery mob attacked him. While defending his property, he was killed.

John G. Whittier, the Quaker anti-slavery poet, whose burning lyrics flew across the country and moulded sentiment against slavery, narrowly escaped death at the hands of a mob at Concord, N. H., in 1836, while attending an anti-slavery meeting.

Of the literary forces that aided in directing sentiment against slavery, the most weighty was the book "Uncle Tom's Cabin," written by Mrs. Harriet Beecher Stowe. It first appeared as a serial in the "National Era," an anti-slavery newspaper at Washington, D. C., but attracted little attention. The great book houses were afraid to publish it lest it should hurt their Southern trade. A new house in Boston published it, in 1852. It at once attracted great attention, and became one of the most popular novels ever written. Whittier wrote to Garrison: "What a glorious work Harriet Beecher Stowe has wrought! Thanks to the Fugitive Slave Law. Better for slavery that that law had never been enacted, for it gave the occasion for 'Uncle Tom's Cabin.'" The sale of the book was almost without limit, at home and abroad. Its greatest success, however, was its moral weight in unifying and antagonizing the Northern conscience to the iniquities of the slave-power.

"The Impending Crisis of the South" was an argument against slavery on moral and economic grounds. Its author, Hinton Rowan Helper, was one of the non-slaveholders of the South, who pleaded for the rights of his class. The book at the time created quite a strong sensation.

The constant discussion and agitation aroused fears and animosities. The mails were regularly searched in many Southern postoffices, and any anti-slavery literature was taken out and burned. "Abolitionist" became the severest term of reproach in the South. The churches became violently agitated over the burning issue. Methodist, Baptist and Presbyterian denominations separated, North and South, on the subject of slavery.

From the influence of platform, pulpit, society, and press, arrayed against the encroaching steps of slavery upon the territory formally dedicated to freedom, there came a crystallized sentiment expressed in the principles of the Republican party in its platform of 1856.

ANTI-SLAVERY PARTIES.—In 1840 the " Liberty Party " put a national ticket in the field. James G. Birney was nominated, but received only a small vote. Four years later he received more than 62,000 votes on the same ticket. The party favored the abolition of slavery in the District of Columbia and in all national territory. It favored the repeal of the Fugitive Slave Law, favored the prohibition of slavery in new Territories and new States, was opposed to the internal slave trade, and opposed the annexation of Texas. Its adherents joined fortunes with the Free-Soil party in 1848.

The " Free-Soil party " was organized by bolting Whigs and Democrats, who held advanced views on the slavery question. It was joined by the followers of the old Liberty party. Among some of its leaders were Charles Francis Adams, Salmon P. Chase, Charles Sumner, William H. Seward, John P. Hale, John A. Dix, and Henry Wilson.

The Presidential candidates in 1848 and 1852 received a considerable popular vote, but not sufficient to carry the electors in any State.

It advocated non-interference with slavery where it already

existed, but opposed all compromises with slavery, or the formation of any more slave territory, or the admission of any slave State.

THE REPUBLICAN PARTY.—The constant and resolute aggressions of the slave-power called forth an equally aggressive free-soil movement in the North. Whigs, Wilmot-Proviso Democrats, and the Free-Soilers united to form a new party, to prevent the spread of slavery into new territory. The various elements opposed to slavery were thus skillfully and smoothly kneaded into the new Republican party. John C. Frémont was the first candidate for President. He received 114 electoral votes; Buchanan, 174; and Fillmore, 8. This formidable vote might well have carried dismay into the pro-slavery columns. The election of Buchanan on a pro-slavery platform gave the South little ground for complaint, but as events have shown, it afforded them an opportunity to prepare for war. Through the treachery of the Secretary of War, John B. Floyd, and the indifference of the administration at Washington, large amounts of arms, ammunition and stores were transferred to the South.

When the time came to choose a President, the people were divided into four parties. The Republicans nominated Abraham Lincoln on the platform that there was no law for slavery in Territories, and no power to enact one, and that Congress was bound to prohibit it in or exclude it from all Federal territory. John C. Breckinridge was nominated by the Southern Democracy, on a platform distinctly favoring the extension of slavery. Stephen A. Douglas was nominated by the Northern

Democracy, on a platform which would leave the people free to decide the slavery question for themselves in each Territory.

The Constitutional Union party nominated John Bell, of Tennessee, on this platform: " The Constitution of the country, the Union of the States, and the enforcement of the laws." The popular vote decided against the extension of slavery. In the electoral college, Lincoln received 180 votes, Breckinridge 72, Bell 39, and Douglas 12.

The slavery question was the issue in the campaign.

JOHN BROWN'S RAID, 1859.--John Brown was an abolition- ist. He moved to Kansas in 1855, in time to become a conspic- uous figure in the thrilling scenes of that State. Five of his sons had settled near Osawatomie the year before, and all took up the cause of freedom. Slavery would no doubt have tri- umphed over legal and legislative skill, had not the sword been thrown into the balance by such bold and resolute men as Brown.

After peace had been restored in Kansas, he conceived the idea of freeing the slaves of the South. Settling on a small farm near Harper's Ferry, he began secretly to collect material for executing his designs. He with twenty-one associates appeared before Harper's Ferry on the night of October 16th, 1859, and easily overpowered the guards and took possession of the ar- mory there, belonging. to the United States. He expected to create an uprising among the slaves, arm them with the guns stored there and liberate the negroes of the South.

Between forty and fifty citizens were captured and confined in the armory by him. Some slaves were liberated. The people of the town, arming themselves, made an attack on the insur-gents. The U. S. Marine, commanded by Col. Robert E. Lee, arrived. The militia commenced to pour in. Thirteen of Brown's men were killed, two of whom were his sons. Two of his men escaped, and the rest were captured. Brown himself was dangerously wounded.

He was speedily tried before a Virginia court, and was exe-cuted on December 2, 1859. His execution for this wild and erratic scheme reflects little credit upon the elements of human-ity and generosity of the officers of Virginia, when we consider that Jefferson Davis and his followers suffered no such fate for conducting the stupendous campaign of the great Rebellion.

Brown died a martyr to the cause of liberating an enslaved people. His spirit was present in many a battle which followed, and many a regiment was stirred by the words of the popular war song—

"John Brown's body lies a-mouldering in the grave,
But his soul is marching on."

SECESSION.—As soon as it became known that Lincoln was elected, South Carolina called a convention to consider an ordi-nance of secession, which was unanimously passed on December 20, 1860. Commissioners were sent to the other cotton States to urge them to follow in the same course.

President Buchanan gave encouragement to the Southern cause by his vacillating action. His message to Congress in December, 1860, which was strongly disunion in character, con-tained these words: "After much serious reflection, I have arrived at the conclusion that no power has been delegated to Congress, or to any other department of the Federal Government, to coerce a State into submission which is attempting to withdraw or has withdrawn from the Union." He might well have profited by Jackson's vigorous measures a third of a century before, when South Carolina threatened to secede.

Mississippi, Florida, Alabama, Georgia, Louisiana, Texas, Virginia, Arkansas, Tennessee, North Carolina, withdrew from the Union in the order named. Four slave States—Delaware, Maryland, Missouri, and Kentucky—did not secede. In these, sentiment was divided between the North and the South, with the preponderance in favor of the former.

The ordinances of secession were followed quickly by the seizure of the United States forts, arsenals, and custom-houses in the seceding States, and by the formation of a Confederate Government. The capital was located at Montgomery, Alabama. Jefferson Davis was chosen President and Alexander H. Stephens Vice-President. Southern officers resigned their places in the Congress and the Cabinet, and in the Army and Navy.

The constitution of the Confederate States was a close pattern of that from whose banner they had withdrawn, except that it made slavery the corner-stone of the new system, and forbade a protective tariff.

CRITTENDEN COMPROMISE, DECEMBER, 1860.—A Senate committee, composed of men of different politics and from different sections of the country, made a last effort to patch up a scheme by which slavery and freedom might work out their ambitions together. The patriotic John J. Crittenden, who was a member of the committee from Kentucky, submitted the scheme. It offered guaranties against arbitrary abolition of slavery by Congress in the slave States, or in places once within their limits, such as forts and navy-yards. It restrained Federal interference with the interstate transportation of slaves. It bound the United States to provide payment for fugitive slaves when local violence prevented their return. It advised Northern States to repeal their personal liberty laws. But its main feature was to establish, by constitutional amendment, the Missouri Compromise line (36° 30′), running east and west across the continent, as a permanent barrier between the free and slave States. All efforts to reconcile the conflicting opinions proved futile. The vital points were rejected by members from the North and South alike.

INAUGURATION OF LINCOLN, MARCH 4, 1861.—Abraham Lincoln was inaugurated March 4, 1861. From his home in Springfield, Ill., to Harrisburg, Pa., he was everywhere received with demonstrations of loyalty. He delivered addresses to the people of the capitals and other large cities of the States through which he passed. Baltimore was not only a slaveholding city, but was infested with a large number of persons who were loud and fierce in their denunciation of Lincoln and the principles which he represented. Frequent reports were heard that a plan had been concocted for the assassination of the new President as he passed through the city. His friends persuaded him to go to Washington on a special train, in advance of the one on which his passage had been announced.

Lincoln's inaugural address was an able state paper. It was an admirable effort to calm the ardor of the South for disunion, without compromising any of the principles of the party which had elected him. The following detached sentences will express Lincoln's views on some of the leading issues of that hour:

"I have no purpose, directly or indirectly, to interfere with the institution of slavery in any of the States where it exists."

"The power confided in me will be used to hold, occupy and possess the property and places belonging to the Government."

"I shall take care, as the Constitution expressly enjoins upon me, that the laws of the Union be faithfully executed in all States."

"No State, upon its own mere motion, can lawfully get out of the Union."

"In your hands, my dissatisfied fellow-countrymen, and not in mine, is the momentous issue of civil war. The Government will not assail you."

The olive-branch of peace was accepted by the conspirators as a challenge to war.

CHAPTER II.

OPENING EVENTS OF THE WAR.

CAPTURE OF FORT SUMTER, APRIL 13, 1861.—The seceding States at once began to seize all forts, arsenals, and national property of every description for the use of the Confederacy. Major Anderson, of the U. S. Army, was occupying Fort Moultrie with a force of but ten men. Fearing an attack by the secessionists in Charleston, he withdrew his command, on the night of December 26, 1860, to Fort Sumter, situated on an island in the harbor, a stronger position than the one which he had abandoned. Fort Moultrie was immediately occupied by the authorities of Charleston. The fort was strengthened and batteries erected, and preparations begun for the reduction of Fort Sumter. The national authorities instructed Major Anderson not to interfere with this hostile proceeding. Early in January, an unarmed vessel, the Star of the West, carried troops and supplies to reinforce Fort Sumter. When within sight of the fort it was fired upon from the Confederate batteries, and was obliged to turn back. No effort was made by the Government to avenge this insult to the national flag. The Confederates organized an army, most of whose officers had abandoned the Federal service. Gen. Beauregard was placed in command of their forces at Charleston. All supplies of food from Charleston were cut off from Major Anderson by the Confederates. The National Government began to make prepara-

(29)

tions to replenish the supply of food, without which the fort would soon have been starved into capitulation. Gen. Beauregard was instructed to demand the surrender of Sumter, and in case of refusal, to reduce it.

The powerful batteries which had been thrown up all around it, opened fire upon the fort. The bombardment continued thirty-four hours. Anderson made a spirited defense, but was compelled to surrender after his ammunition was nearly expended, provisions consumed, magazine surrounded by flames, and other damage wrought to the fort. The surrender was made on the 13th day of April.

The next day the fort was evacuated, and the troops embarked for New York.

Not a man was killed on either side during the engagement. But while preparing to salute the lowered flag, as the garrison took its departure, a premature explosion occurred, which killed one Federal soldier and wounded three others. The joy of the South was complete, on receiving the news of the surrender of Fort Sumter.

CALL FOR TROOPS, APRIL 15, 1861.—News of the attack upon Fort Sumter dispelled all hopes for peaceful solution of the slavery question. Hitherto the President had hoped for reconciliation. War was commenced by the military seizure of the national fort. Lincoln accepted the issue of war thus forced upon the country. On April 15th he issued a call for 75,000 troops, to serve for three months, and summoned Congress to assemble July 4th in extra session. News of the fall of Sumter awakened sentiments of the most enthusiastic loyalty in the Northern States, and the response to the President's call was prompt and patriotic. Within two weeks, 300,000 men offered themselves to preserve the Union and defend the flag. The whole North became a great camp of preparation. The loyal States made liberal appropriations for the public defense. Before the lapse of forty-eight hours, a Massachusetts regiment, armed and equipped, was on its way to Washington. Pennsylvania volunteers reached that city on the 18th, and soon troops were on their way to the capital from all Northern States.

The authorities at Montgomery were no less active. The call for additional troops was responded to with great enthusiasm. Only seven of the Southern States had seceded before Lincoln's call for troops. After this, Virginia, North Carolina, Arkansas and Tennessee cast their fortunes with the Confederacy. The Confederate capital was moved to Richmond, as soon as Virginia seceded from the Union.

On the 19th of April, the anniversary of the battle of Lexington, as the Sixth Massachusetts Regiment was on its way through Baltimore, it was attacked by a mob, which killed three soldiers and wounded others. The troops fired into the mob, killing eleven and wounding several. Intense excitement prevailed. Other troops, yet unarmed, were assailed. Baltimore was virtually in control of the secessionists, but the approach of General Butler's command, and the gathering courage of Unionists brought the rebellious city to its senses.

Col. Ellsworth, in command of the New York Fire Zouaves,

moved down the Potomac to Alexandria. No resistance was met at this point. Seeing a Confederate flag waving from the Marshall House in Alexandria, he stepped in with four of his men and took it down. Passing down stairs, he was met by Jackson, the hotel-keeper, who shot Ellsworth dead on the spot. Jackson suffered a like fate, for he was instantly shot by one of Ellsworth's men.

EVENTS IN WEST VIRGINIA.—The northwestern part of the State of Virginia, comprising one-third of its area, had for many years been at variance with the rest of the State on questions arising from the institution of slavery. When Virginia seceded, an opportunity was afforded this portion of the State to separate itself from the dominating influence of slavery. Accordingly, the people of that section called a convention, disavowed the act of secession, established a loyal government, and took steps to be admitted to the Union as a separate State called West Virginia.

Movements were at once set on foot to protect the new-born State in her efforts to aid the Union. Gen. George B. McClellan was placed in command of a Federal force, with Gen. W. S. Rosecrans as his second. The Confederates were defeated at Philippi and at Rich Mountain, and practically lost all power in the State. These events, though at the time important, must be regarded as merely a prelude to the first great battle, which was soon to be fought.

After these successes in West Virginia and the Union defeat at Bull Run, Gen. McClellan was promoted to the command of the Army of the Potomac, and Rosecrans left to confront Robert E. Lee, who was sent to retrieve Confederate losses in that State. Great results had been expected from Lee's presence, but after several minor engagements in which he exhibited none of that vigor which characterized his later campaigns, he was transferred to other fields.

BATTLE OF BULL RUN, JULY 21, 1861.—The South prepared to prevent the advance of the Union troops into Virginia. General Beauregard, fresh from his glories at Fort Sumter, led a strong Confederate column to Manassas Junction, and posted it behind Bull Run creek. Gen. Joseph E. Johnston, retreating from Harper's Ferry, took a position at Winchester, ready to coöperate with Gen. Beauregard. This line of defense was extended to the Potomac.

Gen. Winfield Scott, the hero of the Mexican War, was General-in-chief of the Union forces. He was too old and infirm to take the field for active service. Gen. Irwin McDowell was placed in command of the army, which commenced the forward movement. The Union General Robert Patterson confronted Johnston. Arlington Heights, Lee's old home, opposite Washington, was seized by the Union troops and strongly fortified. The armies of both sides consisted of raw militia and volunteers, hastily brought together and without military experience. Gen. Scott argued for time to drill the new recruits before attempting an advance. Northern newspapers were impatiently calling for the movement of the army. The cry, "On to Richmond!" was taken up by Congressmen and Senators. The

—3

pressure on the Government became too strong to be resisted.
Secretary Salmon P. Chase was the champion in the cabinet
of the intense feeling in the North for a prompt and vigorous
campaign. Public sentiment became irresistible, and in response
to it, the army advanced, about 35,000 strong. The Confederates had at their command about 30,000 men. Patterson was
directed to prevent Johnston's army from going to the rescue
of their comrades at Bull Run, a task which he did not succeed
in doing. On the 18th of July the Union advance found a
Confederate force at Blackburn's ford, on Bull Run, and after
a sharp conflict the Federals fell back to Centreville. On the
21st they resumed their march, and fought the Battle of Bull
Run, or Manassas Junction. The conflict opened at about
10:30 in the morning. McDowell bore heavily on the enemy's
left, hoping to drive it from the stone bridge, to make himself
master of Manassas Gap, and to prevent the junction of Johnston's reinforcements. He did not know that 8,000 of Johnston's men had arrived the day before. By three o'clock the
enemy had been driven back some distance, when the remaining
brigade of Johnston's army, under the immediate command of
Gen. Kirby Smith, arrived by rail. Cheer after cheer burst from
the Confederate forces as their fresh ranks rushed to the front.
The Union columns broke, rushed down the hillside, and all efforts to re-form them were of no avail: the retreat was continued
in confusion to Washington. The three-months men, whose term
of enlistment had expired, went home. A shadow of gloom was

cast upon the North; the spirit of triumph and confidence upon
the South.

The Confederates did not attempt an active pursuit. Their
army was much demoralized, not in a condition to engage in a
campaign against the defenses at Washington. The Confederates lost about 2,000 killed and wounded, while the Union loss
was about 3,000, many of whom were prisoners. The disaster
taught the lesson so many in the North needed to know—that
the war would be long, bloody, and costly. At once movements
were put on foot for a gigantic struggle by both rival governments.

CHAPTER III.

NAVAL WAR.

BRIEF HISTORY OF THE GROWTH OF NAVAL SCIENCE BEFORE THE CIVIL WAR.—Until the year 1840, naval science had made but little progress. Ships were essentially the same as they had been for the last two hundred years, and naval warfare was conducted on the same principle. A few improvements had taken place, but none of any great importance. The introduction of steam as a motive power in 1840 marked the beginning of a new era. The next thirty years witnessed great improvement. Sailing-vessels were abandoned for the improved steamers. The ram again came into use as a powerful weapon of destruction. The Greeks and Romans had used a ram on their galleys with great effect. When sailing-vessels superseded the galleys, this engine of warfare fell into disuse. The introduction of steam again revived the use of the ram, with greatly increased power. The manufacture of guns had undergone a great change. Their caliber was increased. Breech-loading and rifling came into use. Greater range, accuracy and penetration were obtained. The sides of vessels, hitherto unprotected, were shielded by two-inch iron plate, which was gradually improved until the vessels were armored with solid masses of steel, 22 inches thick. In fact, the whole system of naval tactics underwent a change. The improvement began with the introduction of steam as a motive power, but only reached its culmination in the trials and emergencies of the Civil War.

THE NAVY OF 1861.—At the outbreak of the Rebellion our navy was not in a condition to render the effective assistance which the occasion demanded. The total number of vessels in the service of the Government at the time was ninety. Fifty of these were sailing ships, and, splendid as they had been in their day, they had now become almost useless. Forty were propelled by steam. Most of these were in foreign ports, or laid up in the navy yards. Only eight vessels were ready for immediate use— those of the home squadron; and only four of these were steamers. More than two hundred officers resigned their commissions and hastened to join their fortunes with the Southern States.

The Government began the work of collecting a great navy. Six hundred vessels were demanded at once for blockading the Southern coast and for operating against Confederate privateers. Six screw-frigates, constructed in 1855, commanding the admiration of naval men at home and abroad, were the chief reliance of the Government. They proved of little value, however, because they were unable to enter the shallow waters of the Southern coast. The vessels in foreign ports were called home. Those in the navy yards were soon made available. The merchant marines, though of limited facilities, afforded an opportunity for improvising a naval force.

The South entered upon the war without any navy, and with limited resources for creating one. Had it not been for the aid from England, acting contrary to the rights of a neutral nation, but little damage would have been done to the commerce of the North, and little resistance offered to the naval force of the Union. The Confederate government seized several revenue-cutters and lighthouse-tenders, belonging to the United States; but these were of little value. The Merrimac, which was sunk on the abandonment of Norfolk, was raised by Confederates, and for a time threatened much harm.

OBJECT OF THE NAVY.—The navy with its limited resources had a weighty task imposed upon it at the very beginning. Its objects may be included under several heads:

1. It was to blockade the entire coast of the Confederate States, a distance of nearly three thousand miles.

2. It was to aid in the opening of the Mississippi river and its tributaries.

3. It was to acquire control of all bays and sounds from the Chesapeake to the Rio Grande.

4. It was to protect the commerce of the United States, destroy or capture all Confederate cruisers and blockade-runners.

5. It was expected to capture all forts along the coast and seaports, and to aid in the movements and campaigns of the armies within coöperating distance along the coast.

ABANDONMENT OF NORFOLK, APRIL 21, 1861.—Norfolk, located about twelve miles from Fortress Monroe, was abandoned by the Federals in the early spring of 1861. It was the seat of one of the principal navy yards of the Nation. At this time there were four war vessels lying there, which could have been prepared for sea in a short time. One of these was the frigate Merrimac, which, after being converted into an ironclad, made such havoc at Hampton Roads. There were also several old vessels of no great value in the yards. The inhabitants of Norfolk and vicinity had become very hostile toward the Government. Many of the officers were disloyal to the Union. Doubts and indecision characterized the minds of those who were loyal. And without any good reason, the ships and buildings were fired and destroyed, and Norfolk abandoned on the 21st of April. The greatest misfortune to the Union was the loss of at least 1,200 fine guns, which were used to man the forts of the Confederates from the Potomac ￮ the Mississippi. Had it not been for the guns taken at Norfolk and Pensacola, the Confederates could not have armed their fortifications for at least a year after the opening of hostilities. The destruction of the navy yards seems to have been the result of a panic, for there was no imminent danger to warrant this action.

After remaining in possession of the Confederates about one year, Norfolk was evacuated by them with as little reason as that which led to the departure of the Union authority.

THE BLOCKADE.—The first order for the blockade of the Southern ports was issued by President Lincoln April 19, 1861. The blockade was a military measure of great importance. At the breaking-out of the war the South was destitute of ships, machine-shops, rolling-mills, and gun factories. England, on the other hand, was both capable and desirous of furnishing arms, munitions of war, ships, and clothing, in exchange for the raw cotton grown in the South. Without this commercial intercourse between Great Britain and the Confederacy, the Confederate cause would be greatly weakened, and many of the manufactories of England closed.

All available ships of every description and from every source were drafted into service for the momentous task of blockading the coast from the Chesapeake to the Rio Grande. The force thus hastily gathered, though not at first fully equal to the task imposed upon it, became in time entirely efficient, and virtually sealed the Southern ports from foreign commerce. It is true, some blockade-runners escaped the vigilance of our vessels and carried on a contraband trade with the South.

BLOCKADE-RUNNERS.—With the blockade of the Southern ports the price of cotton in the South fell to eight cents a pound, while in England it rose to fifty cents per pound. Commerce between the two countries became a profitable business to those who succeeded in running the blockade. Regular " blockade-runners " were constructed. They were long, low steam vessels of great speed, which drew but little depth of water. Their hulls were only a few feet out of water. They burned anthracite coal, which made but little smoke. Their trips were made between the Confederate States and Nassau, the capital of the Bahama islands, which was the center from which Great Britain carried on commerce with the South. The blockade-runners carried the cotton to Nassau and the West Indies, where it was taken upon vessels headed for England, while they returned with the cargoes of British goods to feed and clothe the Southern armies and equip the Southern troops. Appearing off the coast on a dark night, they would make a dash past the blockading vessels, and land their cargo in a Confederate port.

During the war, 355 of these vessels were sunk, burned, or otherwise destroyed, and 1,119 vessels were captured, many of which were equipped by the Government for blockading purposes. The total number of vessels taken and destroyed was 1,504, valued in a low estimate, at $30,000,000.

CONFEDERATE CRUISERS.—These cruisers were a class of armed vessels sent out to destroy the commerce of the North. They were called "commerce destroyers," and cruised the seas, generally the highways of commerce, in search of the Union merchantmen, which were to be found in all the ports of the world when the war opened. The Confederate cruisers had no ports to which they could take their prizes. Their own officers constituted their courts of admiralty. When a merchantman fell into their hands, it was set on fire and burned.

The adventures of these cruisers began with the escape of the Sumter, which ran the blockade at the mouth of the Mississippi in June, 1861, and entered upon a memorable career. She was under the command of Captain Semmes, who afterward became famous as the commander of the Alabama.

After the Sumter had taken many prizes, the Federal Government sent several vessels in search of her, but only one of these was fast enough to overtake her if sighted. Finding that Federal cruisers were on his track, Captain Semmes left the Caribbean sea and crossed the Atlantic. The career of the Sumter terminated at Gibraltar. Two Federal gunboats were watching for her; her commander was unable to purchase any more coal, and thus the Sumter was finally laid up at Gibraltar, while Captain Semmes and some of his officers went to Southampton, England, in search of a better vessel, with which to renew their depredations. The Sumter afterward became a blockade-runner, and later was wrecked off the coast of China.

THE TRENT AFFAIR, 1861.—The San Jacinto, commanded by Captain Wilkes, was one of the vessels in search of the Sumter. While at Havana Captain Wilkes learned that two Confederate envoys were on their way to arrange, if possible, for the recognition of the Confederate States.

They were Mr. John Slidell, a prominent Southern lawyer, and Mr. James Murray Mason, the author of the Fugitive Slave Law, chosen to represent the Confederacy at France and Great Britain. Escaping from Charleston on a dark night in a small vessel, they arrived at Havana. There they boarded the British mail-steamer Trent, and set out for Europe. Captain Wilkes determined to intercept them. When the Trent arrived in the Bahama Channel, where he had been on the watch for her, he stopped the vessel, boarded her, seized the Confederate envoys Nov. 8, 1861, over the protests of the English captain, and carried them and their secretaries as prisoners on board the Jacinto. The prisoners were taken to Massachusetts, and there confined in one of the forts of Boston harbor.

No law would sanction the seizure of the envoys. It had not

been long since England had claimed the supposed right to search vessels belonging to another nation, and the United States resisted it in the War of 1812. England had formally given up the claim in the Webster-Ashburton Treaty, 1842. Great Britain denounced this act of Wilkes with great vehemence, demanded the surrender of Messrs. Mason and Slidell and an apology from the United States. The House of Representatives extended a vote of thanks to Captain Wilkes for his arrest of the traitors Slidell and Mason, and public clamor heartily approved his course. War seemed imminent between Great Britain and the North. But the wiser councils of Abraham Lincoln prevailed. "We cannot abandon our own principles," said he. "We shall have to give these men up and apologize for what we have done." Accordingly the envoys were released, January 1, 1862, and set sail for Europe.

Public feeling raved a great deal on both sides. The English public believed that the American statesmen had yielded only to avoid an open rupture, while the Americans believed that England had made an offensive and unwarranted display of force. The Confederates had been rejoicing over anticipated trouble between the North and England. By the return of the envoys the whole trouble was settled without an appeal to arms, but it left, for a time, an impression of hatred on both sides, which was intensified by the sympathy manifested by the ruling class of England for the Southern cause.

THE FLORIDA.—Great Britain became the naval base of the Confederacy. Her ship-builders were preparing a privateer navy for the Confederacy as fast as they could work. Nearly all the Confederate vessels of any service were constructed in English dockyards.

The first privateer which became formidable to the commerce of the North was the Florida, called in her early history the Oreto. The Florida was built at Birkenhead, nominally for the use of Italy. The American minister had learned her real destination, and warned the British government against letting her go. The Florida sailed for Nassau (Bahamas) under the British flag, with every preparation for the reception of guns and munitions of war, which were brought on another vessel, and taken to Grand Key (an uninhabitable island of the Bahamas), and equipped for the work of a cruiser. The British flag was hauled down and the Confederate flag hoisted. Within three months she had burnt thirteen vessels, and taken two for use as Confederate cruisers. After roving the sea for more than two years, she was captured by the United States cruiser Wachusett in the neutral harbor of Bahia, Brazil. Both vessels had permission to remain in the harbor for forty-eight hours to coal and for repairs. The Wachusett crashed into the Florida and opened fire upon her, which compelled her to surrender. She was towed out to sea. The capture of the Florida was a violation of the rights of neutral nations.

The Government disavowed the act of Collins, commander of the Wachusett, and offered apologies to Brazil. The vessel and crew were to be returned to Bahia, but she was sunk by an "unforeseen accident," near Hampton Roads.

THE ALABAMA.—-Of all the Confederate cruisers, the Alabama was by far the most famous. She was built at Birkenhead, near Liverpool, by the house of Laird, expressly for Confederate service. While under process of construction she was called the " 290." It was not until she had put to sea and hoisted the Confederate flag, and Captain Semmes appeared on her deck in full Southern uniform, that she took the name Alabama.

During her career she captured sixty-six Northern vessels. Her plan was always the same. Hoisting the British flag, and decoying her intended victim within reach, she would suddenly raise the Confederate colors, and capture her prize. An American captain saw far off in the night the burning flames of a vessel. Hastening to rescue the crew of the burning ship, he was made prisoner by the Alabama, which still remained in the same waters as the ship which he had burned.

The Alabama did not do much fighting. She preyed upon merchant vessels that could not fight. Only twice did she engage in any conflict. The first time was with the Hatteras, a small blockading ship, which was sunk in a short time. The second encounter took place off the coast of Cherbourg, France, June 19, 1864, with the United States warship Kearsarge, whose size and armament were about equal to her own. In an hour the Alabama was completely shattered, and went down with many of her crew killed and wounded. No one was killed on board the Kearsarge—though three men were wounded, one mortally. Captain Semmes and thirty-eight others were picked up by the British ship Deerhound, that had been hovering around to witness the battle. Instead of communicating with Captain John A. Winslow, of the Kearsarge, after the rescue, the Deerhound pursued a hasty flight to England. The destruction of the "terror to American commerce" caused great rejoicing in the North, but the escape of her commander took from the victory a reason for the happiest applause.

MERRIMAC AND MONITOR, BATTLE BETWEEN, MARCH 9, 1862. After the abandonment of Norfolk by the Federals, the Confederates took possession of the navy yard, and began to make use of what had not been consumed by the flames. Among the ships burned was the frigate Merrimac. The lower part of her hull and engines and boilers were practically unhurt. The vessel was raised, and rebuilt as an ironclad. Her sloping sides were covered with a double coating of iron plates, each two inches thick. A cast-iron ram projecting four feet was attached to the bow of the vessel, which was rechristened the Virginia, by the Confederates.

The news of the construction of this formidable ironclad led the Government to exert every effort to complete the Monitor in season to meet the first movements of the Merrimac. Corresponding efforts were made by the Confederates to have the latter vessel completed first, to make a raid upon the wooden vessels of the United States which were blockading the Chesapeake. This extra effort resulted in preparing the Merrimac for use one day in advance of her little antagonist.

In the harbor off Fortress Monroe at that time, were the Union frigates Minnesota, Roanoke, St. Lawrence, and several gunboats. Off Newport News, seven miles above, which was strongly fortified by a Federal garrison, were anchored the frigate Congress and the sloop Cumberland. These vessels carried heavy batteries and were excellent vessels of their kind, but were not calculated to stand against an ironclad. Realizing that he could not be harmed by these war vessels, the commander of the Merrimac, on the 8th day of March, 1862, steamed leisurely into the midst of the Union vessels and began the work of destruction. Steering straight for the Cumberland and Congress, he struck the former vessel in the side at right angles, and made a great opening into which the water poured. The brave crew of the Cumberland continued the unequal contest with as much heroism as was ever seen in naval battle. Driven from the lower deck by the water, they continued to operate the pivot guns on the upper deck, until the vessel went down with colors still flying. The Congress grounded; and, in her helpless condition, she was compelled to surrender, and was consigned to the flames by the Confederates. The ebb tide and approaching night prevented the Merrimac from making an attack on the remaining Union vessels, so she retired to Sewell's Point, a few miles away, to anchor for the night, with the expectation of completing the work in the morning. It is probably no exaggeration to say that the Confederate ironclad could have destroyed all the wooden vessels at that time in the Federal navy, had they been within reach, and unsupported by fort or monitor.

At 9 P. M. the Monitor made its appearance. An atmosphere of gloom pervaded the fleet. The pygmy aspect of the "cheesebox," as the Monitor was called, did not inspire much confidence among those who had seen the destruction of the Cumberland and the Congress. She took a station amid wreck and disaster, near the Minnesota, which was aground. On Sunday morning, March 9, the Merrimac moved from anchor to attack the Minnesota. The little Monitor moved forward to meet her, while the wooden vessels turned and fled. Then commenced one of the greatest naval combats recorded in history. It revolutionized the navies of the world, and introduced a class of ironclads in place of the vulnerable wooden vessels.

The conflict was long, furious, and at close quarters; neither vessel was very seriously injured. The Merrimac withdrew, however, to Norfolk in a leaking condition, while the Monitor remained in possession of the field. The former guarded the James river, the latter protected the Chesapeake. On the evacuation of Norfolk by the Confederates, in May, 1862, the Merrimac was destroyed. The Monitor went down in a storm at sea while on her way to Charleston, and only a few of her crew were saved.

The Monitor was designed by Captain John Ericsson, who was a native of Sweden. He served in the army and navy of that country, pursued the profession of an engineer in England, and came to America in 1839. The Monitor consisted of a small iron hull 124 feet long, 34 feet wide. On the top of the hull was a boat-shaped raft, covered with iron plates. On the top of the deck there was mounted a turret, 20 feet in diameter and nine feet high, covered with eight one-inch iron plates riveted together. She carried two 11-inch guns, which, as the turret revolved, could be used to fire in any direction. The Merrimac carried ten guns.

The Monitor was built at New York for coast defense, but when news of the formidable character of the Merrimac was received, her construction was hastened to meet the Confederate ironclad. The voyage to the Chesapeake was a tempestuous one. Again and again she was almost sunk, but after an exciting trip, in which she heard the booming cannons at a distance, and saw the sky lit up by the burning Congress, she entered Hampton Roads in time to end the destructive career of the Merrimac.

CHAPTER IV.

COAST OPERATIONS.

HATTERAS INLET SURRENDERED, AUGUST 29, 1861.—Gen. Benjamin F. Butler and Commodore Stringham were sent from Fortress Monroe with sealed orders, on an expedition against Hatteras Inlet. Butler was in command of the land forces, and Stringham directed the naval expedition. This was the first of a series of movements against the Southern coast. Hatteras Inlet commanded the entrance to Pamlico Sound, whose waters became a favorite rendezvous for traders engaged in blockade-running. The Inlet was defended by Forts Hatteras and Clark. The bombardment of these was commenced August 28, 1861, and renewed the next day, when the Confederates hoisted the white flag. The secrecy of the expedition had been so well kept, that for several days the blockade-runners, seeking Confederate shelter, fell an easy prey to the Union troops who had taken possession of the forts. The 615 prisoners who fell into Union hands were taken to New York harbor. The commands of Hawkins and Weber were left to garrison the forts, and Gen Butler returned to the North and commenced the organization of an expedition directed against New Orleans.

CONFEDERATE ATTACK UPON FORT PICKENS, OCTOBER, 1861. At the breaking-out of the war, Pensacola was seized by the Confederates without a struggle. Lieutenant Slemmer was ordered to surrender Fort Pickens, on Santa Rosa Island, commanding the main entrance to Pensacola harbor. By the fidelity of this officer, the fort was saved to the Union. Soon after the fall of Fort Sumter, reinforcements were sent to the defenses of Pensacola. Gen. Braxton Bragg assembled a formidable force there during the early part of the war, and threatened an attack upon Fort Pickens. Finally after months of delay a Confederate force left Pensacola on the night of Oct. 9, 1861, and, crossing the bay, made an attack upon Fort Pickens. The movement was unsuccessful, and the invaders were driven from the island.

EXPEDITION AGAINST PORT ROYAL AND THE SEA ISLANDS, OCTOBER AND NOVEMBER, 1861.—On October 29th a naval and military expedition numbering 10,000 men left Hampton Roads for the Southern coast. Thomas W. Sherman (not William T. Sherman) commanded the land forces and Commodore S. F. Dupont was in command of the fleet. After a stormy passage, in which four transports were lost and two disabled, they arrived at Port Royal, South Carolina. Fort Walker, on Hilton Head, was captured by the fleet, and Beaufort, South Carolina, was abandoned by the enemy. By the combined efforts of the fleet and army, the whole chain of islands which form the coast of South Carolina and Georgia fell into Federal possession.

THE FALL OF ROANOKE ISLAND, 1862.—Another land and naval force, against Roanoke Island, North Carolina, was fitted out early in the year 1862. Gen. Ambrose E. Burnside and

Com. L. M. Goldsborough were in command of the 12,000 men
sent on this expedition. Gen. H. A. Wise commanded the Confederate forces. Much delay was occasioned by the fact that
many of the transports were of too great draft to permit a
passage through the shallow waters of the Sound. This delay
afforded the enemy an opportunity to strengthen the fortress.
At length, after the loss of several vessels, which were grounded
and wrecked by a storm, an entrance to Pamlico Sound was
effected. The Confederate fleet was pursued to Elizabeth City,
and destroyed. The forts of Roanoke Island were taken, Feb.
7th and 8th, after some desperate fighting. The Union men
waded waist-deep through a pond of water that protected one of
the batteries. The Confederates abandoned their work and attempted to retreat, but were overtaken, and 2,500 were compelled to surrender. The Federal loss was 50 killed and 250
wounded.

Edenton, Wintom, and many of the settlements on the Sound
yielded to Union authority. Newbern, one of the most important seaports of North Carolina, was taken March 14th, after a
vigorous defense. Beaufort yielded without resistance. Fort
Macon, after a bombardment, surrendered April 25th. Nearly
the whole of the coast of North Carolina thus lay at the mercy
of the victors. The chief result was the closing of the Confederate ports and the suppression of their commerce.

Gen. Burnside's forces were eventually taken, for the most
part, to Alexandria, to aid Gen. Pope in his campaign against
Lee. Gen. John G. Foster was left in command of the depart-

ment of North Carolina, with barely sufficient forces to hold the points which had been taken.

Soon after the recovery of Port Royal and the adjacent islands, Gen. Quincy A. Gillmore was directed to move against Fort Pulaski, on Cockspur Island. After a bombardment of a day and a half, the fort surrendered, April 11, 1862. Gen. Hunter, who succeeded to the command of Sherman, on May 9th proclaimed South Carolina, Georgia, and Florida to be under martial law, and the slaves of these States free. This declaration was overruled by President Lincoln, as was Frémont's proclamation in Missouri.

GEN. WRIGHT IN FLORIDA, MARCH, 1862.—While Gillmore was before Fort Pulaski, Commodore Dupont and Gen. H. G. Wright were making conquests in Florida. St. Augustine, Jacksonville, and other places were abandoned by the enemy on the approach of the Union forces. Pensacola was evacuated, and everything of a combustible character was burned before the departure of Gen. Jones, its commander.

A strong Union sentiment was manifest in the State after the departure of the 10,000 men who joined the Confederate army. A convention was called to assemble at Jacksonville, April 10, 1862, to organize a Union State Government. To the dismay of those who were engaged in it, Gen. Wright prepared to withdraw his forces two days before the day on which the convention was called. In consequence, the Union feeling made little manifestation, and the Confederate supremacy was maintained to the close of the war.

EXPEDITION INTO NEW MEXICO BY THE CONFEDERATES, FEB-
RUARY, 1862.—The Confederate Gen. Sibley led an expedition,
early in 1862, against the Federal forts of New Mexico, these
forts being under the command of Gen. Canby. He advanced
up the Rio Grande with considerable physical difficulty, and
defeated Canby's regulars in several combats. He found that
he could not maintain himself in that desert region; so he
abandoned Albuquerque, Santa Fé, and other places he had
taken, and conducted a disastrous retreat.

MOVEMENT AGAINST CHARLESTON, 1863.—Charleston remained in undisputed possession of the Confederates until the
spring of 1863. The engagements of the turret monitor led to
the belief that a fleet of these could force a passage through
Charleston harbor. Accordingly, in April, Admiral Dupont
and Gen. Hunter led a fleet of seven of these ironclads in the
experiment. The vessels carried 32 guns; the opposing forts
possessed an aggregate of 300 guns. Torpedoes and other obstructions were placed in the harbor. The heavy fire concentrated upon the vessels compelled them to return. One of them
was sunk after being struck 99 times, of which 19 were below
the water-line. All the rest were more or less damaged. The
forts suffered but little damage. All effort to pass them was
now abandoned, and operations were directed against the harbor
and adjoining islands. Gen. Hunter was superseded by Gen.
Q. A. Gillmore, and Admiral John A. Dahlgren soon relieved
Admiral Dupont. Gen. Gillmore and Admiral Dahlgren at once
set on foot operations looking to a systematic campaign against

Fort Sumter and Charleston. A landing was effected on Morris Island in July, and the enemy was driven to Fort Wagner. Several furious assaults were made upon it, at great cost to the Union arms, as they left 1,500 dead and wounded upon the treacherous sands. The Confederate garrison, however, evacuated the island in September.

The army and the fleet opened fire upon Charleston, Sumter, and the other forts. Fort Sumter was practically demolished. Many shells were thrown into the city of Charleston, and many buildings greatly injured by the slow bombardment which was kept up to the end of the year. Further operations were suspended, and Charleston remained in possession of the enemy until the approach of Sherman's victorious hosts in the spring of 1865.

MOBILE BAY, SUMMER OF 1864.—Mobile was the only seaport of importance on the coast of the eastern part of the Gulf. There were several channels in the bay, the entrances to which were protected by Forts Morgan, Gaines, and Powell. The coast was of such a character as to make blockade-running easy, and many blockade-runners escaped the vigilance of the blockading fleet by passing along the shallow waters of the coast. The city of Mobile became an important rendezvous for their traffic.

After the fall of Vicksburg, Farragut was directed, in June, 1864, to prepare his vessels for an attack on Mobile bay. In addition to the forts the bay was defended by four vessels, one of which was the ironclad Tennessee, the most formidable vessel the Confederates ever built by the Confederates. Torpedoes and obstructions rebellion. been placed in the water.

Farragut arranged his fourteen wooden vessels, two abreast, lashed them together, supported on their flanks by four monitors. As they neared the forts every gun that could be brought to bear upon the approaching fleet thundered forth its echoes. The concentrated fire from the vessels was directed toward the forts, and many of the gunners were either killed or driven to cover. The monitor Tecumseh, in the lead, was struck by a torpedo and sunk. Except this single loss, the fleet succeeded in passing the forts and obstructions without serious damage. No sooner was the combat with the forts at an end, than a new one began with the Tennessee. Steaming from the protection of Fort Morgan, she was met by the vessels from the Union fleet. She was pounded by the guns from the monitors, and rammed at full speed by the larger vessels, in a terrific struggle, until her case became hopeless. She raised the white flag and left Farragut in control of Mobile bay. Five thousand troops under General Gordon Granger had already been landed to the rear of Fort Gaines, which surrendered August 7th; and Fort Morgan on the 23d. No immediate attempt was made for the capture of Mobile city, for the surrender of the forts served the purpose of the Government,—to close the bay to blockade-runners.

Operations were again resumed, in the spring of 1865, by General Canby and Admiral Thatcher, and after a month the defenses held by General Taylor were taken, April 12, 1865, Q. ¹ the Union Army entered the city, ignorant of the fact that Admi. ·rmy had surrendered three days before. set on fo.

CHAPTER V.

WAR IN MISSOURI.

THE ORGANIZATION OF THE ARMIES, 1861.— In Missouri, as in several slave States, a majority of the people were loyal. The Legislature refused to pass an ordinance of secession, but invested the Governor, Claiborne F. Jackson, with despotic power. He was determined to take the State out of the Union, and used every means at his command in the interests of the Confederacy. He established camps of instruction in different parts of the State. One near St. Louis he named Camp Jackson. About twelve hundred men stationed here and armed by the Confederate Government were surprised on the morning of May 10, 1861, surrounded by Captain Nathaniel Lyon with 6,000 men, and the whole garrison was compelled to surrender. A mob following Lyon's men heaped insult and then violence upon them. One regiment finally fired upon the assailants, killing twenty-two persons.

Governor Jackson was active in carrying out his designs at Jefferson City. He called for 50,000 State militia to repel Federal invasions, and divided the State into nine military districts. Sterling Price, who was appointed commander of the State forces, urged officers commanding in the districts to make haste to organize the militia, and assemble them at Boonville and Lexington. A Confederate force entered the State from Arkansas and Texas to assist in the work of rebellion.

(57)

BOONVILLE AND CARTHAGE.—Union troops were being assembled at the Federal arsenal at St. Louis under the command of General Lyon. He gave the enemy little time for preparation. Steaming up the Missouri from St. Louis to Jefferson City, he found the Governor had fled to his adherents at Boonville. On the 17th of June, Lyon reached Boonville, where some two or three thousand men, under the command of Colonel Marmaduke were assembled. They were dispersed after a sharp engagement, and fled toward the southwest, through Warsaw, receiving reinforcements as they went.

Colonel Franz Sigel, a veteran German officer, had been dispatched with 1,500 men farther south. He had pushed on near to Carthage, hoping to prevent a junction between Jackson and some other forces which his Confederate brigadiers were hurrying to him. A spirited engagement took place, July 5th, in which the flanking cavalry of the enemy compelled Sigel to retreat to his baggage trains. The Confederate loss was much greater than the Federal. Jackson's forces were greatly augmented during the night and morning by the arrival of Price with his Arkansas and Texas troops. Sigel, thus greatly outnumbered, continued his retreat to Springfield, where General Lyon joined and outranked him.

The State convention reassembled at Jefferson City July 20th, and by a vote of 52 to 28 declared the offices of Governor, Lieutenant-Governor, Secretary of State, and of legislators, vacant because of the acts of treason of those officials. Their acts opposed to the Federal Government were declared null and

void. New officers were elected and inaugurated, who administered the affairs of the State.

WILSON'S CREEK, AUGUST 10, 1861.—Major General John
C. Frémont was appointed to the command of the Western
Department July 9, but did not reach St. Louis until the 25th.
Efforts were made to obtain reinforcements for Lyon, but the
disaster at Bull Run made it necessary to send all aid to that
quarter. Meantime the Confederate troops were forming, and
advancing upon General Lyon in two columns. Lyon determined to strike a blow before they could perfect a junction. A
skirmish occurred at Dug Spring, in which he had the advantage; but he could not prevent the columns from uniting. His
force numbered 5,500, while the enemy numbered 12,000.
Even with this disparity of numbers he fell upon the foe encamped at Wilson's Creek, August 10th. This battle, next to
Bull Run, was the most important of the year 1861. Lyon
was twice wounded, once in the head; his horse was shot from
under him. In a final charge, as the Colonel of the Second
Kansas regiment lay severely wounded, General Lyon headed
the column, calling out " Come on, brave men! I will lead you."
At that moment a bullet struck him in the breast, and the
heroic leader fell mortally wounded; but the enemy was driven
from the field. Sigel, who assaulted the Confederate rear, had
met a repulse. With the loss of their leader, and in the face
of a great disparity of numbers, the Union troops, having made
an effective assault, retreated from the contest, as the enemy
were again forming to renew the battle. The Confederates

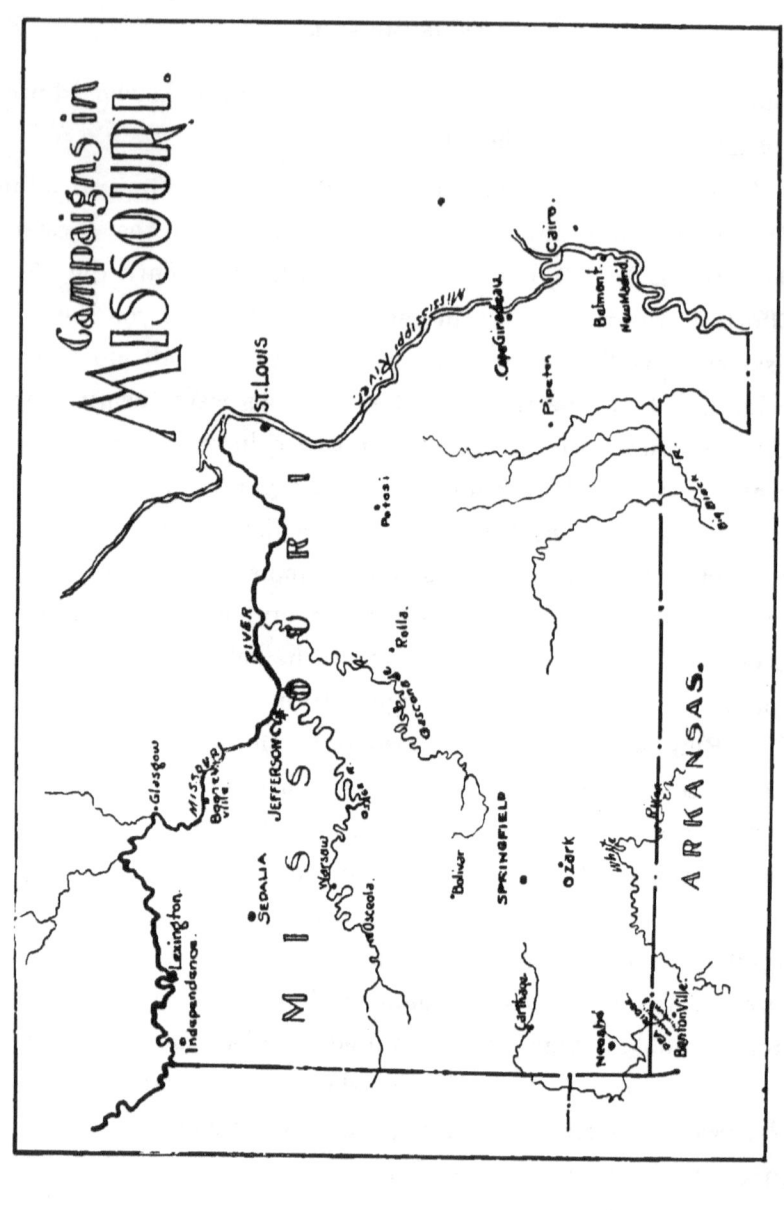

claimed the victory, as they held the field and took six guns, but they had been so severely punished that no pursuit was attempted. Each army had lost more than a thousand in killed, wounded, and missing.

Major Sturgis assumed command of the Union troops, and conducted the retreat.

THE FALL OF LEXINGTON, Mo., SEPT. 20, 1861.—General Price moved from Wilson's Creek battle-field northward to Lexington, where Colonel James A. Mulligan was garrisoned with a force numbering 3,500. The attempt by Frémont to reinforce Mulligan did not succeed. The water-supply was cut off from the beleaguered troops, who, with parched lips, repelled repeated assaults. The enemy constructed movable breastworks of hemp, which they rolled before them as they advanced toward the Union troops. Price had increased his forces until they reached 18,000. With this number he appeared before Lexington and opened a terrific fire upon the little Union garrison, which answered with determined spirit. The Federal troops had exhausted all ammunition, consumed all rations, and had been without water for days. Finally, after three days of fighting, the Union troops were compelled to yield to an unconditional surrender, September 20, 1861.

MOVEMENT OF OFFICERS AND ARMIES.—Frémont at once left St. Louis with the intention of attacking Price, but that officer retreated after the capture of Col. Mulligan, to the southwest part of the State, where he was rejoined by Gen. McCulloch, who had separated from him after the battle of Wilson's Creek.

Frémont proclaimed martial law in Missouri, August 31, and promised freedom to the slaves of all persons who should take up arms against the United States Government. It was feared that this proclamation would lead many Unionists in the border States, especially Kentucky, to side with the Confederacy, if indorsed by the National administration. President Lincoln issued an order modifying Frémont's proclamation so as to restrict it to the slaves who were actually engaged in rebellion by the direction or persuasion of their masters.

After organizing his army, now numbering 30,000, Frémont marched toward Springfield in pursuit of the foe. A battle between his army and the Price forces became imminent. But on the 2d of November an order from Gen. Scott arrived, which relieved Frémont of his command and placed Gen. Hunter in his place. The removal of Frémont for the purpose of securing more efficient service caused much complaint in Missouri and throughout the country among the anti-slavery men. It proved an unfortunate affair, as Gen. Hunter with a force superior in number and discipline to his opponents, retreated to Rolla without a battle. The campaign, inaugurated with great expense, was a flat failure, and the southwest part of the State was abandoned, for the time, to Confederate pillage and guerrilla outrages.

Gen. Hunter was superseded in the command of the Department of Missouri by Henry W. Halleck, on the 12th of November, 1861.

Gen. Price pushed his force northward unresisted. He entered and occupied Springfield, Osceola, Lexington, burned Warsaw, and established Confederate supremacy over the greater portion of the southern and western parts of the State. At length Gen. Pope, who had conducted a successful campaign against the guerrillas in northern Missouri, but now in command of the central district of the State, moved against the enemy. A detachment of Pope's forces, under Jefferson C. Davis, surprised the enemy's camp at Milford, near Warrensburg, and took over 1,000 prisoners and much baggage and supplies. Before Price had time to concentrate his forces, he had been so roughly handled that he retreated rapidly southward through Springfield and across the Arkansas line.

Gen. Pope was then sent with a land force to coöperate with Commodore Foote in the reduction of New Madrid and Island No. 10. He had thus commenced the building of that reputation which soon placed him in a position in which he showed but little ability as a commander of a great army.

BATTLE OF PEA RIDGE, MARCH 7–8, 1862.—Late in December, Gen. S. R. Curtis was placed in command of National troops in southwestern Missouri. He advanced from Rolla in pursuit of Price, who retreated before him to the Boston Mountains, Arkansas. Gen. Albert Pike, with a number of Cherokee Indians and Gen. Benj. McCulloch in command of a division of Texas and Arkansas troops, joined the forces of Price, increasing them to about 20,000; and Gen. Earl Van Dorn was sent to take command of the whole Confederate force. Curtis had but little more than one-half the force which opposed him.

Van Dorn resolved to give battle, and he fell upon the advance division of Federal troops at Bentonville, under Gen. Sigel, who succeeded in conducting a masterly retreat until reinforced by the main body. Then, in a severe engagement March 7th and 8th, the Confederates were driven to the ravines, and finally put to rout. The National loss in this engagement, called by the Federals the battle of Pea Ridge (named by the Confederates Elk Horn), was over 1,300 killed, wounded, and missing. The Confederate loss was heavy, but the numbers are unknown.

GUERRILLA WARFARE.—No important military operations were undertaken in Missouri and Arkansas for some time after the engagement at Pea Ridge. The more important events farther East drained the resources of the West, and led to a withdrawal of the troops from this State. Van Dorn and Price were called to Tennessee, and participated in the engagement around Corinth. Curtis sent a large part of his army to assist in the siege of Corinth, and led the rest in a march across the State of Arkansas to Helena, on the Mississippi.

The withdrawal of these forces encouraged the formation of guerrilla bands. They became very numerous in the interior of Missouri, where they carried on a desperate and sanguinary guerrilla warfare. The encounters were many and fierce. Gen. J. M. Schofield, who was left in command in Missouri, organized the loyal citizens into a State militia. He had 50,000 names on his rolls, of whom 20,000 were ready for effective service by July, 1862.

The Confederate Gen. Hindman gathered a large force in Arkansas in the fall of the year 1862. IIis troops were poorly armed and disciplined, but commanded by a general who was determined to engage in battle. The opportunity was afforded him at Prairie Grove, in December, where he was defeated by a force much smaller than his own, under Generals Blunt and Herron. The losses were about equal on each side. The Confederates retreated south to the protecting barriers of the Boston Mountains.

QUANTRELL RAID ON LAWRENCE, KAN., AUG. 21, 1863.— After the fall of Vicksburg, many Confederate soldiers returned to their homes in Missouri. A season of renewed activity was imparted to the guerrilla bands that continued to roam about in their plundering excursions. One of the most atrocious outrages of the war was committed by one of these bands led by the notorious Quantrell, who had for some weeks been threatening various Kansas towns. Assembling about 300 picked and well-mounted followers, at a place of rendezvous near the State line, and skillfully avoiding several detachments sent in pursuit of him, he crossed into Kansas, and pushed directly for Lawrence. He entered the defenseless city in the early morning of August 21. Stores and banks were robbed, 185 buildings burned, and 150 to 200 inhabitants murdered in cold blood. The work was completed in three or four hours and the marauders were on the retreat, pursued so closely that more than 100 of the band were killed.

—5

CONFEDERATE REVERSES.—Gen. Holmes's attack on Helena, Ark., was gallantly repulsed by Gen. Prentiss July 4th; and the Confederate Gen. Marmaduke met reverses at Springfield, Mo., January 8th; at Hartsville, January 11th; and at Cape Girardeau, April 26th, 1863.

PRICE'S LAST RAID IN MISSOURI, 1864.—The last important operation in the West was a raid conducted by Gen. Sterling R. Price through Arkansas and Missouri. In the West it is called the "Price Raid." Several engagements between his raiders and Federal authority occurred in Arkansas. Price then, organizing his forces to the number of about 15,000, into three divisions, entered Missouri and ravaged the State for two months—September and October. At Pilot Knob he attacked a small Federal force, which, after administering severe punishment to him from behind intrenchments, was forced to retreat. The raiders at once threatened the depots at St. Louis, Rolla, and Jefferson, and for a week or more they seemed to have their own way.

Gen. W. S. Rosecrans, now in command of the Department of the Missouri at St. Louis, sent Pleasonton's cavalry and the Kansas militia under Blunt and Curtis, to cope with Price's veterans. Engagements occurred at St. Louis, Jefferson City, Independence, and Westport. The marauders were put to flight southward. They crossed into Kansas near West Point, Mo., closely pursued in their southern movement by the Union troops. There was an engagement at the crossing of the Marais des Cygnes (called the Osage, farther down-stream) river, and on Oct. 25th the Confederates were overtaken, and the decisive battle of Mine Creek was fought on Kansas soil, in Linn county. The enemy lost nine pieces of artillery, and 800 prisoners, among whom were Generals Marmaduke, Cabell, and Slemmons, the latter being mortally wounded. General Graham, also of the Confederate army, was killed. The pursuit was conducted with such vigor that the enemy abandoned the project of attacking Fort Scott, fled from Kansas, and soon after departed from the State of Missouri with his forces greatly demoralized, and his army reduced by captures and dispersions to perhaps 5,000 men.

Most of the noted guerrilla bands followed Price out of Missouri, and their raids and depredations came to an end.

These operations, of a secondary nature, bore little relation to the general strategy of the main campaigns. Their chief importance consisted in the moral weight added to the Federal cause by the preservation of national authority in this section, and in the protection of the rights of loyal citizens.

CHAPTER VI.

GRANT'S CAMPAIGN IN THE WEST.

BELMONT, GRANT'S FIRST BATTLE, NOVEMBER 7, 1861.—
Gen. Ulysses S. Grant, who was in command of Cairo, moved
down the Mississippi with 3,000 men for a demonstration
against Belmont, Mo., opposite Columbus. Two Union gunboats accompanied the transports. These engaged the batteries
of Columbus, while the troops landed on the Missouri side,
Nov. 7, 1861. After a spirited conflict, the troops fought their
way through the abatis surrounding Belmont, and succeeded in
driving the enemy over the bluff to the bank of the river.
Heavy reinforcements were sent from Columbus to cut Grant's
troops off from their gunboats, and with superior numbers compel them to surrender. His exhausted troops valiantly fought
their way back to the boats, and re-embarked for Cairo. The
Confederate loss was more than 600, while the Union loss was
much less.

BATTLE OF MILL SPRINGS, JANUARY 19, 1862.—While General Grant was preparing to move against Forts Henry and
Donelson, General Thomas, who commanded the Union forces
in eastern Tennessee, began operations against the extreme east
of the Confederate line of defense. Gen. Felix K. Zollicoffer
was at the head of the enemy's forces. His principal camp was
at Mill Springs, on the Cumberland river, in a thinly settled

and poorly cultivated region.   One small steamboat brought supplies up the river from Nashville, to feed the army, which numbered 5,000 men.

Gen. Geo. B. Crittenden joined Zollicoffer, and superseded him in command.   Fearing an attack from Thomas, he resolved to anticipate it, and sallied forth to surprise several Union regiments at Logan's Crossroads.   The Confederates were utterly defeated Jan. 19, 1862.   Gen. Zollicoffer was killed.   The Union loss was 250 to the enemy's 500.   The engagement was called by the Confederates Fishing Creek; by the Federals, Mill Springs or Logan's Crossroads.   Crittenden withdrew his troops across the Cumberland, abandoning eastern Kentucky.

In the early part of January, Gen. James A. Garfield defeated the Confederates, commanded by General Marshall, at Prestonburg, Ky.

FORT HENRY, FEB. 6, 1862.—A few miles south of the Kentucky line, the Tennessee and Cumberland rivers approach within eleven miles of each other.   The Confederates had erected Fort Henry, on the east bank of the Tennessee, commanding the passage of that stream, and Fort Donelson, on the west bank of the Cumberland, controlling its waters.   A dirt road connected the two forts, by means of which the garrisons were expected to support each other if assailed.

To Gen. Grant, with the aid of Commodore Foote and his seven gunboats, was assigned, by order of Gen. Halleck, the task of taking these forts.   Leaving Cairo with some 15,000 troops on steam transports, they moved up the Ohio and Tennessee to

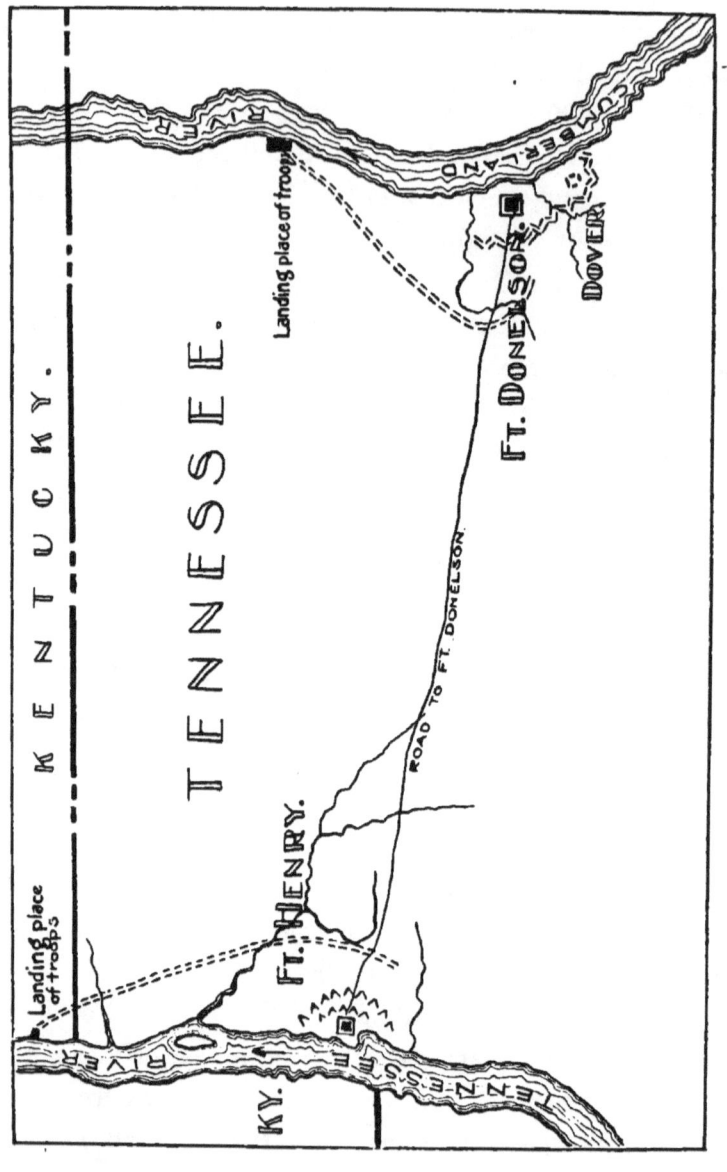

within four miles of Fort Henry. The troops were landed, and the main force under Gen. J. A. McClernand moved south to occupy the road leading to Fort Donelson. Commodore Foote steamed up the river and commenced a fierce bombardment of the fort. In less than two hours the guns of the enemy were silenced, and the fort compelled to surrender. Gen. Tilghman, Confederate commander at Fort Henry, had previously sent nearly all of his troops under Col. Heiman, who was second in command, to Fort Donelson, a portion of whom were overtaken by McClernand's cavalry, and twenty captured. Gen. Tilghman and about one hundred men who remained in the fort, surrendered Feb. 6th, 1862, while the rest escaped to Fort Donelson.

Gen. Albert Sidney Johnston, perhaps the most promising of the Southern officers, was in command in the West, with headquarters at Bowling Green. Gen. Buell lay in Johnston's front.

SURRENDER OF FORT DONELSON, FEB. 16, 1862.—While McClellan was still engaged in drilling, organizing and disciplining the Army of the Potomac, the army in the West commenced active operations. After the capture of Fort Henry, Grant prepared to invest Fort Donelson. It was here that Grant earned his first laurels as a staunch soldier. Fort Donelson was strongly fortified and garrisoned. The reinforcement from Fort Henry increased the numbers to about 21,000 men. From his victory on the Tennessee, Grant moved against Fort Donelson with 15,000 troops, and appeared before it on Feb. 12th. Commodore Foote steamed down the Tennessee and up the Ohio and Cumberland, and appeared before Fort Donelson with his gunboats and transports on the evening of Feb. 13th, bringing more than 10,000 reinforcements.

The gunboats had done so well at Fort Henry that they were again permitted to open the assault. They did so the next day, but, after desperate fighting, they were forced to retire from the range of the fort. Two of the vessels were disabled and others were badly damaged. The land forces then began a vigorous movement against the place. For two days there was severe fighting. An effort by the Confederates to cut their way out had failed. The Union lines were closing in upon them. The weather, which was pleasant and mild when the campaign commenced, became inclement and cold. Rain began to fall, followed by snow, which was accompanied by intense cold. The suffering on either side was fearful and almost universal, as the soldiers lay in their snow-clad beds without fire or tent. Great preparations were made by the Union forces for a concentrated attack on the morning of the 16th. The hopelessness of the Confederate situation brought a letter from Gen. Buckner asking for terms of surrender. Gen. Grant replied in these words:

"*No terms, except an unconditional and immediate surrender, can be accepted. I propose to move immediately upon your works.*"

The garrison was surrendered the same day (Sunday) unconditionally. The capture included about 15,000 men, 65 cannon, and 1,760 small arms. The Confederates had lost about

2,500 in killed, wounded, and missing, while Grant's loss was 2,041.

Gen. John B. Floyd was in command at Fort Donelson. He had been Secretary of War under Buchanan, and was under indictment at Washington. Fearing to surrender the command himself, he resigned in favor of Gen. Pillow, who for like reason turned the command over to Gen. Buckner. Both Floyd and Pillow escaped up the river on two Confederate steamers, and left Buckner to surrender the garrison. Floyd filled the steamers with men, estimated at 3,000, of his own brigade, who escaped with him to Nashville. Col. Forrest also escaped, with 800 cavalry. The conduct of Floyd in deserting his troops was on a par with his treachery as Secretary of War in supplying the South with arms and ammunition. For his conduct at Fort Donelson he was reprimanded by Jefferson Davis, and dismissed from service.

The victory was of great importance to the National arms. It opened up two navigable rivers, and left the enemy no stronghold in Kentucky and northern Tennessee. The whole Confederate lines, extending from Bowling Green on the east to Columbus on the west, had to be abandoned. A new line of defense was selected, along the Charleston & Memphis Railroad.

As Grant marched toward Fort Donelson, Gen. Buell moved against Gen. Johnston, whose forces at Bowling Green were greatly diminished by the detachment sent to Gen. Floyd at Donelson. Bowling Green was evacuated by Johnston, who retreated to Nashville, and soon continued his march south to

Corinth, Miss. Buell moved forward, took possession of Nashville, and established his headquarters there, while his army was
quartered around the city.

BATTLE OF SHILOH, OR PITTSBURG LANDING, APRIL 6–7,
1862.—The Confederate line of defense was bounded by Memphis on the west, Chattanooga on the east, with Shiloh in the
center.

Gen. Halleck was placed in command of all of the armies of
the Mississippi Valley early in 1862, with headquarters at St.
Louis. They embraced the Army of the Ohio, afterward called
the Army of the Cumberland, under Gen. D. C. Buell; the
Army of the Tennessee, under Gen. U. S. Grant; the Army of
the Mississippi, under Gen. John Pope; and the Army of
Southwest Missouri, under Gen. S. R. Curtis.

Gen. Grant's victorious army, after a brief rest at Fort Donelson, crossed to the Tennessee, and prepared for a new movement against the Confederates, who were now concentrating at
Corinth. While adopting vigorous measures for the execution
of the movement upon the center of the new line of defense
along the Memphis & Charleston Railroad, Grant received an
order from Gen. Halleck, instructing him to turn over his command to Gen. C. F. Smith, March 4, 1862.

Grant was relieved of his command because of supposed disobedience. The temporary change of commanders did not retard the preparation for the movement of the army. Transports arrived, and the troops were taken up the Tennessee river,
and disembarked at Savannah in safety. The illness of Gen.

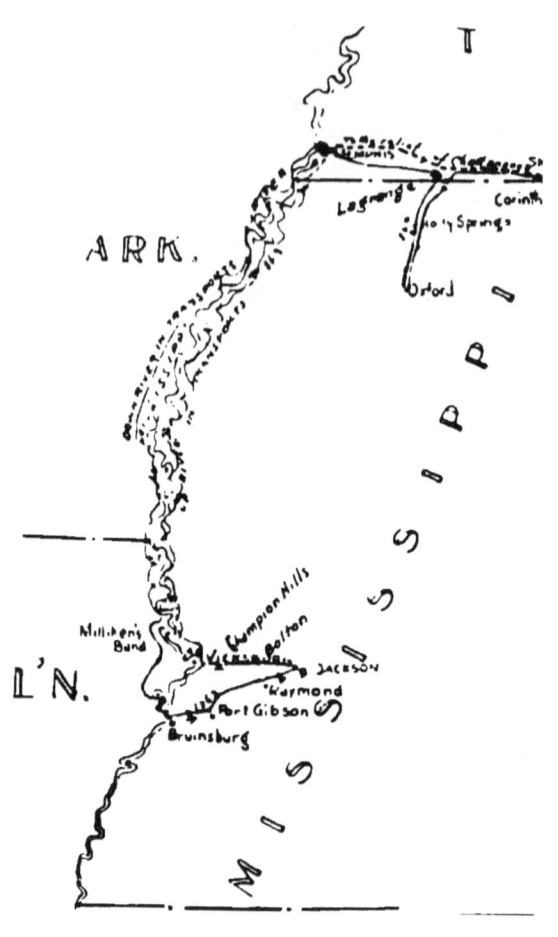

_____ Grant's Route
.... Buell's Route
.... Grant to relief of Chattanooga

GRANT'S Campaign
IN THE WEST.

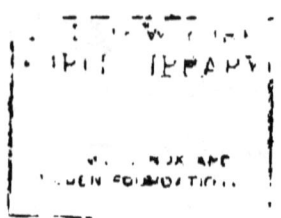

Smith, which resulted in his death, and the discovery that Grant had not been guilty of disobedience, resulted in reinstating him to his former command, March 13th. Much was expected from the army that had gained the signal victory at Forts Henry and Donelson. Public gaze was now concentrated upon it. No time was lost. Gen. Buell was ordered from Nashville to join Grant, who moved his troops from Savannah to Pittsburg Landing, nine miles farther up the river.

Buell at the same time sent Gen. O. M. Mitchell southward, with instructions to destroy as much of the Memphis & Charleston Railroad as possible. He passed through Shelbyville, and on the 11th of April he surprised and captured Huntsville, where he destroyed a large amount of supplies and railroad stock. He moved to Decatur and Tuscumbia. It was his intention to move eastward to Chattanooga and Rome, to destroy the machine-shops and foundries there; but he was compelled to retire before the superior force of Gen. Kirby Smith. Later he joined the command of Gen. Buell in his campaign against Bragg, when this officer conducted his invasion of Kentucky.

Gen. Albert Sidney Johnston had collected an army of 45,000 men around Corinth. Grant's force numbered about 40,000 men in and around Shiloh. Five thousand of these, under Gen. Lew Wallace, did not arrive on the scene of conflict until at the close of the first day's action. Gen. Buell was approaching with a force of 20,000 to coöperate with Grant. Gens. Price and Van Dorn were on their way from Missouri with a large force to swell Johnston's numbers.

As early as the 3d of April there had been skirmishing among
the pickets. An attack upon the Union army was not expected,
however. No defenses had been erected, on the theory that the
army would move upon Corinth to attack the enemy as soon as
Buell should arrive. Johnston, however, determined to strike a
blow before reinforcements could come to Grant. Moving silently forth from Corinth to within a few miles of the Federal
pickets, he encamped for the night, and early on Sunday morning, April 6th, his army came like an avalanche upon the Union
pickets, who were driven back in confusion. Soon the enemy
was upon the main body. Grant was not, for the moment, present. The troops were not prepared for the onslaught. The
lines fell back, and were re-formed. Beauregard, Bragg and
Hardee were able seconds to Johnston. Sherman, McClernand,
McDowell, Prentiss, and on the second day Lew Wallace and
Buell, rendered their best service to Grant.

Prentiss was surrounded, and compelled to surrender with
2,200 men. The Union army had been badly shattered during
the day. Not less than 5,000 men were huddled under the bank
of the river, resisting every effort to bring them out to lines
again by the statement, " Our regiment is all cut to pieces."
The lines fell back from one position to another until late in
the afternoon, when they were formed along the slopes and crest
of the bluff along the river. In this new position, with a deep
ravine in front of the left, with a raging river behind the army,
arrayed in a semi-circle they beat back the march of the then
triumphant army. The gunboats Tyler and Lexington swept

the ravine, which extended to the river, and hurled shells into
the Confederate columns. Here the enemy made the last desperate effort to take the Union batteries and to capture the
troops or drive them into the river. Every effort failed. The
ravine became a death-trap, and was soon filled with the bodies
of the dead and wounded. The onward march of the Confederates was stopped. They had lost heavily during the day.
Gen. Johnston was killed. Gen. Lew Wallace arrived with
5,000 effectives, after the firing had ceased for the day. Buell's
forces arrived, and were ferried across the river during the
night. Twenty-five thousand fresh troops were thus brought
upon the Union field.

With the early light of the morning the conflict was resumed.
Gen. P. G. T. Beauregard, who succeeded to the command of
Johnston's army, made a desperate attempt to hold his ground.
His decimated troops responded nobly, but it was all in vain.
The little old log church, which constituted Shiloh, again be-
came a conspicuous object in the battle-field. The enemy was
overpowered, and driven from the field, back to the place which
he had so stealthily left a few days before.

The Union loss was 1,754 killed, 8,408 wounded, and 2,885
missing, most of whom were prisoners. The Confederate loss
was 1,728 killed, 8,012 wounded, 959 missing.

CORINTH EVACUATED, MAY 30.—Gen. Halleck arrived at
Pittsburg Landing April 11, and took command of the army in
person. The way in which Grant had conducted the battle of
Shiloh was not satisfactory to him. Grant was given a sort of

second command, without any real duty. Pope's army of 30,-000 men arrived a few days later, fresh from the capture of Island No. 10. Other accessions from various quarters increased Halleck's army to 100,000 men. Great preparations were at once begun to move against the enemy at Corinth, where Beauregard had strongly fortified himself after his defeat at Shiloh.

Corinth was then an insignificant village, about twenty-two miles southwest of Pittsburg Landing, by the nearest wagon-road, or nineteen miles as the bird flies. It owed its military importance to the fact that it was located at the intersection of two great railroad systems—the Mobile & Ohio and the Memphis & Charleston.

Beauregard's army was reinforced by the troops from Missouri under Price and Van Dorn, and by the troops that had a short time before evacuated New Orleans. His force now numbered more than 50,000 men.

The forward movement of Halleck's army from Shiloh to Corinth was commenced on April 30th. The movement was a siege from the start: slowly but gradually the troops advanced, always behind intrenchments. Three weeks were consumed in marching fifteen miles. Finally, Halleck's troops reached a position from which assault was practicable. Beauregard held out as long as possible, without attacking the besieging columns, and when his position became untenable he abandoned Corinth and retreated to Tupelo. Halleck won a bloodless but barren victory. His troops took possession of Corinth **May**

30th, and commenced erecting fortifications on an elaborate scale.

Gen. Buell was detached on the 10th of June, and sent toward Chattanooga to oppose Gen. Bragg, who succeeded Beauregard in the command of the Confederate army driven from Corinth. In order to strengthen Buell, many of the best and most experienced soldiers were taken from Corinth and placed under him. The Union division which continued at Corinth remained comparatively inactive from June to September.

Some important changes were soon to take place in the distribution of the troops and in the change of officers. The reverses of the Army of the Potomac led the authorities to look around for a new general-in-chief in place of McClellan. Halleck was looked upon as the coming man. He was accordingly summoned to Washington to assume the responsible position of commander of all the forces in the United States. Grant succeeded to the command of his old army, while Pope was ordered to Virginia, and Rosecrans was placed in command of Pope's forces under Gen. Grant.

IUKA, SEPT. 19.—Generals Price and Van Dorn were left to confront the Union troops under Gen. Grant. Perceiving the reduced condition of the Federal army, they began maneuvering for the possession of Corinth. Price moved northeasterly, apparently with the view of joining Bragg in his Kentucky campaign, expecting thus to draw Grant from Corinth while Van Dorn would move forward and occupy the place. Price took possession of Iuka, driving out a small Federal force stationed there. Gen. Rosecrans was sent by a southern route to attack Price at Iuka, while Gen. Ord went by a northern route to intercept the retreat. Bad roads and imperfect maps of the country prevented a simultaneous attack. Rosecrans's division of 9,000 met the enemy near Iuka, and in an engagement in which each side lost about eight hundred men he succeeded in defeating the force under Price. During the night the Confederates made their escape, and formed a junction with Van Dorn.

Gen. Grant had counted on the destruction of Price's army. As it was, Iuka was a victory without much gain. Rosecrans returned to Corinth after this engagement, and Grant moved his headquarters to Jackson. The enemy under Van Dorn, having failed in the attempt to get possession of Corinth by strategy, determined to take it by assault, and recover northern Mississippi to the Confederacy.

BATTLE OF CORINTH, OCTOBER 3-4, 1862.—Gen. Grant had under his command at various points about forty-eight thousand men. Of these, 7,000 were under Sherman at Memphis, 12,000 under Ord at Bolivar, 23,000 under Rosecrans at Corinth, and 6,000 at Grant's headquarters in Jackson.

While occupying a position at Corinth, Rosecrans was attacked by Generals Price and Van Dorn, in command of a Confederate force numbering 38,000 men. On the 3d, the engagement consisted of skirmishing, and fragmentary charges and repulses on both sides, with the advantage in favor of the Confederates. The next day witnessed a ferocious struggle. The enemy made three furious attempts to capture Robinette's battery, which had already inflicted heavy damage upon them. Each time they were repulsed with great loss. In the third charge the Confederate banner was twice placed on the parapet and twice shot away. Col. Rogers of the Second Texas sprang upon the embankment with colors in his hand. In an instant he and five others who followed him fell, mortally wounded.

The defeat of the enemy became complete. They retired from Corinth in disorder.

On the 5th the retreating foe was struck by Hurlbut and Ord, at the crossing of Hatchie river, about ten miles from Corinth. They were again thrown into confusion, but by maneuvering they made good their escape.

The Union loss was 2,359 in killed, wounded, and missing. The enemy lost about three thousand killed and wounded, besides 2,225 prisoners.

Soon after his defeat at Corinth, Van Dorn was superseded by Gen. Pemberton, and Rosecrans was promoted to Buell's command. Gen. Grant began preparations to move upon the only remaining stronghold of the enemy in the Southwest—Vicksburg.

CHAPTER VII.

THE OPENING OF THE MISSISSIPPI.

THE CONFEDERATE LINE OF DEFENSE MOVES SOUTH.—When the Civil War commenced, the Mississippi, from the mouth of the Ohio to the Gulf, fell into the hands of the Confederates. Every effort was exerted by them to retain this great commercial highway. As the Confederate line of defense fell back before the advancing columns of Grant's victorious veterans, from Donelson to Shiloh, from Shiloh to Corinth, and from Corinth to Vicksburg, so all places on the upper Mississippi dwindled and faded away before the combined movement of the land and naval forces. With the fall of Forts Henry and Donelson came the abandonment of Columbus; with the Confederate defeat at Shiloh came the surrender of Island No. 10; with the evacuation of Corinth came the abandonment of Fort Pillow. New Orleans and Vicksburg were the only places on the river that offered serious resistance to the Union forces. All other places above Vicksburg were weakened as the Confederate line of defense was pushed southward, and thus they were abandoned, or fell an easy prey to the assailing forces. The following pages in this chapter will narrate the events of the struggle for the opening of the " Father of Waters."

COLUMBUS ABANDONED, MARCH 4, 1862.--Commodore Foote collected a flotilla at Cairo, apparently for use at Nashville.

When all was ready, he drifted down the Mississippi to Columbus, followed by troops on transports under Gen. William T. Sherman, while a supporting force moved overland from Paducah, under Gen. Cullum.

Columbus, Ky., was a Confederate stronghold, commanding the navigation of the Mississippi. Gen. Leonidas Polk, Episcopal bishop of Louisiana, was in command. He abandoned the city before the Union troops arrived, and fell back to the stronger defenses of Island No. 10.

FALL OF NEW MADRID (MARCH 14) AND ISLAND No. 10 (APRIL 7).—The islands of the Mississippi are numbered from the mouth of the Ohio river down to the Gulf. Island No. 10 lay in a sharp bend in the Mississippi, about thirty miles below Columbus, Miss. New Madrid, on the Missouri side, is a few miles farther down-stream, though on account of the great bend in the river it lies northwest of the island.

The opening of the Mississippi was one of the objective points of the Federals. To resist this purpose the Confederates had strongly fortified Island No. 10. Forty guns had been mounted. Gen. Beauregard was in command, but he left for Corinth, April 5th, and transferred his command to Gen. Makall.

Gen. John Pope, who commanded in eastern Missouri, appeared before New Madrid with some 20,000 men, while Commodore Foote was preparing a fleet to assail Island No. 10 from the north. He intrenched three regiments at Point Pleasant, to command the passage of the river directly back of Island No. 10, and sent to Cairo for large siege guns to bombard New

Madrid. Gen. McCown, seeing the danger of capture, abandoned the place at night during a heavy thunder-storm, and re-

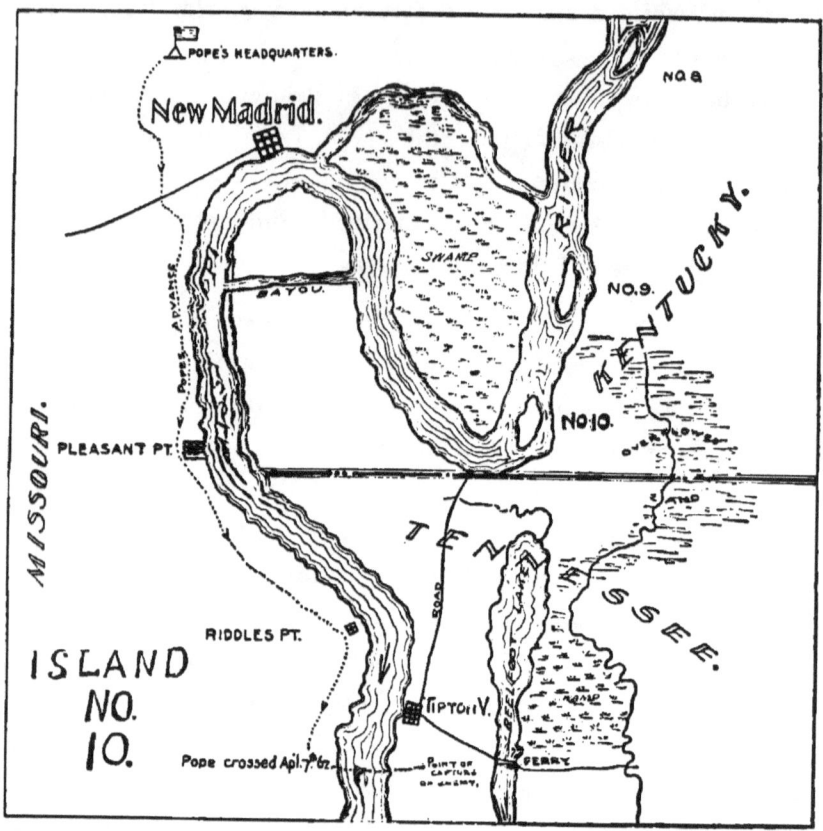

moved his troops to Island No. 10, leaving most of their equipage in camp.

About the time of the surrender of New Madrid, Commodore Foote left Cairo with a fleet of seven ironclads and other boats for the purpose of aiding Gen. Pope in his attack on Island

No. 10. Commodore Foote bombarded the Confederate works many days without any damage to them. Gen. Pope wished to approach the enemy from the unprotected south. He could not take his troops across the river, as his boats were all above the island. He conceived the plan of digging a canal across the loop of the river, so as to be able to take his transports below the enemy's batteries and convey his troops across to the Kentucky side. The canal was dug through James bayou, a swampy peninsula formed by the bend of the river. It was twelve miles long and fifty feet wide. About ten miles was through a timber district, much of which had to be sawed under the surface of the water. The remarkable feat was accomplished in nineteen days.

The transports passed through the canal to a point below the island, while two of Foote's ironclads ran past the batteries. Pope's troops crossed the river, took Tiptonville, and closed the only avenue of escape for the beleaguered troops, as the swampy and flooded lands to the east precluded retreat in that direction. Entirely cut off from retreat or succor, the whole Confederate force on the mainland and on the island, 7,000 in number, surrendered April 7th,—the day on which the battle of Shiloh was fought.

Island No. 10 has since disappeared. The water, constantly wearing at the upper end, has little by little swept it entirely away.

SURRENDER OF NEW ORLEANS, APRIL 29, 1862.—The attempt to open the Mississippi was not confined to the operations from the north. Early in the year 1862, a combined land and naval force was prepared to move against New Orleans from the south. For this purpose forces were congregated at Ship Island, which is located in the Gulf of Mexico, about 100 miles north and east of the mouth of the Mississippi river. Commodore David Farragut was chosen to command the fleet, and General Benjamin F. Butler was placed in charge of the land forces.

New Orleans was the largest Southern city, with a population at the outbreak of the war of 170,000. It possessed the greatest export trade, prior to the war, of any city in the world. It contained the resources of modern warfare, having workshops where machinery of the most powerful kind could be built, and having artisans capable of building ships, casting guns, and making small arms. Its people were as hostile to the United States as any in the South. The city is one hundred miles above the mouth of the Mississippi. Fort Jackson on the west side, and Fort St. Philip on the east side of the river, guarded the approaches to the city.

Immense wealth in coin and produce was furnished in great abundance by New Orleans to support the military operations directed from Richmond. Regiment after regiment had been raised and equipped here, and dispatched to meet the pressing exigencies on the Potomac, the Tennessee, and the upper Mississippi. When the hour of peril came to New Orleans, only a small military force, poorly drilled, remained to defend the city.

Gen. Mansfield Lovell was in command of the Confederate forces stationed here. He exhausted every energy to defend and

protect the city. Forts St. Philip and Jackson were strengthened, and all the land approaches to the city were fortified and
guarded.

The river was obstructed by strongly braced piles and green
live-oaks. A strong chain was extended across the river within
range of the guns of the forts. It was supported by eight dis-
mantled vessels and a large raft. Fire-rafts were prepared, to
drift toward the Union fleet and ignite the vessels.

Farragut with his powerful fleet of 47 vessels, carrying the
land forces of 14,000 under Butler, steamed up the river. The
mortars and gunboats approached within range of the forts and
opened fire upon them. For six days and nights the mortars
kept up an unremitting fire, mainly upon Fort Jackson; 16,800
shells were thrown without much effect upon the enemy's defenses. Finally, Farragut determined to run past the forts.
Captain Bell was sent on the night of the 20th of April with
two gunboats on the dangerous mission of making an opening in
the chain obstruction, for the passage of the fleet. The whole
fire of Fort Jackson was concentrated upon them, but the cable
was successfully separated near the left bank, and a sufficiently
large opening made to admit the passage of the fleet, which was
waiting below. At 3:30 in the morning of April 24, the bold
attempt to pass the forts was begun. On they steamed, in the
face of a terrific fire from the forts, past the chain, through
sunken hulks, amid burning rafts, encountering the Confederate
fleet of fifteen vessels, two of which were ironclads. The fleet
kept up a continuous rain of shot and shell upon the forts as it

passed by them. It captured or destroyed every Confederate vessel, and accomplished the mission for which it set out with the loss of but a single vessel. Thus was achieved a feat in naval warfare which had no precedent, and which is still without a parallel except the one furnished by Farragut himself at Mobile, two years later, and the one furnished by Dewey at Manila, which, though not entirely similar, was in some respects more remarkable in results.

Commodore Porter, who kept up the mortar-fire while Farragut was forcing his way up the stream, says:

"No grander or more beautiful sight could have been realized than the scenes of that night. From silence, disturbed now and then by the slow fire of the mortars,—the phantom-like movement of the vessels giving no sound,—an increased roar of heavy guns began, while the mortars burst forth in rapid bombardment, as the fleet drew near the enemy's works. Vessel after vessel added her guns to those already at work, until the very earth seemed to shake from the reverberations. A burning raft added its lurid glare to the scene, and the fiery attacks of the mortar-shells, as they passed through the darkness aloft, and sometimes bursting in midair, gave the impression that heaven itself had joined in the general strife. The succeeding silence was almost as sudden. From the weighing of the anchors, one hour and ten minutes saw the vessels by the forts, and Farragut on his way to New Orleans, the prize staked upon the fierce game of war just ended."

Gen. Lovell, who was in command at New Orleans, came down the river to observe events, and narrowly escaped capture. He hastened to the city and withdrew his soldiers on the evening of the 24th, leaving the town at the mercy of the Union fleet. When news reached New Orleans that the Confederate flotilla had been destroyed and the triumphant fleet was approaching the city, a strange scene followed. Hopeless panic seized the good people of the city, and ruffians, cut-throats and thugs went about pillaging houses, shops, and stores. Public materials were heaped in the streets and burned. Twelve thousand bales of cotton were consumed by the flames. The mob swayed back and forth in the streets, hooting, yelling, cursing, and urging the people to resist the landing of the Federals.

Farragut appeared before New Orleans on the 25th of April, and demanded the surrender of the city. The mayor was power-less to control the mob, and could not surrender the city while the people were swayed by their passions. But on the 29th the militia landed and took possession of the public buildings. The forts had surrendered the day before. Gen. Butler had worked his way through bayous and bays in the rear of Fort St. Philip, landing his men from row-boats on the first firm ground reached. Realizing the uselessness of protracting the contest, the enemy surrendered the forts to Captain Porter. Gen. Butler took military command of New Orleans, and in-augurated stringent methods for cleansing and pacifying the unclean and turbulent city. Almost one-half of the population of the city were of foreign birth. A large number of the poorer element belonged to a dangerous and desperate class. Severity alone would answer in controlling them. Wm. B. Mumford was hanged for tearing down the National flag which was raised over the mint by one of Farragut's officers. This event had a healthful effect upon the turbulent and lawless.

The total loss to the Union forces in achieving the brilliant victory at New Orleans was 40 killed and 177 wounded.

BATON ROUGE, NATCHEZ, AND THE FIRST ATTACK ON VICKS-
BURG, 1862.—After New Orleans had been secured and handed
over to Gen. Butler, Farragut pushed up the Mississippi, taking
Baton Rouge, Natchez, and every town of any importance as
far as Vicksburg. On June 28th a general attack was made
upon this city. Farragut succeeded in running the batteries
with two frigates and six gunboats, and bombarded the enemy's
works from above; but little or no effect was produced upon
them. The bombardment was continued at intervals, while
General Williams was attempting to cut a canal across the
isthmus formed by the bend of the river, and while an applica-
tion to Gen. Halleck at Corinth was pending, for a corps of his
army to aid the fleet. The work of the canal, the first of three
attempts, proved unsuccessful, and no troops were sent to aid
Farragut. The siege of Vicksburg was abandoned by order
from Washington, and Farragut dropped down the river with
the greater part of his fleet. Gen. Williams with his soldiers
returned to Baton Rouge in time to repulse an attack made upon
that place, August 5th, by the Confederates under Gen. J. C.
Breckinridge.

FORT PILLOW EVACUATED, MAY 10.—Not long after the
brilliant victory of Commodore Farragut before New Orleans,
a Federal fleet under Com. H. C. Davis prepared to attack Fort
Pillow, located on the Mississippi in the vicinity of Memphis.
But on the approach of the fleet, the enemy evacuated the place,
May 10th.

MEMPHIS TAKEN, JUNE 6, 1862.—Commodore Davis proceeded with his fleet toward Memphis. A formidable Confederate flotilla awaited his approach, commanded by Commodore Montgomery. The fleets met at half-past five in the morning, when the engagement began. The inhabitants swarmed in multitudes upon the bluff, levee, and house-roofs, to witness the battle. Disaster came thickly upon the vessels of the enemy. Their entire fleet was either captured or destroyed in an hour and a half after the beginning of the engagement, with the exception of the flagship Van Dorn, whose superior speed enabled her to escape. The enemy's loss was heavy—nearly 100 men killed and wounded; while Col. Ellet, jr., commander of the Union rams, was the only man wounded on the Federal fleet. He died afterward from exhaustion and from the effect of the wound. The Queen of the West was the only Federal vessel severely injured.

Commodore Davis then took possession of the city, and the supremacy of the Federal Government was again established in one of the chief towns of Tennessee.

The ultimate effect of this victory was great. It assisted in effectively clearing the Mississippi from the presence of the powerful Confederate gunboats.

With the single exception of Vicksburg, every other stronghold of the foe had been taken. The conquest of Vicksburg alone was necessary to open the channel of the great highway of the West, and sever one of the leading arteries of the Confederacy.

SECOND MOVEMENT AGAINST VICKSBURG, DECEMBER, 1862.
Vicksburg, located on the Mississippi river about midway between its mouth and Cairo, was the natural center and chief
stronghold of the slaveholding States in the West after the fall

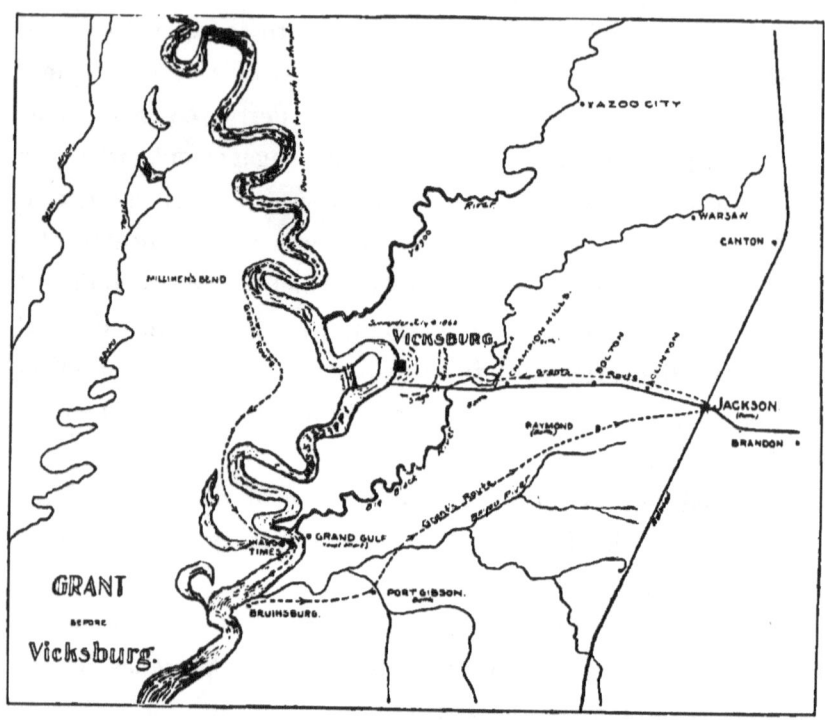

of New Orleans. Its natural strength and importance as commanding the navigation of the Mississippi river were early
appreciated: and it was so fortified and garrisoned as to make
the storming of the works a dangerous task and the capture of

it well-nigh impossible. The naval demonstration against Vicksburg after the victory at New Orleans, had proved a failure.

After Halleck was promoted and transferred to Washington,
Grant was put in command of the district of western Tennessee.
His command was extended Oct. 16, 1862, to include the State
of Mississippi. He had gradually driven the enemy southward
at Forts Henry and Donelson, Shiloh, Corinth, and Iuka. He
now commenced preparations for an active campaign against
Gen. John C. Pemberton in his front, with the hope of ultimately taking Vicksburg. Pemberton had established his headquarters at Jackson, Mississippi, while Van Dorn, second to him
in command, occupied the Confederate front at Holly Springs.
Grant moved his own headquarters from Jackson, Tenn., to Lagrange, and arranged with Rear Admiral Porter to convey Sherman's men from Memphis to Vicksburg. He himself moved
with nearly 60,000 men by way of the Mobile & Ohio Railroad.
He pushed through Grand Junction and Holly Springs to Oxford. While at the latter place preparing to move on Jackson
and Vicksburg, Van Dorn struck a damaging blow to Grant's
communications. Col. R. C. Murphy was left in command of
Holly Springs, which had been the temporary depot of arms,
munitions and provisions for the Union army. He ignomin-
iously surrendered the place and men under his command Dec.
20, 1862, to a band of Confederate raiders, while other places
with a less number of men in garrison valiantly repelled the
invaders. Grant had dispatched 4,000 men by rail for the relief of Holly Springs, but they arrived only a few hours after

the enemy had departed. Col. Murphy was dismissed from service in a stinging order by Gen. Grant.

Thus by the cowardice or perversity of one man, were not only 2,000 men surrendered, and several million dollars' worth of property sacrificed, but the fair promise of an important expedition was blighted. By the loss of his stores Grant was completely paralyzed. He decided to fall back to Grand Junction, to move westward to Memphis, and to descend by the river to Vicksburg. A courier was at once sent to notify Sherman of this disaster.

The day after the Holly Springs surrender, Gen. Sherman had left Memphis with the right wing of the Army of the Tennessee, about 30,000 strong, and passed down the Mississippi, on transports, and twelve miles up the Yazoo. Debarking his men, he commenced an assault upon the defenses of Vicksburg from the north. Grant's recoil from Oxford was unknown to Sherman, as Grant's courier failed to reach his destination, and the Confederates under Gen. Pemberton, previously confronting Grant, now faced about and concentrated their energies in opposition to Sherman, who expected Grant to engage the attention of the main body. Expeditious as were Sherman's movements, all of the Confederate forces, with the exception of Van Dorn and his cavalry, were on hand to receive him.

Vicksburg is built on a range of bluffs whose average height is about 200 feet, and quite precipitous from Vicksburg to Haines Bluff, a distance of about thirteen or fourteen miles. Beyond the bluffs there is low ground of swamps and bayous,

the chief of which is Chickasaw Bayou. The enemy had constructed an abatis and dotted the swamps with rifle-pits. The
bluffs frowned with rifle-trenches and hostile batteries. Coming
from the north, Sherman was compelled to pass through the low
lands, and then ascend the abrupt bluffs, though at the time he
set out on the expedition he had not realized the seriousness of
the obstacles afforded by the character of the soil.

Sherman's army was uniquely Western. They were fighting
for a Western advantage, and entered into the campaign with
a grim determination to carry the approaches to Vicksburg.
Admiral Porter, in command of the Union fleet, gave prompt
and hearty coöperation to the land forces. The impediments
were too great to be overcome. An assault was made, in which
about 2,000 men were lost, including prisoners and wounded.
The news of Grant's failure to come overland, the consequent
concentration of about 40,000 Confederates to oppose his troops,
and the strong fortification of the enemy, induced Sherman to
abandon the undertaking for the time. He knew that any further attempt to capture the place would result in a useless and
disastrous loss of life. He accordingly embarked with his troops
Jan. 2, for Milliken's Bend. While on the point of leaving,
Gen. John A. McClernand, Sherman's senior, arrived and took
command. He acquiesced in Sherman's plans for the return
expedition, and at once began active measures for the reduction
of Fort Hindman, called also " The Post of Arkansas," fifty
miles from the Mississippi, where a French settlement had been
made in 1685. After a gallant defense, the fort fell into the

hands of Gen. McClernand. The 5,000 prisoners were sent to St. Louis, and the Union forces, pursuant to the order of Gen. Grant, returned to Milliken's Bend.

THIRD AND FINAL MOVEMENT AGAINST VICKSBURG, 1863.— Gen. Grant, having reorganized and refitted his army at Memphis, descended the river with his troops in transports to Young's Point, nine miles above Vicksburg. Here was the head of the canal project commenced and abandoned some months before by Gen. Williams. Gen. Grant concluded to complete the canal. By means of this he expected to isolate Vicksburg, and take his transports down below the city to convey his men across the river. A large number of men were employed at this work. The heavy rains flooded the district, making work at the canal impossible, and induced Grant permanently to abandon the undertaking. He had also attempted to flank the Confederates by passing with his transports through a network of bayous, lakes, and connecting streams to a point below Vicksburg; but he found the impediments too great to accomplish this.

The character of the Confederate defense and the nature of the country convinced Gen. Grant that Vicksburg could not be successfully assailed from above unless he had full control of the Yazoo river, for which he had persistently but vainly struggled. He now decided on an entirely new line of operations. In pursuance with this plan he recalled the various expeditions looking to the control of the Yazoo valley. He set out from Milliken's Bend, marched down on the west side of the river to a point below Vicksburg, intending to cross the river in transports, and assail the enemy from the east, instead of from the west as he had intended to do. In the meantime Commodore Porter, at the suggestion of Gen. Grant, had made preparations to run the Vicksburg batteries with his ironclads and transports. The ironclads passed without harm, but of the nine transports attempting to pass the batteries, one was set on fire and burned to the water's edge, one was disabled and sunk, while the rest passed with comparatively little damage.

GRIERSON'S CAVALRY RAID.—Grant determined to retaliate for the destructive cavalry raids of Morgan, Forrest, and Van Dorn. Col. B. H. Grierson, starting from Lagrange, Tenn., with a brigade of 1,700 cavalry, swept rapidly southward through Mississippi and Louisiana, and entered Baton Rouge in sixteen days, after having traveled 600 miles, destroyed much property, and captured and paroled some prisoners.

GRANT'S MOVEMENT UPON VICKSBURG FROM THE SOUTH. APRIL TO JULY, 1863.—On the 29th of April Grant directed a naval attack upon *Grand Gulf,* which was gallantly made by Admiral Porter with his gunboat fleet. But as no decided advantage could be gained, owing to the elevated position of the Confederate batteries, the attack was soon abandoned. Learning that there was a good road leading from Bruinsburg to Port Gibson in the rear of Grand Gulf, Grant placed his men on transports and crossed the river at Bruinsburg. His army had marched seventy miles on the west side of the river, over muddy roads, scarcely above the river-line. Grant crossed the river

—7

with 10,000 men, April 30th. They did not carry a tent or take a wagon. It has been said that Grant's only baggage was a tooth-brush. Other divisions followed soon after. On the 3d of May they left the river. They did not march directly on Vicksburg, but pushed inland to cut off communications with the city.

Gen. J. E. Johnston was in supreme command of all Con-federate forces west of the Alleghanies. He had been at Chat-tanooga, but came to the relief of Pemberton when his situation became critical. Pemberton's troops, about 50,000 in all, were stationed from Haines Bluff on the north to Grand Gulf on the south, and to Jackson and Granada on the east. As Grant advanced toward *Port Gibson,* the enemy was encoun-tered and defeated May 1st in quite a severe battle. Grand Gulf fell as a result of this engagement.

Sherman, who was conducting a feint against the enemy's works in the north, was ordered to join Grant's forces, while Grant changed his base of supplies from Bruinsburg to Grand Gulf. Grant then continued his march toward Jackson, en-countering no obstacles until near *Raymond,* where he met and defeated two of the enemy's brigades (May 12th). At *Jackson* the Confederates were again defeated (May 14th), and driven from the city.

The Confederate main body, numbering 25,000 men, under Gen. Pemberton, marched out from Vicksburg to meet Grant's invading army. At *Champion Hills* they were defeated with considerable loss, May 16th, and retreated toward the works of Vicksburg, pursued by the Union troops. Making a stand near

the *Big Black river,* the Confederates again met with defeat
(May 17th), and then fell back to the friendly shelter within
the fortifications of Vicksburg.

- An immediate assault on the land defenses of Vicksburg was
determined upon by Grant, who apprehended an attack on his
rear by Johnston, strongly reinforced from Bragg's army.
Accordingly, a general assault was made on the afternoon of
May 19th, which resulted in no advantage to the Union troops.
The next two days were devoted to bringing up and distributing
provisions and to a preparation for a more determined attack.
The assault upon the well-fortified defenses of the Confederates
was made with great spirit, but resulted in the decimation of
the ranks as they advanced. The troops were finally recalled
from the advanced and imperiled positions which they had
taken, and settled down to the siege of the Confederate stronghold. The Union loss was about 3,000 killed and wounded in
this wasteful assault.

SIEGE OF VICKSBURG, AND SURRENDER ON JULY 4, 1863.—
Vicksburg was now completely invested. Porter's gunboats
prevented escape by water, or succor from the Louisiana side.
And Grant, keeping a sharp lookout for Johnston in the rear,
commenced digging his way into Vicksburg from the east, with
a force not much superior in number to that which he had beaten
at Champion Hills and the Big Black. Pemberton was notably
short of both provisions and ammunition; 6,000 of his men were
in the hospital, sick or wounded; his hopes of relief were slender.
Grant's men were in good spirits, and, since the day of the un-

lucky assault, he had received reinforcements. Mines were sprung under Confederate forts, and breastworks thrown up in advance of the Union army as it gradually worked its way toward Vicksburg. But while the troops were digging mines from without, famine silently at work within the Confederate ranks was more persuasive than bullet-shot or saber-cut.

Finally, after forty-five days of siege, Pemberton, hopeless of relief, and at the end of his resources, hung out the white flag, and surrendered his army and the city on the 4th of July.

As a result of this campaign in and about Vicksburg the enemy lost about 10,000 men killed and wounded, and 37,000 prisoners, which includes those taken before the siege.

Gen. Grant reports his losses in this memorable campaign, from the day he landed at Bruinsburg until that of the surrender, at 945 killed, 7,095 wounded, and 537 missing.

This was by far the most disastrous blow to the Confederacy that had yet been given. No other campaign of the war exceeds this in brilliancy of conception and in successful prosecution.

Gen. Johnston had been using every exertion to raise an army strong enough to fall upon the rear of Grant's army and raise the siege of Vicksburg. Gen. Sherman was sent with a force to hold Johnston in check. Not being able to meet Gen. Sherman in a pitched battle, Johnston began operating down along the Big Black river, with the probable intention of forming a junction with Pemberton, and of cutting a way out for him. But before this could be attempted, Pemberton surrendered his famished army. Gen. Johnston, hearing of the surrender of the

Confederate army, marched eastward, pursued by Sherman, to Jackson, where a small engagement occurred. During the night he hurried across the Pearl river, and continued his retreat through Brandon to Morton.

On June 6th a force of Confederates from Arkansas made an unsuccessful attempt to take Milliken's Bend. Just prior to the fall of Port Hudson, Confederate General Holmes with 9,000 men tried to take Helena, held by General Prentiss with a force less than one-half as large as that of his assailant, but failed.

Sherman pursued Johnston's army as far as Brandon, but realizing that the enemy had escaped, he returned to his old position about Vicksburg. Thus ended one of the greatest, and in many respects most important campaigns of the Civil War.

SURRENDER OF PORT HUDSON, JULY 8, 1863.—General Nathaniel P. Banks assumed command of the department of the Gulf, Dec. 11, 1862, with a force of 30,000; but he sent detail after detail until his available troops to operate against Port Hudson was only 14,000. He was expected to coöperate with Gen. Grant in his efforts to open the Mississippi and expel the Confederates bearing arms in Louisiana and Texas. Gen. Gardner was in command of Port Hudson, with a force equal to that under Banks. He was well fortified. Two spirited attacks were made upon the Confederate defenses, on May 27th and June 14th. Banks, having gained no permanent advantage, settled down to the employment of the same methods for the reduction of the place as Grant was using at Vicksburg, namely, digging his way to the breastworks of the enemy, and reducing the efficient defense by cutting off all supplies and succor.

About 2,500 of the enemy's cavalry were in the rear of Gen. Banks's army. Gen. Jos. E. Johnston, at Jackson, was in danger of swooping down at any moment. Fresh reinforcements from Alabama and Georgia sufficient to raise the siege might be expected. Gen. R. E. Lee, so recently victorious at Chancellorsville, might send a relief corps by rail to Gardner. In vain the garrison looked for reinforcements. The ammunition for small arms was gradually expended, until but twenty rounds per man remained; and but little more for the artillery. The meat gave out, and mules were killed and served as food. Rats were cooked and eaten, and pronounced as good as squirrels. Considering the enervated condition of the troops, the enemy made a gallant defense. Suddenly, on July 6th, the Union batteries shook the heavens with tremendous salutes, while cheer after cheer from behind the works, and from the gunboats, rolled to the hills, reverberating the good tidings that Vicksburg had surrendered. The news of this disaster to the Confederacy made it folly to resist any longer. Gen. Gardner accordingly opened negotiations with Banks, and under the terms of capitulation the garrison became prisoners of war July 9th. The Union troops took possession of the city. The loss to Banks's army in this campaign of forty days was about 3,000 men. The number of prisoners taken at the Port was 6,408, but the number captured in the whole campaign was 10,584 men, besides many guns, arms, etc.

Gen. Banks, after his victory at Port Hudson, led an expedition of 6,000 into Texas by way of the Rio Grande. After taking Brownsville and Point Isabel, and leaving Gen. Dana in command at the former place, he returned to New Orleans.

With the fall of Vicksburg and Port Hudson came the undisputed navigation of the Mississippi. Only local and partisan hostilities were conducted on it after this. One of the objective points of the war was accomplished. The great river remained open to the close of the war, in undisputed possession of National authority.

CHAPTER VIII.

BRAGG'S INVASION OF KENTUCKY.

MOVEMENT TO CHATTANOOGA, 1862.—The Confederate veterans that had confronted Grant at Shiloh and Corinth retreated to Tupelo. After the fall of these places the enemy's efforts were directed to the defense of two strongholds—Chattanooga on the east, and Vicksburg on the west. The events of the struggle for possession of the latter place have already been given. Gen. Braxton Bragg, now in command of the Confederate armies west of the mountains, abandoned his position at Tupelo, and moved his troops via the Mobile railroad to Chattanooga. His army had been increased by conscription to 45,000 men, and was organized in three corps, under Hardee, Bishop Polk, and Kirby Smith, respectively. Gen. Buell left Corinth on the 10th of June for Chattanooga by way of the Memphis & Charleston Railroad, which had been destroyed by the enemy. The rebuilding of the road under instructions from Gen. Halleck consumed much time. The Confederates profited by this delay, and on the 29th of July they entered Chattanooga before the arrival of the Union army, and established headquarters there.

INVASION OF KENTUCKY, 1862–63.—The Confederates conceived the bold plan of carrying the war farther north. McClellan's campaign before Richmond had proved a failure, and led to the invasion of Maryland by Lee. Simultaneous with Lee's movement north, Bragg started on his invasion of Kentucky. He had been assured that many Kentuckians were awaiting an opportunity to join the Southern cause. He expected a general uprising in favor of the Confederacy to attend his march north, and hoped finally to recover Tennessee and west Kentucky from National authority.

Louisville with its immense resources was the immediate object of his gigantic raid, though Cincinnati was thought also to be within his purview. Buell supposed that Bragg would endeavor to get possession of Nashville. To avoid this, Buell concentrated the bulk of his forces at Murfreesboro. While he was doing this, Bragg stole a march on him, and set out for Louisville.

GEN. KIRBY SMITH AT RICHMOND, KY., AUGUST 29, 1862.— As Grant was conducting his magnificent campaign in the West, driving the enemy farther and farther south, portions of Kentucky and Tennessee became exposed to the Confederate raiders,—Morgan, Forrest, and other chieftains who overran the State. Gen. Kirby Smith, who played an important part in the Battle of Bull Run, uniting these bands, marched forward from Knoxville as the advance guard of Bragg's army. Passing through Big Creek Gap of the Cumberland mountains, he pushed rapidly northward through London to Richmond, Ky. Here he encountered, August 16, 1862, a Union force under Gen. Nelson. In the battle which followed, the Federal troops were badly defeated, with a loss of several thousand prisoners.

Nelson himself was killed. After his success at Richmond, Smith found little opposition at Lexington, Frankfort, Paris, and Cynthiana. He was within one day's march of Cincinnati, whose citizens, under the direction of Gen. Lew Wallace, were making vigorous efforts to receive him, when he again fell back to Frankfort and Lexington to effect a junction with Bragg.

BUELL'S MARCH TO LOUISVILLE, SEPTEMBER, 1862.—When Buell discovered that the true object of the Confederates was Louisville, and not Nashville, as their first movements seemed to indicate, he set out on a great race for that place. He left a garrison at Nashville, and by forced marches he succeeded in reaching Louisville, Sept. 25th,—about one day in advance of his competitor, who had been delayed on account of a burnt bridge at Bardstown. At Louisville Buell received large reinforcements. Most were in the shape of raw troops, but some were veterans sent up the Mississippi and Ohio from Grant's army. His forces had thus been augmented, until they numbered 100,000 men.

BATTLE OF PERRYVILLE, OCT. 8, 1862.—Buell had failed to gain possession of Chattanooga, and permitted Bragg to invade the State of Kentucky. His delays were very distasteful to the authorities at Washington. Orders were issued in the latter part of September relieving him of the command of the army. Thomas was appointed to succeed him. But this able and magnanimous soldier pleaded earnestly for the retention of Buell, with the effect that the order was suspended and Buell retained.

Campaigns of
BUELL & BRAGG
Route of Union Army shown in Red.
" " Bragg's . " — ▸ —
" " Smith " " ⟶
at Harrodsburg where they united
with Bragg

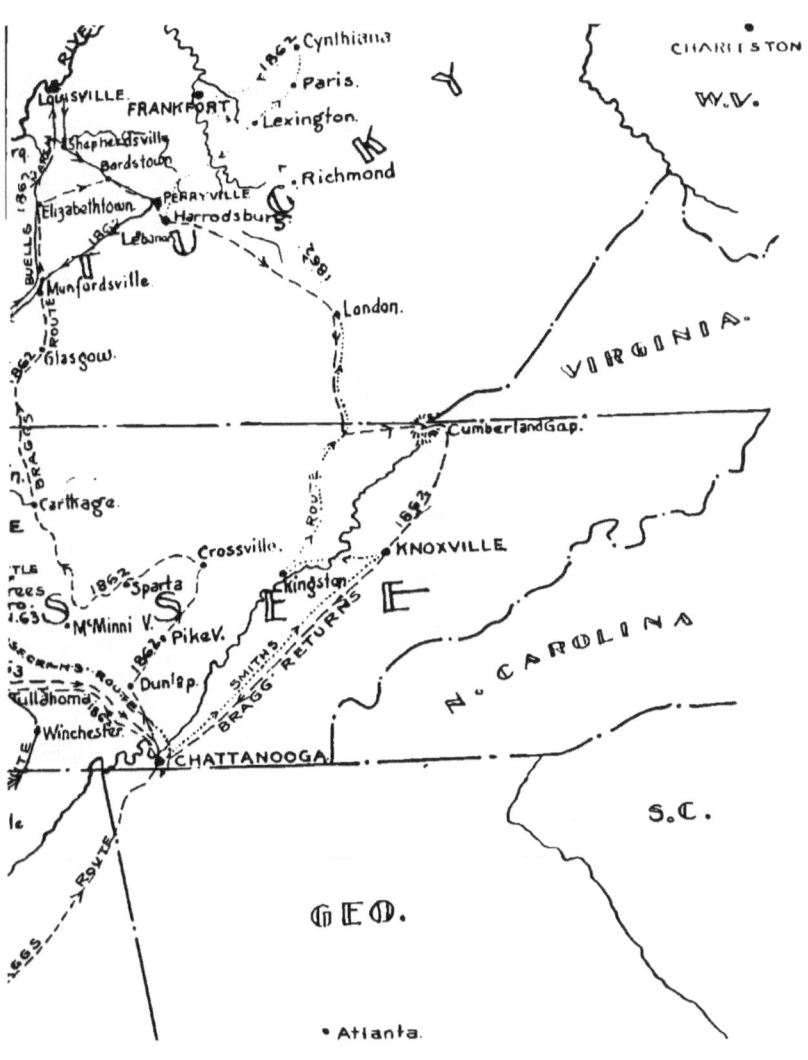

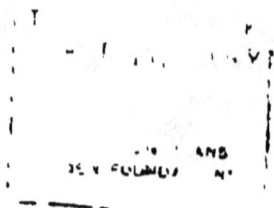

This reminder of the desires of the Federal authorities awakened Buell to a determination to meet the enemy. He accordingly set out to find his opponent.

Gen. Bragg in his march north passed through Pineville, Carthage, Glasgow, and Munfordsville, to Bardstown. Leaving Bishop Polk temporarily in command of the troops, Bragg went to Frankfort, which had been occupied by Smith's command, to witness the inauguration of Richard Hawes as Confederate Governor of the State. The booming of cannon announced the near presence of Union troops, and cut short the inaugural address of the pretended Governor, who was obliged to seek safety by a hasty departure. Buell moved forward to attack the enemy, now posted at Bardstown. Bragg commenced a slow retreat, and Buell came upon Hardee's division at Perryville. Polk soon joined Hardee and both fell heavily upon McCook's division of Buell's army. The battle continued during the day of October 8th, with great severity. But during the night the enemy decamped, and retreated to Harrodsburg, where they were joined by Kirby Smith. The Union loss in this battle in killed, wounded and missing was about 3,300, while the Confederate loss was about 2,500.

The Federal army did not pursue the retreating army at once. The battle was little better than a drawn engagement. No decided advantage had been gained. Bragg had, of course, failed to reach Louisville, and now he was made to retreat southward, but in no great fear of disaster to his troops. His retreat was conducted through Cumberland Gap, and ended at Chattanooga.

He succeeded in carrying off hundreds of wagon-loads of provisions, clothing, and other necessaries for the army. He drove with him thousands of beeves, horses, and mules, and carried away an immense amount of groceries and domestic goods gathered from the stores of Lexington, Frankfort, Danville, and other places.

In consequence of Buell's slow pursuit, Bragg was permitted to conduct a safe retreat without having been attacked more than once in a period of five months. Gen. Halleck desired Buell to undertake a campaign in eastern Tennessee, still occupied by the enemy. Buell believed it utterly impossible to supply the army with food, at places remote from the railroad. The project was abandoned, and the Union troops again concentrated at Nashville.

The Federal Government, much displeased with the inactivity and dilatory movements of Buell, removed him from the command, Oct. 30th, 1862. Gen. Rosecrans, who had figured prominently at Corinth and Iuka, superseded him.

The result of the Kentucky campaign was no more satisfactory to the Confederate government than to the National authority. Both sides expected decisive results, and neither obtained them. Scarcely had Bragg reached Chattanooga, when he was ordered to move northward again. He moved his headquarters to Tullahoma, and then to Murfreesboro.

BATTLE OF MURFREESBORO, DECEMBER 31, JANUARY 2, 1863. Gen. Rosecrans on assuming command of the Army of the Ohio (hereafter to be known as the Army of the Cumberland) found it greatly demoralized by long marches and indecisive results. Of the 100,000 men on the muster-rolls, 26,482 were absent by authority. Most of these, but not nearly all, were sick or wounded and in the hospitals; 6,484 were absent without authority,—or in other words, had deserted. His effective force numbered about 65,000 men. His cavalry was inferior in number and efficiency to the troops of Forrest and Morgan, who rode around at will, stripping posts and supply trains. The two armies lay watching each other, the one at Nashville, the other at Murfreesboro. Rosecrans had given the impression that he would remain in winter quarters at Nashville. Bragg sent a strong cavalry detachment under Morgan and Forrest to work upon the supply trains and break the Union communications. Rosecrans was busily engaged in collecting a supply of food. Suddenly, on the 26th of December, he broke camp and moved forward. His march was commenced in the rain. The Confederates had celebrated Christmas with much gayety at Murfreesboro. Their outposts retreated before the Union advance. Their cavalry, supported by some militia, skirmished with the advancing patriots. The immediate object was the defeat of Bragg's army, and the ultimate object was to get possession of Chattanooga. The Union troops present on the eve of battle numbered 43,000 strong. The Confederate army was reported by Bragg as 38,000, though their number is placed as high as 62,000 by some authorities.

Gen. Bragg had placed his army along the bluffs of Stone river, near Murfreesboro. Here, on the last day of the year,

commenced one of the most sanguinary battles of the war—
called the battle of Murfreesboro, or Stone river.

Rosecrans' plan of battle was to throw his left under Crittenden across Stone river, and assail the Confederate right in
force while his own right should stand on the defensive. Cu-
riously enough, Bragg had planned precisely the same tactics.
He placed his right on the defensive, and sent his left to crush
the Union right. Under such circumstances the army moving
first on a vigorous attack upon the opposing forces would carry
the day. While Rosecrans' left was crossing the river to open
battle, his right was furiously assailed, and so unexpectedly
that two batteries were taken before a gun could be fired. The
Confederate success was decisive. The onslaught paralyzed
Rosecrans' aggressive movement. He had to withdraw his left
for the purpose of saving his right. The Union troops were
driven back. Rosecrans re-formed his lines. His artillery was
posted on a knoll surrounded by a plain. Against this new line
the Confederates dashed themselves desperately but vainly.
Four times the hitherto victorious army was hurled back with
great loss. But the result of the first day's conflict was, on the
whole, decidedly in favor of the Confederates. They had taken
one-half of the ground on which the Union army had encamped
in the morning, and had seized twenty-eight of the Union large
guns. The enemy's cavalry had committed much havoc upon
Rosecrans' baggage and supply trains, and the Union army had
lost heavily in killed and wounded.

Many a general would have calculated at the close of the day

how best to get back to Nashville. Gen. Rosecrans, however,
took stock of his ammunition, and found that he had sufficient
left for another battle. The assault of the enemy upon the
position to which Rosecrans' army had retreated in the afternoon, had demonstrated his ability to hold his ground here.
Giving orders to issue all the ammunition, and marshalling his
troops for every advantage, he lay down with his army to await
the arrival of New Year's Day. He had expected to keep the
holiday quietly unless Bragg should desire to renew the
conflict. Both armies maintained their respective positions
throughout the day, with only an occasional artillery duel or a
random skirmish encounter.

On Jan. 2d the Confederates opened fire with great vehemence from batteries which they had planted before the Union
center and left. At first their strength was overwhelming, but
reinforcements being thrown upon them, they were hurled
back in disorder, with heavy loss in killed, wounded and prisoners. Darkness had now set in, which prevented Rosecrans
pressing the advantage he had gained. A pouring rain next day
softened the earth, and impeded the movements of the artillery.
Gen. Bragg however concluded to leave, and commenced the
movement as stealthily as possible, near midnight. He gathered up his men and guns so cautiously that even the Federal
pickets knew nothing of his movements until daylight next
morning, Sunday, the 4th.

The manner in which the operations upon the rear of the
Union army were resisted reflected little credit on the skill and

energy of those who commanded. About two thousand prisoners, mostly stragglers and fugitives, were taken by the Confederates, and a large amount of baggage and army trains was taken or destroyed, which no doubt greatly impaired Rosecrans' ability to pursue successfully the retreating foe.

Rosecrans made no movement in pursuit of the Confederates until the next day. In his official report he says: " We learned that the enemy's infantry had reached Shelbyville by 12 M. on Sunday; but owing to the impracticability of bringing up supplies, and the loss of 557 artillery horses, pursuit was deemed inadvisable."

Rosecrans reported his losses at 1,533 killed, wounded 7,000, and 3,000 prisoners. Bragg reported his losses at 10,000, of whom 9,000 were killed and wounded. The Union losses were some greater than those of the Confederates, but the great disaster of the first day was turned into a dearly purchased victory the second, by the gallantry, obstinacy and heroism of Rosecrans and his men.

Among those who figured prominently in the Union army were Gen. McCook, in command of the Union right division; Gen. Thomas, in command of the center; and Gen. Crittenden, in command of the left.

Bragg retreated to Shelbyville and Tullahoma. Rosecrans remained inactive at Murfreesboro until late in the summer of 1863.

MORGAN'S RAID INTO INDIANA AND OHIO, 1862.—While Gen. Rosecrans at Murfreesboro was accumulating wagons, muni-

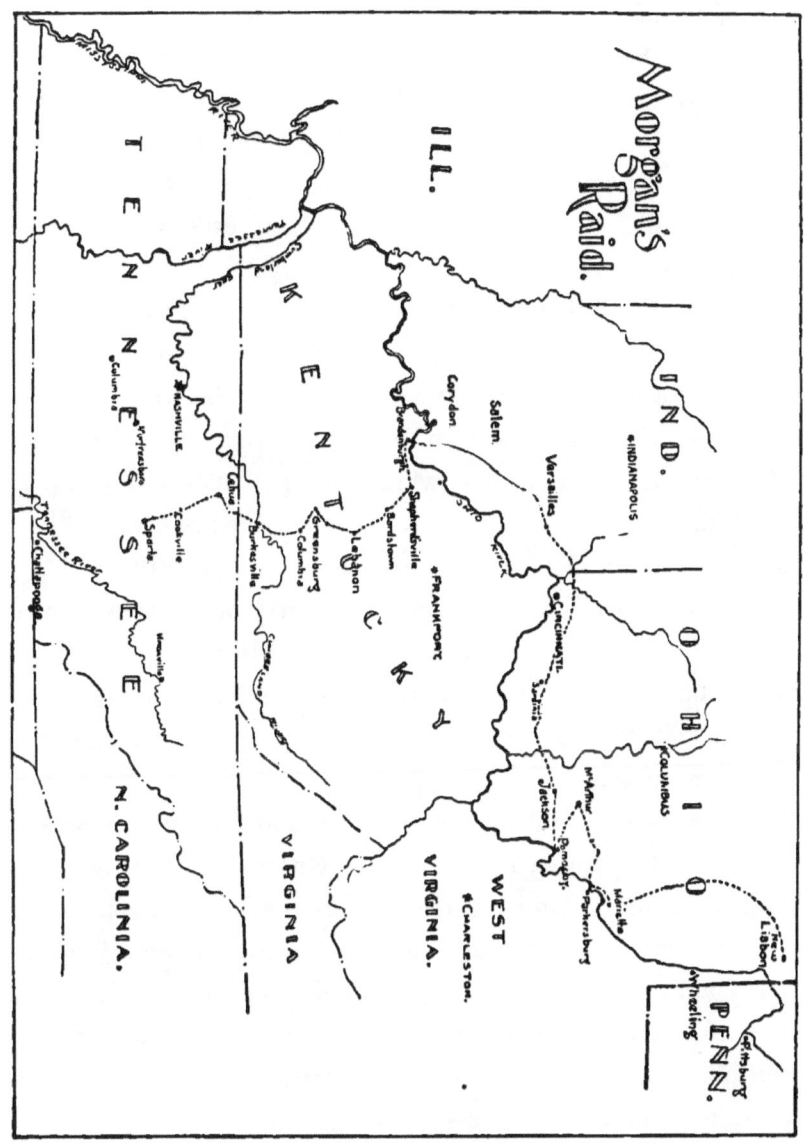

tions and supplies for an advance against Gen. Bragg's army confronting him at Shelbyville, the noted and generally successful cavalry leader, Gen. John H. Morgan, was preparing for a more extended and daring cavalry raid than he had yet undertaken. Setting out from Sparta, east and a little north of Murfreesboro, June 27, 1862, Morgan crossed the Cumberland river at Burkesville with a force of 2,028 effectives, and four guns. Columbia was partially sacked by his subordinates, contrary to orders. Col. Moore, hastily intrenching himself with a force of 200 men, by constructing an abatis, at Green river, valiantly repelled the invaders on the "glorious Fourth."

After attacking Lebanon, which was gallantly defended by Col. Hanson with 400 men until the town was fired, compelling him to surrender, Gen. Morgan moved to Shepardsville.

He struck the Ohio at Brandenburg, forty miles below Louisville, and, seizing three steamboats, crossed to the Indiana side. During his progress through Kentucky he had increased his command, by the addition of Kentucky sympathizers, to 4,000 troops and ten guns.

Morgan sped inland through Corydon and Palmyra to Salem, Ind., where he captured 350 " Home Guards." Passing on in zigzag lines in an easterly direction through Vienna, tearing up railroads, cutting telegraphs, burning factories, and inciting dismay among the inhabitants, he passed Versailles, Harrison, and within seven miles of Cincinnati; then by Williamsburg, Sardinia, Piketon, and Jackson. He struck the Ohio at Buffington Island, not far below Parkersburg, whence he expected an easy escape through the poor and thinly settled region of West Virginia and eastern Kentucky, to the more congenial shades of southwestern Virginia. His troops levied on granaries, barns and kitchens as they marched, but the pursuit was so warm at times along the route that they found comparatively little time for predatory mischief.

There had been some skirmishes from day to day, but the raiders were too strong for any force that could be assembled on the instant, while their route could not be foreseen; and their movements were too rapid for the pursuing forces, over roads on which bridges had been destroyed and obstacles cast to impede the progress of the pursuers.

Gen. Hobson, who had been following from the Cumberland river, arrived at Brandenburg just after the last boat which aided in conveying Morgan's troops across the Ohio had disappeared. He had foreseen that Morgan would again return to the Ohio, and sent at once to Louisville to have the river patrolled by gunboats. As soon as it became evident that he was making for Pomeroy or Gallipolis with intent to cross, the inhabitants felled trees across the roads, and imposed obstacles to impede the celerity of their progress.

The weary raiders struck the Ohio just at daylight, at a ford a little above Pomeroy. Preparations for crossing the river were hastily made, but a volley of musketry upon the advance companies attempting to cross, followed by the roar of cannon down the river from the gunboats, and supplemented by the appearance of three heavy columns of infantry at the bluffs and in the rear and on their right, put the fugitives to flight. They left their guns and wagons; dismounted men and the sick and wounded to the number of 600 were taken prisoners, while the rest took a precipitous flight up along the river in pursuit of an avenue of escape.

Passing up the river about fourteen miles to Belleville, Morgan and his remaining men had fairly begun, at 3 P. M., to swim their horses across (330 having gotten away), when Generals Hobson and Shackleford, in command of a division of pursuers, were again upon them. The gunboats also appeared, bringing several regiments to share in the hunt. As there was no hope in fighting, all that now remained (over 1,000), excepting Morgan and a few adherents who escaped, capitulated without further resistance.

Morgan, now stripped of his guns and wagons and miscellaneous plunder which he had collected, passed inland with the remnant of his force to McArthur, making a forlorn attempt to cross the Ohio at Marietta. They then passed to Eastport, thence to New Lisbon. Here they were driven to a high bluff and surrounded by the home guards and their pursuers, ever on their track.

Gen. Morgan and several of his officers were taken to Columbus, and confined in the penitentiary. Their heads were shaved, like those of ordinary felons, for which no reason has been assigned, nor does it appear by whom it was ordered,— certainly not by the Government. No labor was required of them, but they were confined in cells. Seven of them, including Morgan, dug their way out and escaped. Morgan and Captain Hines, after changing their clothes, proceeded at once to the depot, got on the train, which they knew would start at 1 A. M., and were carried by it very near Cincinnati, when they put on the brakes at the rear of the train, checking its speed, and jumped off and ran to the Ohio river. They were ferried across to Kentucky, and went at once to a house where shelter and refreshments awaited them.

Morgan made his way through Kentucky and Tennessee to northern Georgia, losing his companion by the way. Thence he went to Richmond, where he was received in great ovation, and again entered the Confederate service in east Tennessee, where he was killed the next year,—thus ending a daring and brilliant career which was directed against the perpetuity of the Union.

CHAPTER IX.

CHATTANOOGA.

CAMPAIGN AGAINST CHATTANOOGA, 1863.—Gen. Rosecrans remained in Murfreesboro until late in June. His supplies had been mainly drawn from Louisville, through a semi-hostile country, over a single railroad. It required a heavy guard at every depot, bridge, or trestle, to protect them from destruction by the enemy's raiders. His cavalry was no match, as had been proven by past experiences, for the Confederate horse, commanded by such vigorous and audacious partisans as Morgan, Forrest, and Wheeler. Though Rosecrans' best efforts were given to the strengthening of his cavalry, he could hardly obtain horses fast enough to replace those destroyed by the enemy or worn out by service.

Bragg had 18,000 infantry under Bishop Polk at Shelbyville, strongly intrenched and formidably fortified behind five miles of earthworks. Eighteen miles back of this, in a mountain region traversed by bad roads, was another intrenched camp, at Tullahoma. Hardee's corps of 12,000 was at Wartrace, to the right of Shelbyville. Besides these, Bragg had troops at Knoxville and Chattanooga. Perhaps 40,000 was the number he could concentrate upon the field of battle, while Rosecrans had not less than 60,000. If Bragg fell back, destroying railroads and bridges, he would be strengthened; while Rosecrans would be compelled to extend and protect his communications, and thus his available force for battle would be reduced.

Gen. Rosecrans began his advance on June 24th, and, in a series of brilliant flank movements, succeeded in dislodging the enemy from his intrenched camp at Tullahoma and Shelbyville; and in nine days, without any serious engagement, he had cleared middle Tennessee of the Confederate army, at a cost of barely 560 men. The Confederates lost as many killed and wounded, besides 1,634 prisoners who fell into the hands of the Union troops.

Bragg retreated toward Chattanooga, a Confederate strong-hold, the key to eastern Tennessee and northern Georgia. Having obtained a fair start while Rosecrans was preparing to fight, and having the use of a railroad whereon to transport his guns and supplies, Bragg easily made good his flight over the Cumberland mountains and across the Tennessee river at Bridgeport, where he destroyed the railroad bridge behind him.

Rosecrans was expected by the authorities at Washington to follow him sharply. Considerable delay occurred from the time he commenced his movement in pursuit of the fugitives until he appeared before Chattanooga. Bragg's devouring host had left in that rugged and sterile region no vestige of food for the Union army. To supply men and beasts with subsistence in that mountainous district was no easy task. After the railroad had been repaired to Stevenson, and the East Tennessee road to Bridgeport, and a considerable quantity of supplies accumulated at Stevenson, the army moved on toward Chattanooga. It

crossed the Tennessee river at Bridgeport and Shell Mound on
September 8th, and the several corps pushed forward across
high and steep mountains, to concentrate at Trenton, Ga., in the
valley of Lookout creek, which runs northeasterly into the Tennessee just below Chattanooga.

Gen. Bragg was in a quandary. He could hold Chattanooga
against an assault by Rosecrans' larger army, but if his communications should be cut off from his rear it would be only a
question of time when his army would be starved into capitulation. To *divide his forces,* or *to remain cooped up* in Chattanooga, were both suicidal. *To abandon Chattanooga* was to
evacuate the only remaining Confederate stronghold in Tennessee. He chose the latter, evacuated Chattanooga, and saved
his army,—what Pemberton attempted to do at Vicksburg when
it was too late. Bragg retired southward into Georgia, posting
his divisions along the highway from Gordon's Mill to Lafayette,
facing Pigeon Mountain, through whose passes the Union army
was expected to come from McLamore's Cave. Gen. Crittenden of Rosecrans' army took peaceful possession of Chattanooga,
and, stationing a garrison there, pursued the enemy up along
the East Chickamauga creek to Ringgold and Dalton. The rest
of the Union army should, according to plans, pass through Dug
Gap of Pigeon Mountain, and swoop down upon the enemy at
Lafayette.

CONCENTRATION OF CONFEDERATE TROOPS, SEPTEMBER,
1863.—While these preparations and movements were going on
in the Union camp, Bragg was silently collecting around La-

fayette the most numerous and effective army west of the Alleghanies, which had ever yet supported the Confederate cause. Gen. Buckner had been called from Knoxville, abandoning eastern Tennessee to Burnside; Johnston sent a strong division under Walker from the region of the Mississippi; and Lee, having satisfied himself that Richmond was in no danger from Meade, dispatched Longstreet's heavy corps of veteran troops from the Rapidan. All available troops that could be gleaned in Georgia were sent to the front. Rosecrans estimated Bragg's entire force as thus strengthened at 92,000—a great excess over his own forces. Making all allowance for incorrectness of estimates, there is scarcely any doubt that the Confederate force outnumbered the Federal.

Rosecrans, believing that the Confederates were on the retreat toward Rome, separated his divisions for the purpose of intercepting the retreat and of crushing the enemy between his columns,—the same tactics which proved fatal to Hooker's army at Chancellorsville.

Whatever may have been Bragg's intention before he received the reinforcement, he afterwards determined to meet his adversary in battle.

Rosecrans had not been informed, as he should have been, by Meade or Halleck at Washington, that a heavy corps had been sent from Lee's army, probably to reinforce Bragg. On the contrary, Gen. Halleck had informed Rosecrans that deserters had reported to him that a part of Bragg's army was reinforcing Lee.

BATTLE OF CHICKAMAUGA, SEPTEMBER 19 20, 1863.—Gen. Rosecrans by this time was aware that the situation had become serious, and began a concentration of his army, which numbered 55,000 strong, while the Confederate army now confronting his was estimated by the best authority at 70,000.

The battle opened on the morning of September 19th, by Gen. Bragg's attempt to gain possession of the road to Chattanooga, and it continued during the day. The Confederates had doubtless suffered a greater loss of men thus far and had gained no ground for which the Federal army contended. But the Union soldiers were clearly outnumbered; and now they felt it. Every brigade had been under heavy fire during the day, while the Confederates had several yet in reserve. Rosecrans had no reinforcements at hand, and could not expect any. Five Confederate brigades, fresh from Virginia, came up during the night, and were placed where the experience of the day showed they were most needed. Gen. Longstreet came up and took command of their right wing. He was himself worth a whole regiment. The two armies, equally brave, equally well disciplined, and equally well handled, but unequal in number, lay facing each other for the inevitable conflict on the morrow.

A fog having obstructed the operations of the armies, the conflict opened late next morning, Sunday, September 20th, and raged with great fury during that day. Though the gallant defenders of the Union made a valiant and persistent effort to drive off the foe, they were assailed with equal valor and fortitude, and finally driven from the field of action.

Rosecrans retreated to Chattanooga and intrenched his army behind the formidable fortifications. Gen. Bragg followed next day, taking quiet possession of Lookout Mountain and Missionary Ridge, whence he looked down into the coveted stronghold, never again destined to fall into Confederate hands.

Gen. Bragg has been assailed by the Confederates for not pursuing the Union army into Chattanooga on the evening of the 20th. But human endurance has a limit. His men had been marching their hardest and fighting their best for two days, with scarcely a pause. He had lost two-fifths of his army. Bragg in his official report tersely says: "The darkness of the night and the density of the forest rendered further movement uncertain and dangerous; and the army bivouacked on the ground it had so gallantly won."

Gen. Thomas did not retreat to Chattanooga, but stopped at Rossville with 25,000 men to intercept the advance of the enemy upon the former place. It seems as though Bragg might have improved his victory by dislodging the Union troops at Rossville, and by driving them into Chattanooga.

Gen. Longstreet, seeing the army in full retreat, urged Gen. Bragg to order a general advance in pursuit of their adversary, just as Gen. Pleasonton, after the battle of Gettysburg, had urged Gen. Meade to do,—and with the same effect.

The Federal losses in battle are officially stated at 16,351 in killed and wounded. Mr. Greeley in his "American Conflict" adds that it is perfectly safe to increase this number by stragglers and imperfect returns to 20,000. Bragg admits a loss of 18,000, of whom 16,000 must have been killed and wounded.

Gen. Bragg had won an unmistakable victory, but its fruits had ended with the battle-field. His arms had triumphed, but he had lost the strategic point of the campaign,—the possession of Chattanooga. When he advanced in force and appeared before the Federal fortifications, not even the fiercest fire-eater was ready to storm the defense behind which Rosecrans stood, ready to repeat the lesson he gave Price and Van Dorn at Corinth.

Bragg could not carry the coveted stronghold by storm. He was urged to move across the Tennessee and advance to Nashville.. He perceived the folly and probable ruin of his army in this. His recent reinforcements, constituting half his army, had come by rail, without wagon or horse. One-third of his artillery horses had been lost on the field of battle. A formidable river had to be crossed without pontoons, railroads had been destroyed, and the offensive movement was pregnant with difficulties sufficient to bring apparent ruin to the army.

On the other hand, with the Union army in Chattanooga too weak in its present state to meet him in open battle, he commanded the undisputed navigation of the river, and controlled all the railroads radiating from that city. Union supplies had to be brought in wagons over mountain roads of inconceivable badness. Forage and food were very scarce, and for a time the troops were put on short allowance, while thousands of horses starved, or were worked to death in wagoning supplies over the mountains. So Bragg settled down to the siege of Chattanooga, expecting to starve the Union army into capitulation.

While Rosecrans was cooped up in Chattanooga, he received, October 19, an order relieving him of the command of the army. Gen. George H. Thomas succeeded him.

EXPEDITION FOR THE RELIEF OF EASTERN TENNESSEE, SUMMER OF 1863.—Burnside, who had been relieved of the command of the Army of the Potomac and placed at the head of the Department of the Ohio, proceeded through Kentucky for the liberation of the crushed and suffering loyal people of eastern Tennessee. In July and August he collected an army of 20,000 men at Camp Nelson, near Richmond, Ky., and commenced his march on Knoxville, at the same time that Rosecrans moved on Chattanooga. He met with little resistance. At passes where a regiment and battery might have temporarily repelled a corps, not a shot was fired. The flight of the Confederates at all points which the Union army touched was unexpected and misconstrued. Burnside believed that the recent National triumph at Vicksburg, Port Hudson and Gettysburg had disheartened the enemy, and collapsed the Rebellion in that region.

This was a mistake: Buckner was simply withdrawing his force from east Tennessee to reinforce Bragg. This should have been discovered, and averted or counteracted by the addition of Burnside's forces to Rosecrans' army. Burnside should have been under the orders of Rosecrans, but he had no superior except Halleck, who failed to concentrate forces at the time concentration was needed. Rosecrans could not give any orders to Burnside, who in turn had no idea of the former's danger, which in fact was not in line of his prescribed duty. He proceeded for the recovery of eastern Tennessee. His appearance was hailed with delight by the Unionists who had been forced into Confederate service, or into a manifestation of Southern allegiance under penalty of death. Long-hidden National flags now waved from many a house. Bounteous supplies of food, unsolicited, and cheers and rejoicings, welcomed the return of National authority and protection.

While the army of the Cumberland remained quietly in Chattanooga, the Confederates conceived the idea of sending a force under Longstreet for the recovery of Knoxville, recently taken by Burnside. Advancing silently and rapidly with a force estimated at 7,000, he fell upon and captured the outposts of Philadelphia, Ky. The enemy advanced through Lenoir, London, and Campbell's Station. Gen. Burnside retreated to his intrenchments in Knoxville. Longstreet pursued him, and on November 17th commenced a siege on the city. Shelling and skirmishing served to break the monotony for ten days. On the arrival of reinforcements, Longstreet delivered an assault upon the works, and met a repulse.

While these events were occurring in and around Knoxville, Gen. Bragg met a disastrous defeat from the combined forces under Gen. Grant; and a relief corps was sent from Chattanooga under Gen. Sherman to raise the siege of Knoxville, which was

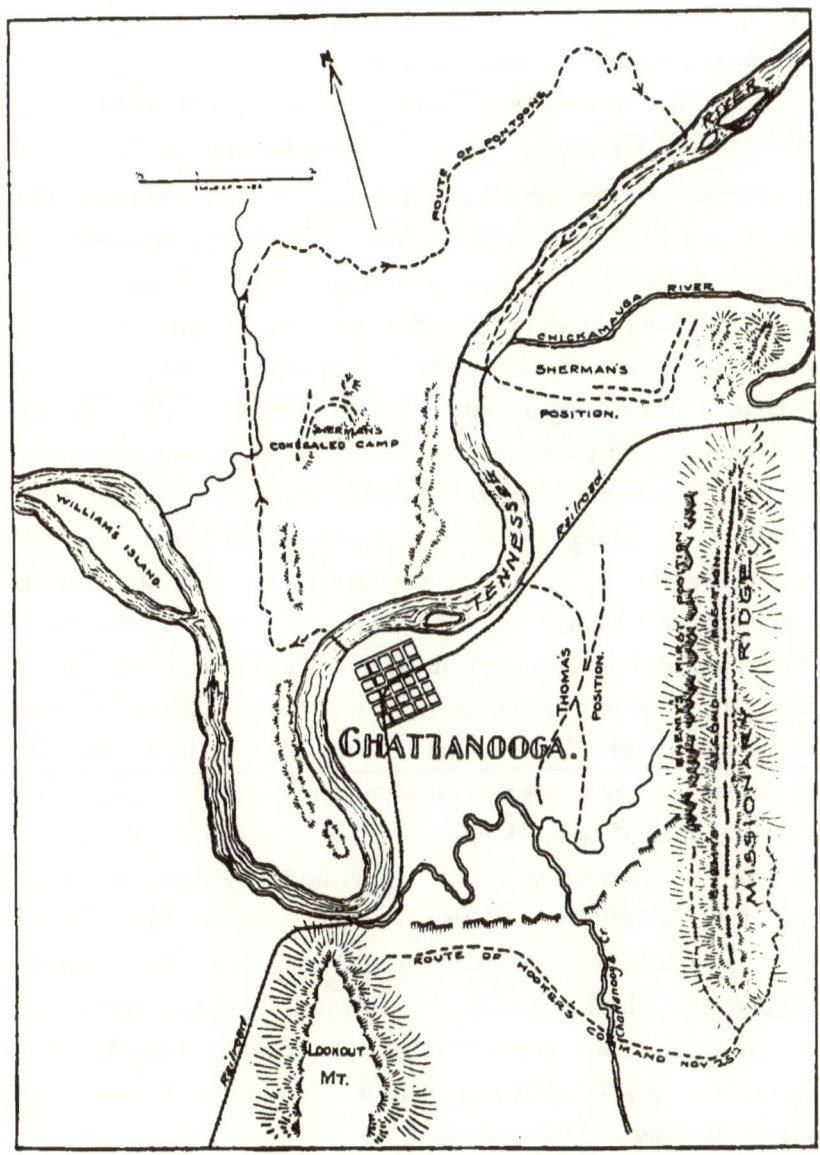

promptly done. When Longstreet heard of Sherman's approach, he moved rapidly eastward to Russellville, Va.

The Union entire loss in this side campaign was about 1,000, while that of the enemy was two or three times as great.

CONCENTRATION OF UNION FORCES AT CHATTANOOGA, OC-TOBER AND NOVEMBER, 1863.—Gen. Halleck became thoroughly alarmed at the peril of Rosecrans' army at Chattanooga, too late to save it from the defeat at Chickamauga, but just in time to prevent starvation forcing an unwilling capitulation.

Gen. Halleck telegraphed to Burnside at Knoxville, Hurlbut at Memphis, and Grant at Vicksburg, to move troops to the support of Rosecrans. Before Burnside made his appearance at Chattanooga, Bragg had defeated Rosecrans, and sent a force to operate against him. Grant was sick at New Orleans, out of reach of the telegram; and Sherman, who represented him at Vicksburg, did not receive it until it was a few days old. Hurlbut's corps was put in motion eastward. Gen. Halleck, learning of the reverse at Chickamauga and not hearing from Grant or Sherman, on September 23d dispatched about 20,000 men, under the command of Gen. Hooker, to Tennessee to hold Rosecrans' line of communication from Nashville to Bridgeport. They were sent by rail from Washington through Wheeling, Cincinnati, Louisville, and Nashville, to the Tennessee. Gen. Hooker concentrated his forces at Bridgeport, preparing to dispute with Bragg the right to use the river and the highway along its bank as an avenue for the transportation of supplies to the Union troops inclosed at Chattanooga.

The road across the mountains used for this purpose imposed a most laborious and difficult task upon the troops. It is estimated that not less than 10,000 horses were used up in this service, and that it would have been impossible to supply our army a week longer, by reason of the exhaustion of the horses, and the increasing badness of the roads caused by autumn rains.

Gen. Bragg had sent a large force of cavalry under Wheeler across the Tennessee river to cut off Thomas's supplies. In the Sequatchie valley he captured or burned from 700 to 1,000 wagons with supplies. He next struck McMinnville, in the heart of Tennessee, where he captured 600 men and a large quantity of supplies. He was pursued by Union cavalry in this raid, and attacked in several sharp engagements, in which he lost about two thousand men, killed and captured. The Union loss must have been greater, while the property destroyed was worth millions.

Gen. Grant was placed in command of all forces now concentrated around Chattanooga. He assumed nominal command at Louisville, Oct. 18, 1863. Telegraphing to Gen. Thomas to hold Chattanooga at all hazards, he received the answer, " I will hold on till we starve," and proceeded at once to the scene of action.

Gen. Sherman reported to Gen. Grant at Chattanooga Nov. 15. The troops which he had brought from Vicksburg as reinforcements were speedily arranged to aid in the final assault upon the enemy's stronghold.

—9

ATTACK UPON LOOKOUT MOUNTAIN AND MISSIONARY RIDGE, NOVEMBER 24–25, 1863.—On November 24 Gen. Hooker's division made a brilliant assault on Lookout Mountain, upon which the enemy had fortified itself. Hooker's men pressed forward in the face of a terrific fire, driving the enemy before them from their rifle-pits. On up the mountains, over boulders and ledges, crests and chasms, they went. Hooker had ordered his men to be halted and re-formed on reaching the summit of the mountain. The tide of victory carried them on over the summit without halting, until they had taken many prisoners and driven the remainder down the precipitous eastern declivity of the mountain, when darkness arrested the progress of the victorious army. The enemy passed across Chattanooga valley and concentrated their forces on Missionary Ridge, posting their front behind breastworks erected by the Union troops after the sanguinary battle of Chickamauga.

The next morning Hooker moved down Lookout Mountain and began to coöperate with Sherman and Thomas in the final assault upon Missionary Ridge. As the Union skirmishers advanced, two abreast, with the whole army in easy supporting distance, the enemy, seized with panic, abandoned the works at the foot of the hill and retreated precipitately to the crest, closely pursued by their conquering adversary. In less than an hour the victorious troops had taken the summit of the ridge. The Union troops seized the abandoned and yet-smoking guns of the enemy, and turned them upon their panic-stricken owners.

The fall of the night ended the pursuit of the retreating foe by the Federal troops, but next day Hooker resumed pursuit as far as Ringgold, where he remained until Dec. 1st.

Immediately after the battle Gen. Sherman went to the relief of Burnside, who was shut up in Knoxville, and compelled Longstreet to raise the siege and decamp.

Gen. Grant estimated his loss in the series of struggles at 757 killed, 4,529 wounded, 330 missing; total, 5,616.

Bragg's loss in killed and wounded was comparatively light, since his fighting was mainly behind breastworks. On the whole, his army was weakened by the struggle and its results by about 10,000 men, and Chattanooga remained in undisputed possession of the Union troops.

CHAPTER X.

SHERMAN'S MARCH ON ATLANTA.

SHERMAN'S MARCH ON ATLANTA, 1864.—When Gen. Grant was promoted to the rank of Lieutenant-General, commanding all the forces of the Union, Gen. W. T. Sherman was assigned to the command of the military division of the Mississippi, comprising the Departments of the Ohio, the Cumberland, the Tennessee, and the Arkansas. He received the order March 4th, 1864, at Memphis, and proceeded to Nashville at once, where he met Gen. Grant, who unfolded his plans in full to his most trusted subordinate, and discussed at length the great campaigns soon to be inaugurated against Richmond and Atlanta. These campaigns were to begin simultaneously on the Rapidan and on the Tennessee. They were to be pressed so vigorously that neither of the Confederate main armies could spare any troops to reinforce the other, as they had done at Chattanooga to the discomfiture of Gen. Rosecrans.

When Gen. Sherman received final instructions from Grant, it was decided that the campaign should be inaugurated in the beginning of May. Accordingly, with the opening of May, Sherman left his winter quarters around Chattanooga, with an army now augmented to nearly 100,000. In every other way but in cavalry it was superior to the one which confronted it.

As Sherman advanced into Georgia, the necessity of maintaining his communications greatly reduced the force in front, which was probably 70,000. Johnston had about 50,000, but was in time considerably reinforced.

The country from Chattanooga to Atlanta is rough and irregular. There are rugged mountains and deep narrow ravines, and broad valleys traversed by two considerable rivers, succeeded again by a rugged mountain region with narrow and bad roads.

Gen. Bragg was relieved of the command of the Army of the Tennessee in December, and called to Richmond, where he acted for a time as military adviser for Mr. Davis. Gen. J. E. Johnston, who had been wounded in the battle of Seven Pines, and afterward commanded the Confederate forces in Mississippi, was transferred to his command Dec. 18, 1864, with headquarters at Dalton. Johnston's position at Dalton was covered by an impassable mountain. Sherman preferred not to hazard an engagement by an attack upon this position. While Thomas was feigning an attack upon the front, McPherson flanked the enemy by moving on Resaca through Snake Creek Gap. Johnston was compelled to evacuate his stronghold, and he fell rapidly back to Resaca. The Union troops occupied Dalton on the heels of the departing foe, and pressed sharply toward Resaca.

Sherman's tactics were uniform through this campaign, though they varied in detail as exigencies arose. He marched with his center upon the enemy, while he sent a right or left flanking party where the nature of the country afforded best opportunities for success.

Johnston avoided an engagement unless advantages were strongly in his favor. Sherman by skillful maneuvers forced Johnston from his stronghold. Each strove to gain an advantage in bringing about a conflict. Johnston hoped to be able to fall upon Sherman's troops and crush them after they had moved into the heart of the Confederate country. Sherman hoped, by flank movements to bring the enemy from behind earthworks, and then defeat him. The result of the campaign shows how well Sherman succeeded. His marches on Atlanta stand in glaring contrast with those bloody conflicts between Grant and Lee in the Overland Campaign.

A second flanking movement was sent out by Sherman's right, to turn Johnston out of Resaca. This was met by an attack upon Hooker and Schofield still in his front. The enemy met a repulse, and lost about 3,000. Sherman's loss was some less. Johnston retreated, and attempted to make a stand at Adairsville against the Union center, but on the approach of the main body he continued his retreat to Cassville and Kingston. Upon being pressed here, he again retreated to Allatoona, where the country is again mountainous. He doubtless had expected to fight in earnest here.

Another flanking movement by Sherman far to the right, on Dallas, brought an engagement at New Hope Church, May 25 to 28, four miles north of Dallas. The Confederates lost 3,000 and Sherman 2,400.

Johnston meantime had been gathering his detachments and receiving reinforcements, until his army numbered 62,000. He fell back to Marietta, with Bush Mountain on his right, Kenesaw Mountain on his center, and Pine Mountain on his left. There were skirmishes between the opposing forces for a series of days. On the 27th of June, Sherman ordered an assault. Sherman says: " I ordered an assault with the full coöperation of my great lieutenants, Thomas, McPherson, and Schofield,— as good and true men as ever lived and died for their country's cause; but we failed, losing 3,000 men to the Confederate loss of 630. Still, the result was, that within three days Johnston abandoned the strongest possible position, and was in full retreat for the Chattahoochie river. We were on his heels, skirmished with his rear at Smyrna Church on the 4th day of July, and saw him fairly across the Chattahoochie on the 10th, covered and protected by the best line of field intrenchments I have ever seen, prepared long in advance. . . . We had advanced into the enemy's country 120 miles, with a single track of railroad, which had to bring clothing, food, ammunition, everything requisite for 100,000 men and 25,000 animals. The city of Atlanta, the gate city, opening the interior of the important State of Georgia, was in sight; its protecting army was shaken but not defeated, and onward we had to go."

Gen. Johnston, too weak in force to take the offensive, conducted a masterly retreat. Gen. Sherman, too shrewd to slaughter his men in useless assault upon strongly fortified works, flanked the enemy from his stronghold, as he watched opportunities to inflict punishment upon him. Thus the movement from Chattanooga to Atlanta consisted of a series of retreats on the part of Johnston and flank movements on the part of Sherman, during which a number of engagements took place. Dalton, Resaca, Adairsville, Cassville, Kingston, Allatoona Pass, Kenesaw Mountain, Chattahoochie river, and Atlanta, mark the successive retreats of Johnston.

THE DEFEAT OF HOOD AND THE FALL OF ATLANTA, SEPTEMBER 2, 1864.—The "retreating policy" of Johnston was not approved by the authorities at Richmond, and Gen. John B. Hood, an officer of great reputation for energy and impetuous bravery, was appointed to succeed him. With this change of commanders came a change of policy, by which a most valuable service was rendered to the Federal cause. Johnston had not been able to prevent Sherman's persistent, determined, and generally skillful advance. He had lost about 15,000 men in two months by a defensive campaign. He had settled to the defense of Atlanta with the Chattahoochie river to his left and Peach creek on his right, when Gen. Hood assumed command. About 51,000 men were turned over to the new commander, who proceeded to bring them into deadly action at once.

Sherman, after crossing the Chattahoochie river and Peach creek, was vehemently assailed, July 19, by Hood's army, which met a disastrous repulse. The Union loss was about 1,500, while Sherman estimated the loss of his opponent in killed, wounded, and prisoners, at about 5,000.

Gen. Hood fell back to within a couple of miles of Atlanta, behind the strong line of defense consisting of redoubts, abatis, and rifle-pits, constructed in 1863. Leaving a small force behind his works, he made a long night march with his main body, expecting to fall upon the Union left and to crush the successive divisions before they could support one another.

Gen. Hardee struck an unexpected blow at Smith's division of Blair's corps. Gen. McPherson, while riding in fancied security through the woods to the rear of that division, was shot dead as he gave an order to fill up a gap into which the Confederates were pouring like a torrent. McMurry's battery was surprised and taken. But after Sherman massed his forces, and when the first shock of surprise had disappeared, the triumphant beginning of the enemy's assault was turned into defeat, and then a rout to his defenses.

The Union loss in this stubborn contest of July 22d was 3,722, of whom 1,000 were prisoners. The Confederate loss during the day as estimated by Gen. Sherman was 8,000, of whom 1,000 were prisoners.

Gen. Stoneman was dispatched with 5,000 cavalry on a raid against the railroads in Hood's rear. He was to be joined at Lovejoy by a division under Gen. A. O. McCook, numbering 4,000. Stoneman did not arrive at the appointed time; and McCook's force, being confronted by militia brought from Mississippi to aid in the defense of Atlanta, and being pursued by the Confederate cavalry, was compelled to flee for safety, after having destroyed a considerable quantity of Hood's supplies.

Gen. Howard succeeded to the command of the Army of the Tennessee on the death of Gen. McPherson. Gen. Hooker, considering himself disparaged, was relieved from the command of his corps at his own request, and Gen. Slocum succeeded him.

The Army of the Tennessee was now shifted from Sherman's extreme left to his extreme right, in a movement to flank Hood out of Atlanta by cutting the railroad in the rear. Gen. Hood detected the movement, but not until the Federal army had sufficient time to hastily construct a breastwork of rails and logs before being assailed by the enemy. Hood, expecting to catch the army in disorder, or at least unprepared, hurriedly brought his forces from the west of Atlanta, and impetuously charged upon the Union forces, July 28th. But the Confederates were swept down by a murderous fire as they approached, and were driven back. Again and again they were re-formed and led to the assault, only to have their brave ranks decimated by their vigilant opponents. Finally the foolish assault was abandoned. Sherman estimated the Confederate loss at 5,000, while his own was only 600; but Hood admits a loss of 1,500 only.

Gen. Hood divided his forces to guard his communications from Kilpatrick's cavalry raid. He sent Hardee with half of his men to Jonesborough, while he remained at Atlanta. Several engagements occurred between Hardee's and Howard's divisions, to the discomfiture of the former.

On the night before Sept. 1st, ominous sounds indicated to Sherman, who was about twenty miles away, that something momentous was happening at Atlanta. Supposition pointed to the truth, that Hood, completely outgeneraled, and at his wit's end, was blowing up the magazines, burning stores, and preparing to leave Atlanta with the little he could carry with him, deprived as he was of the use of the railroads.

Gen. Sherman occupied Atlanta Sept. 2d. Establishing headquarters in the city, he ordered the removal of the remaining inhabitants to the North or to the South as each preferred. This order was considered an act of great inhumanity and cruelty, by the Confederate officers; but in truth it was a deed of kindness, prompted by nobility of spirit toward a helpless people in a region which was stripped of food and every avenue for furnishing an immediate supply. Every one who could shoulder a musket or drive a team had been conscripted into the Confederate army. All the machine-shops, factories and foundries which had done good service to the Confederates had been destroyed by Hood before leaving Atlanta. No food had been left by his army in Atlanta, and none could be sent from the adjacent country, whoever might perish. It would have cost great sums for the Government to feed these helpless people, even if it had been at all practicable. To let them stay and starve would have been cruel and barbarous. The order for the removal was therefore wise, provident, and humane. The removal was effected quietly, at National cost. Those preferring to go South, numbering 2,035 persons, were taken in wagon to a camp called "Rough and Ready." Those who preferred to go North were taken by rail to Chattanooga.

Gen. Grant, speaking of Sherman's memorable march to Atlanta, says: " The campaign had lasted about four months, and was one of the most memorable in history. There was but little if anything in the whole campaign, now that it is over, to criticize at all, and nothing to criticize severely. It was creditable alike to the general who commanded and the army which had executed it. Sherman had on this campaign some bright, wide-awake division and brigade commanders whose alertness added a host to the efficiency of his command. The news of Sherman's success reached the North instantaneously, and set the country all aglow. It was followed later by Sheridan's campaign in the Shenandoah Valley; and these two campaigns probably had more effect in settling the Presidential election of the following November, than all the speeches, all the bonfires, and all the parading with banners and bands of music in the North."

In the campaign from May 7th to September 1st, the Confederate loss in killed and wounded, as recorded in the War Records, was 22,400; besides these, Sherman took 13,000 prisoners. The Union losses during the same period of time were nearly 32,000 men.

HOOD'S MARCH NORTH, SEPTEMBER, 1864.—The task of supplying any large army with food is momentous. But the task of supplying Sherman's army on this campaign was extremely difficult, passing as he did into the heart of the hostile territory, through mountainous districts, over bad wagon-roads, with but a single railroad connecting him with the North.

Nashville, his principal depot of supplies, was 130 miles away from Chattanooga, which is more than 100 miles from Atlanta. The supplies were brought from Louisville over a single railroad by way of Nashville and Chattanooga, to Atlanta. All the bridges, trestles and culverts along the railroad had to be guarded from the depredations of the enemy's cavalry and from the vandalism of a hostile population.

Gen. Hood, after being driven from Atlanta, decided to take advantage of Sherman's long line of supplies. Being reinforced, he moved around Atlanta, and pushing rapidly north, he began tearing up the railroad, breaking down the telegraph, and threatening Sherman's line of communication. He expected to be able to draw the Union army from Georgia. A division of Hood's army, under Gen. French, marching up through Dallas, attacked Allatoona, Oct. 5, 1864, which was defended by about 2,000 men under Gen. John M. Corse. Gen. French had in his command about 5,000 men, who furiously assaulted the works, but were repeatedly driven back. Gen. Corse and men valiantly held out until aid came. This brave commander himself was wounded in the face, and 707 of his men—being more than one-third of his whole number—were killed or wounded.

While the battle was raging, Gen. Sherman stood on Kenesaw Mountain, eighteen miles south, and, by means of signal flags, conveyed from peak to peak, over the heads of the enemy, the glad tidings of approaching aid in the famous message which

has been perpetuated in the well-known song, " Hold the Fort,"
by P. P. Bliss:

> "Ho! my comrades, see the signal
> Waving in the sky!
> Reinforcements now approaching—
> Victory is nigh."
>
> *Chorus*—"Hold the fort," etc.

Gen. Sherman pursued the enemy through Rome, Resaca,
Villanow, Lafayette, to Gaylesville, Alabama. After the lapse
of a week he became convinced that his adversary was endeavoring to draw him out of Georgia, and refused to follow him
who would not fight, and whom he could not overtake,—unin-
cumbered as Hood was, without any heavy wagon-trains. He
directed Stanley with the Fourth corps and Schofield with the
Twenty-third to march to Chattanooga and thence report at
Nashville, to Thomas, who had been dispatched thither Sept.
28, to meet the retreating foe.

After Sherman had become assured that Thomas was strong
enough to meet Hood's army, which now consisted of 35,000
infantry and 10,000 cavalry, he turned his army southward.
Gathering up his garrison, and sending some to Chattanooga
to aid in the defense of Tennessee, destroying foundries and
mills at Rome, cutting loose from all communications, and
drawing around him all his remaining forces, Sherman made
preparations for the great " March to the Sea," which became a
potent factor in hastening the downfall of the Rebellion.

HOOD'S TENNESSEE CAMPAIGN, NOVEMBER TO DECEMBER,
1864.—Gen. Geo. H. Thomas had been detached from the main

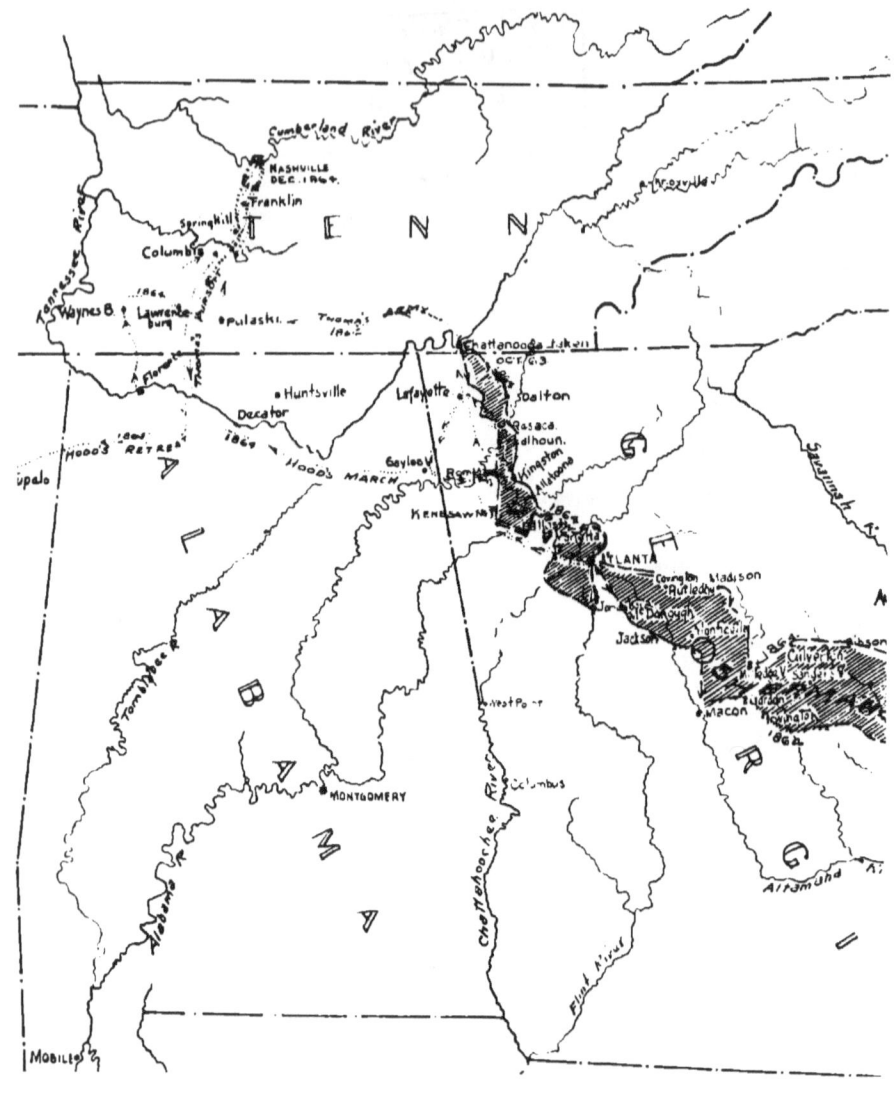

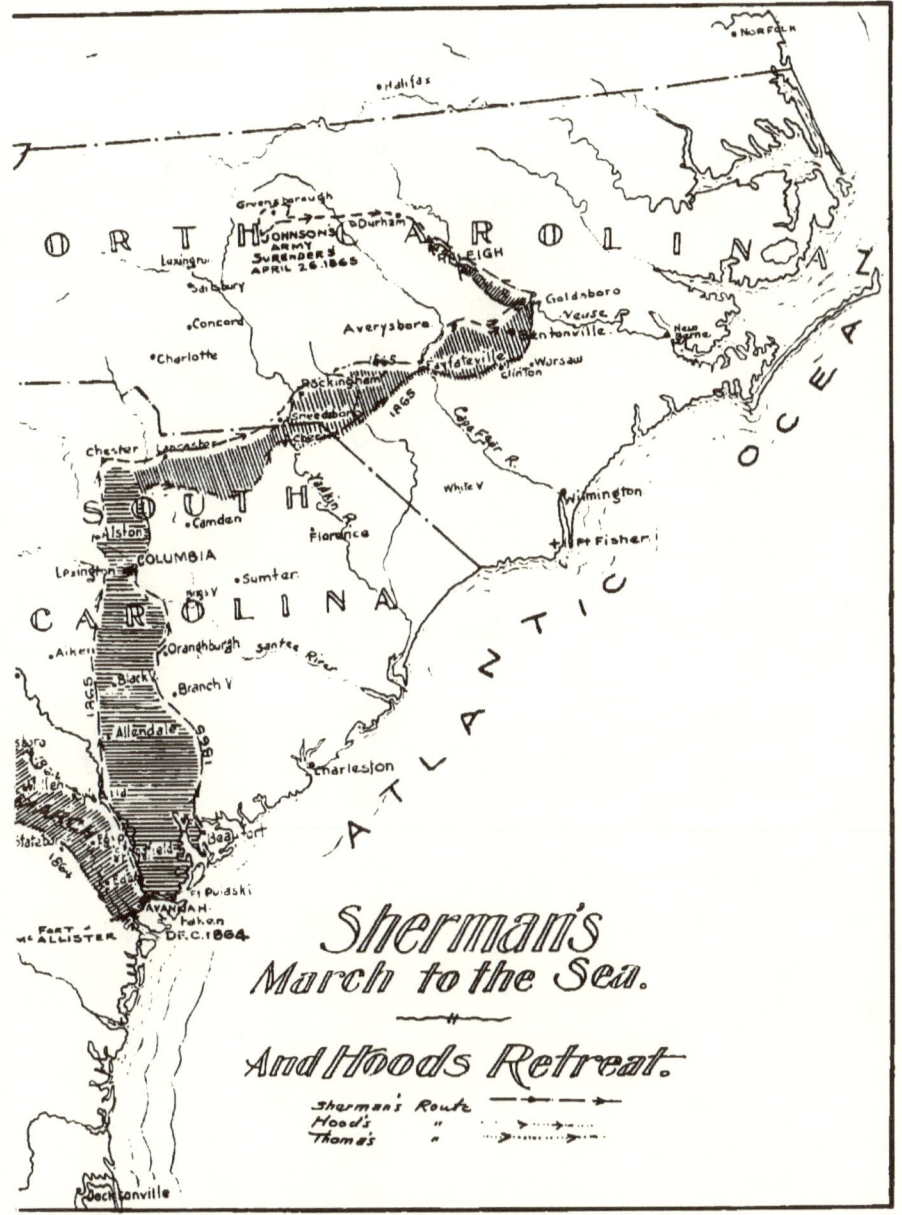

Sherman's
March to the Sea.

And Hoods Retreat.

Sherman's Route
Hood's   "
Thomas   "

army in Georgia, and given command of the Army of the Tennessee with the widest discretionary powers in the conduct of the campaign against Hood. Gen. Grant, in his camp before Richmond, could hardly believe that Hood was moving on Nashville, " which," as he said, " seemed to be leading to his certain doom."

Gen. Hood was reinforced by part of Gen. Dick Taylor's army from the South. His entire force thus augmented was near 55,000 men.

Gen. Thomas had as many men now under his command as Hood had, and probably more, counting all from Knoxville to Memphis, stationed at various posts and depots. They were chiefly fragments of regiments and brigades guarding supplies. bridges, etc. To abandon these points might involve the loss of all that had been gained in the campaign in Tennessee. Not to abandon them greatly reduced the available force to actively oppose Hood. Excluding those guarding posts and depots, he had no more than 30,000 men.

Gen. Forrest, leading a large body of cavalry, preluded Hood's advance. Crossing the Tennessee near Waterloo, he suddenly fell upon and took Athens, Alabama, (September 23,) invested by 600 colored troops. Skirmishing heavily at Pulaski and Tullahoma, he passed through Columbia, Mt. Pleasant, and Lawrenceburg. He crossed the Tennessee safely, after having done much damage and captured about one thousand prisoners. He moved to Corinth and thence to Johnsonville, where some sharp fighting ensued, and then set off to join Hood in his march upon Nashville.

Gen. Hood did not attempt to cross the Tennessee while Sherman remained at Kingston. After making a feint on Decatur, Hood passed on to Tuscumbia and then to Florence. After hearing that Sherman had cut loose from his base at Atlanta and started southward on his "Great March," Hood made preparations for a movement into Tennessee to retrieve his shattered record by a brilliant stroke against Thomas. On Nov. 17, the division of Hood's army stationed on the south bank of the Tennessee, at Florence, effected a crossing, and set out with the rest on their march into Tennessee. Passing through Waynesboro, Lawrenceburg, Columbia, and Spring Hill, his army moved toward Nashville.

Gen. Thomas had been apprised of the departure of Gen. Sherman from Atlanta, and, relying upon his own resources, he began a campaign against the approaching foe, which resulted in the destruction of Hood's army.

Gen. Thomas, keeping a firm front, gradually fell back toward Nashville, gathered strength as he retreated. On the 30th of November Gen. Schofield halted a few miles south of Franklin and threw up a slight breastwork, intending to stop while his wagon-trains, which blocked the road for many miles, should be gotten across the Harpeth river.

Franklin is situated eighteen miles south of Nashville, in a bend of the river, which forms a rude square when united with the line of the Union defenses. Gen. Schofield's command numbered about 20,000 men, a part of whom had already crossed the stream to guard the trains and the flanks of the Union position. The number that confronted the Confederate advance was not much above 10,000. The enemy's charge was so impetuous and heavy that, scarcely checked by the outworks, they broke through the Union center, took eight guns, and planted their flag in triumph on the Union breastworks. But a valiant and brilliant charge by Opdycke's brigade drove the enemy back, recovered all that had been lost, and took a number of prisoners. All efforts to retake the lost breastworks by the enemy proved vain, and assault after assault was repulsed with great loss to the assailants. The conflict continued until about ten o'clock at night. A little after midnight, after the trains were well on their way to Nashville, the Union men quietly drew out of their defenses, and by noon next day the sleepless heroes were safe within the defenses at Nashville.

In the report of the battle Gen. Thomas gives 189 killed, 1,033 wounded, and 1,104 missing,—nearly all of the latter prisoners. He reported the enemy's loss at 1,750 killed, 3,800 wounded, and 702 prisoners; total, 6,252. Gen. Hood admits a loss of only 4,500.

ASSAULT ON NASHVILLE, DEC. 15, 1864.—Hitherto, Gen. Thomas had encountered considerable odds; but when on Dec. 2 Hood settled down before Nashville, the case became reversed. With his losses at Franklin, and casualties and hardships of an offensive and unseasonable campaign, his numbers were reduced to about forty thousand.

—10

Gen. Thomas had received Gen. A. J. Smith's command from Missouri, 5,000 of Sherman's men from Chattanooga, under Gen. J. B. Steedman, and the garrison at Nashville and other reinforcements, until his army numbered 55,000. His infantry clearly outnumbered that of Hood's, but his cavalry was inferior to that confronting him. He paused to mount a few thousand more men before challenging Hood to a decided conflict.

Gen. Grant, now General-in-chief of all the Federal forces, perplexed at the threatening dangers of the strong Confederate army in the heart of Tennessee, left his camp on the James to inspect affairs in the West. He became convinced that his commander in Tennessee, like Sheridan in the Shenandoah Valley, needed no supervision. He returned to his own immediate command for the prosecution of his momentous campaign against Lee and Richmond.

Gen. Hood established his lines south of Nashville, a part of which were within six hundred yards of the Union center. A week of cold weather ensued, wherein both armies became inactive. Hood's men, poorly clad and sheltered, suffered more than the Union men. When at length the temperature softened, Gen. Thomas issued orders, Dec. 14th, for a general advance upon the Confederate lines the next day. The morning broke auspiciously; a dense fog concealed the movements of the Union troops. The assault was made with great vigor and determination. The close of the first day found 16 of the enemy's guns, 1,200 prisoners and 40 wagons in possession of the Union troops, while its losses had been light. Never had men fought with greater alacrity and more steadiness. The next day the Confederates were completely routed, and Hood's invasion ended. He began a disorderly flight south, his army utterly demoralized.

In the two-days battle Thomas had taken 4,462 prisoners, including 287 officers, many small arms, and 53 guns.

The next day the cavalry under Wilson pursued the retreating foe vigorously. They made a stand at Franklin, attempting to defend the crossing at the Harpeth river, but they were forced to decamp, leaving behind 1,800 of their wounded in the hospital, and 200 of ours formerly taken, besides 400 prisoners. Another stand was made by the enemy's rear guard four miles south of Franklin, but it was soon routed and dispersed by Wilson's cavalry. Rain fell almost incessantly, until the brooks became raging rivers. Hood destroyed the bridges, after crossing them, making pursuit very difficult. After several partial engagements, he succeeded in making his escape with the remnant of his army. The pursuit was continued as far as Lexington, Ala. When learning that Hood had crossed the Tennessee at Bainbridge, Thomas ordered a halt.

Gen. Forrest, who had been sent on a cavalry raid, rejoined Hood at Columbia.

Brig. Gen. Lyon, who had been sent by Hood while at Nashville, with 800 cavalry to tear up the Louisville railroad, had his entire command destroyed or taken prisoners. After surrendering, he escaped in the darkness by seizing a pistol and shooting a sentinel.

Hood's army had almost ceased to exist. What remained of it was stationed at Tupelo, Miss., when Hood was " relieved of its command at his own request," Jan. 23, 1865.

In this campaign, from Sept. 7, 1864, to Jan. 20, 1865, Gen. Thomas had lost in killed, wounded and missing about 10,000 men, which was less than one-half the loss of the enemy. He had taken as prisoners nearly 1,000 officers, from Major General down to the lowest rank, and 10,895 non-commissioned officers and privates. He had administered the oath of submission and amnesty to 2,207 deserters, and exchanged 1,332 men, and had taken a large number of small arms and large guns.

CHAPTER XI.

SHERMAN'S GREAT MARCH TO THE SEA.

SHERMAN'S GREAT MARCH TO THE SEA, 1864. Gen. Sherman's army, which set out for the "Great March" through the heart of the Confederacy, numbered about 60,000 infantry and 5,500 cavalry. After concentrating these around Rome and Kensington, Ga., and destroying everything which might be used to his injury by the enemy, he sent his parting messages, and set off, Nov. 11th, on his memorable march to the sea. His command moved forward in two grand wings, the right led by Gen. O. O. Howard, comprising the Fifteenth Corps under Gen. P. J. Osterhaus and the Seventeenth under Gen. Frank P. Blair; the left by Gen. Henry W. Slocum, comprising the Fourteenth Corps under Gen. Jeff C. Davis and the Twentieth under Gen. A. S. Williams. Gen. Judson Kilpatrick led the cavalry, which careered in front and on either flank of the infantry, so as to screen, as far as possible, the movements of the army from the detection of the enemy. Moving rapidly to Atlanta, Howard pased through McDonough, Monticello, and Gordon; while Slocum advanced by Covington, Madison and Eaton to Milledgeville. They destroyed railroads and factories as they advanced, meeting thus far with very little opposition. Each subordinate commander was instructed to live on the country so far as possible, and save the twenty days' bread and forty days' beef, coffee and sugar, and three days' forage, contained in the wagons. The cavalry made a dash on Macon, driving off the Confederate cavalry, but was unable to carry the works behind which the enemy's infantry was posted.

At Millen, on the Central Railroad, half-way from Sandersonville to Savannah, was a great prison camp. Many Union men that had been captured were confined here, and subjected to unspeakable privations and hardships. Sherman intended to liberate them. To this end he sent Kilpatrick with most of his cavalry far to his left, so as to convey an impression that the army was making for Augusta rather than for the coast. But this failed of the desired end. Millen was reached on the 3d of December, but the prisoners had previously been removed.

DESTRUCTION OF RAILROADS.—The railroads were destroyed right and left as the army moved south. Bridges were burned and culverts destroyed, while the track was torn up for long distances, and the rails twisted. To do this rapidly, the soldiers would form a line along the road, and, with crowbar and poles placed under the rails, pry up long distances at a time. Others would pile up the ties, place the rails across them lengthwise, and then set fire to the ties. In this manner the rails were heated in the middle more than at the ends, and were easily twisted so as not to be of any further use. Some of the rails were carried to the nearest trees, and bent around them as bands ornamenting the trees of Georgia. Some crews tore up the rails, others piled up the ties; some carried the rails, while others twisted them: so the work progressed methodically and rapidly with the movements of the army.

SUPPLYING THE ARMY.—The organization for supplying the army was very complete. Each brigade furnished a company to gather supplies of forage and provisions for the command to which it belonged. Pillaging was strictly forbidden, but everything in the shape of food for man or forage for beast was taken. These foraging parties—or "hummers," as they were popularly called—went out for miles on either side of the army. Starting in advance of the organization to which they belonged, and gathering great quantities of provisions, they returned to the line of march, where each stood guard over his pile of food till his own brigade came along, when it was turned over to the brigade commissary and quartermaster. When they started out in the morning they were generally on foot, but scarcely any of them returned in the evening without being mounted on horses, which were turned in for the use of the army. The progress of the column was not permitted to be interrupted by the reception of the forage. Everything had to be loaded upon the wagons as they moved.

The South prior to the Rebellion kept bloodhounds to pursue runaway slaves and escaped convicts, and now they were used to capture escaped prisoners. Orders were issued to kill all of these animals as they were found. The imagination of the troops converted every species of dog into the bloodhound, so that even the poodle had no lease on life in the presence of the advancing blue-coats.

ALARM SOUTH AND NORTH.—Sherman's march through Georgia caused great alarm in the South, and to some extent in the North. If words and bluster could avail against heavy battalions, Sherman's army would have been annihilated in a day. As he moved southward, consternation became more pronounced and the people more frantic. Cadets were taken from the military colleges and added to the ranks of the militia. Convicts were released from jails under a promise to serve in the Confederate army. The Legislature of Georgia passed an act levying the population *en masse* into military service, and then fled in great confusion as Sherman's hosts neared the State capital. All efforts to check the advancing columns were futile. Hardee, Wayne and Wheeler collected some forces that hovered around the Union flanks, the most serious of which was the cavalry under Wheeler, whose presence and skirmishes caused some annoyance, but no detention. The foragers were compelled to defend themselves frequently from the scattered forces of the enemy, but the casualties were small.

Southern newspapers, commenting on Sherman's troops, depicted them as in the most deplorable condition, saying that they were greatly demoralized, and aimlessly wandering around, with the hope of reaching the seacoast to come under the protection of the Union gunboats. Some of these papers reached the North. This news caused Lincoln some alarm, as he had not heard from Sherman since he had cut loose from Atlanta. It produced much mental distress among the friends and relatives of those who were serving under Sherman's banners. The confidence which Grant and Lincoln had in Sherman's ability served to bridge over the period of suspense consequent upon the absence of any definite and authentic news from or about him.

CAPTURE OF SAVANNAH, DECEMBER, 1864.--The receipt of the following telegram by President Lincoln on the 22d of December dispelled all doubt as to Sherman's safety, and caused much joy in the North: " I beg to present to you as a Christmas gift the city of Savannah, with 150 guns and plenty of ammunition; also about 2,500 bales of cotton."

No events of special note occurred on the march from Millen to Savannah. This place was found to be intrenched and garrisoned by 10,000 troops under Gen. Hardee. Sherman proceeded at once to invest the place, which was commenced on the 10th of December. Starting with some troops to open communication with the Union fleet in the lower harbor, he encountered Fort McAllister, which was soon taken by an assault made by Gen. Hazen's division. Communications were then opened with the fleet. The hearts of the men were made glad by the message that a vessel bearing the accumulated mail for the army was there with supplies, which the troops were supposed to need. Sherman returned on the 15th, to complete arrangements for an effective siege of that place. When the investment was supposed to be complete, he summoned Hardee to surrender, who replied that he was not completely invested, and refused to surrender. During the dark and windy night of December 20th, Hardee made his escape by crossing the Savannah river on a pontoon bridge, and marching up the causeway road toward Charleston.

The next morning found the National army in possession of the city before the bombardment of it had fairly commenced.

But the Confederate army was beyond the reach of immediate pursuit; so Gen. Sherman remained in the city a month, resting and refitting his army, preparatory to resuming his march through the Carolinas. The loss in the march of 255 miles, which was accomplished in six weeks of time, was 63 killed, 245 wounded, and 149 missing. It resulted in the conquest of Georgia, the capture of 1,328 prisoners and 167 guns, the seizing of a vast amount of provisions, cattle, horses, etc., and the destruction of millions of dollars' worth of shops, foundries and railroads which had helped support the Rebellion.

The promise of freedom to the slaves, which should follow the triumph of the Union cause, brought a swarm of negroes in search of information and to satisfy their curiosity, to the rear of Sherman's army, notwithstanding every effort had been used by Sherman and his officers to induce them to remain quietly at home. About 10,000 accompanied the army on its march to the sea. Many of these were assigned to the lands on the Sea Islands, which were abandoned by the Confederates when Gen. Thos. W. Sherman and Commodore S. F. Dupont directed an expedition against them in the fall of 1861. From the settlement upon these islands developed, after the close of the war, one of the chief sources of employment for the Freedman's Aid Bureau.

SHERMAN'S MARCH THROUGH THE CAROLINAS, SPRING OF 1865.—Gen. Grant had planned to take Sherman and his army

from Savannah to the James river by water, and so informed
Sherman. On receipt of this letter, he at once began prepara
tions for the removal of the army on transports to aid Grant
around Richmond. Seeing that it would take a long time to
collect the transports for his 60,000 men and their equipage, he
suggested marching north through the Carolinas. Grant accepted and approved the plan, as it contained, if only partially
successful, many features of embarrassment to the foe. By
marching north, living upon the country as he went, he would
be able to devastate the sources of supplies for the Confederate
army. The trans-Mississippi region had long ago been cut off.
Sheridan had desolated the Shenandoah Valley. The blockade
of the seaports had become more stringent. Georgia had lost
her ability to render much assistance or furnish many supplies.
Outside of Virginia, which had already been heavily drained
of its resources, North and South Carolina alone remained as
sources for supplies in any quantity. To destroy their ability
to furnish food and munitions to Lee at Richmond, would
render his position untenable.

OBSTACLES TO BE ENCOUNTERED.—The movement of the
army northward was much more difficult and dangerous than the
" March to the Sea." In the march southward the army moved
parallel with the rivers, and on highways between them, so it was
difficult for any but a large force to obstruct or retard his movement south. But the march north would necessitate the crossing
of many streams, some of them rivers. A single man could burn
a bridge and prevent the army from crossing for a couple of

hours. Gen. Joseph E. Johnston had been placed in command of Hood's decimated forces, to which were added all available garrisons and levies. He appeared in the field prepared to dispute the northward movement of his old antagonist. Lee was seeking to slip away from Grant at Richmond, and, with the aid of Johnston, fall upon Sherman and crush him. He was to march through a country that naturally furnished fewer provisions than the region through which he had previously passed, and those were more completely exhausted, being near the seat of greatest action. And the territory had become of such great importance to the very existence of the Confederate army, that the most desperate efforts to save it were to be expected. With a caution that admirably balanced his boldness, Sherman arranged to have the fleet coöperate with him along the coast, keeping watch of his movements, and establishing places where supplies could be reached, and refuge taken in case of necessity.

CAPTURE OF COLUMBIA, FEBRUARY 17, 1865.—On the 18th of January, turning over the city of Savannah to Gen. John G. Foster, who was in command of the coast in that vicinity, Gen. Sherman issued his orders on the 19th for the movement of his whole army. The Seventeenth Corps under Gen. F. P. Blair had previously been taken by water to Pocotaligo, which was about forty miles north of Savannah, for the purpose of threatening Charleston.

The left wing moved up along the Savannah river, concentrating at Robertsville, twenty miles west of Pocotaligo. Sherman was thus pursuing his favorite strategy of dividing the enemy's forces, and drawing attention from his own designs, so as to prevent a concentration of forces to resist him in the inhospitable region through which his course lay.   He had expected to leave Savannah with his whole army on the 15th of January, at the time the Seventeenth Corps was transported to Pocotaligo, but incessant rains and floods caused a delay of a fortnight.   By the first of February all preparations were completed for the final march, the left wing threatening Augusta and the right demonstrating against Charleston.   He had sent out rumors representing both places as his objective points. Augusta, containing many Confederate stores, was in painful apprehension of a visit from Sherman.   Charleston, the hotbed of secession, in a State that had done so much to prepare the public mind of the South to rebel and secede, was fearful of direful results.   Indeed, a feeling was entertained throughout the North that a heavy hand should be laid upon this city, and nothing but the magnificent results that followed Sherman's march deterred the radical portion of the people of the North from condemning the movements because Charleston had been left out.   Sherman, however, chose to move on a route directly between the two places which had been threatened with some ostentation, and struck directly for Columbia, which he entered February 17th.   There was almost constant skirmishing on the road between the cavalry of the opposing forces.   Some time was lost in rebuilding bridges which had been destroyed to impede the progress of the army.   The march was without much incident until he entered Columbia, which was found to be on fire. The main forces of Confederates had been concentrated at Augusta and Charleston in anticipation of an assault, so that but a small force under Gen. Wade Hampton was left to defend Columbia; but he fled on the approach of Sherman's army. Before leaving the city, Gen. Hampton had ordered all the cotton to be moved into the streets and burned. Bales were piled up everywhere and the ropes and bagging cut. A storm was in progress, which blew tufts of cotton against houses, into trees, and around the town, which soon looked as though a snow-storm was in progress. Sherman had given orders for the destruction of arsenals and machine-shops; but before this was done, the burning cotton, blown in every direction, had set fire to the city. As soon as Sherman entered the city, every effort was made to extinguish the flames, which continued from dusk until 3 A. M., and rendered homeless between 4,000 and 5,000 people. It is reasonably certain that Hampton burned his own city,—not with malicious intent, but through the folly of filling the streets with burning cotton.

Sherman destroyed the arsenal purposely, and tons of powder, shot and shell were taken to the river and sunk in deep water. He also destroyed the factory which made the Confederate paper money, large quantities of which were carried away by the Union soldiers.

THE FALL OF CHARLESTON, FEBRUARY 18, 1865.—The fall of Columbia involved the fall of Charleston, including Fort Sumter and its defenses. Hardee, realizing his isolated condition after the capture of Columbia, evacuated the city so famous in war, on the 18th of February. He was resolved, however, to leave as little as possible for the use of his adversary. Before the retirement of Hardee's troops, every building, warehouse and shed stored with cotton was fired by a guard detailed for that purpose. The horrors of the conflagration were heightened by a terrible catastrophe. A spark accidentally ignited the powder in the depot of the Northwestern Railroad, where a large quantity was stored. A tremendous explosion occurred, shaking the city from one end to the other. The building was in a second a whirling mass of ruins, enveloped in a tremendous volume of flame and smoke. About two hundred lives were lost in that fiery furnace. From the depot the fire spread rapidly to the adjoining buildings, and consumed a considerable portion of the town before the flames could be subdued. The destruction of all public property had been as complete as Hardee could make it.

Hardee with 12,000 men made haste to cross the Santee and Peedee rivers before Sherman could turn upon and crush him. But Sherman, having other plans, did not attempt to intercept him. Gen. Foster took possession of the city with the National troops.

While at Columbia, Sherman learned of Johnston's restoration to the command of the Confederate army in the Carolinas. Leaving this place on the 20th, Sherman's army moved toward Fayetteville, the right wing going through Cheraw and the left through Lancaster and Sneedsboro. He reached Fayetteville on the 11th of March without much opposition or any special

incident.   On the 15th he left Fayetteville for Goldsboro, at
which place Gen. Schofield was preparing to reinforce him;
while Gen. Terry, who had recently taken Fort Fisher, also
came to his aid.

Sherman was compelled to move with greater caution than he
had hitherto done, as a formidable army was being concentrated
to oppose him.   Hardee from Charleston, Beauregard from near
Columbia, Chatham from Tennessee, Bragg with forces drawn
from the eastern defenses of North Carolina, and Wheeler's
and Hampton's cavalry,—all united under the able and wary
command of Gen. J. E. Johnston,—made up a body of not less
than 40,000 men.

FORT FISHER TAKEN, JANUARY 15, 1865.—Fort Fisher, at
the mouth of Cape Fear river, guarded the entrance to Wilmington.   This port was of great importance to the Confederates,
as it formed the principal inlet, at this time, for blockade-
runners, who brought such supplies and munitions from abroad
as could not be produced by the South.   Foreign governments,
particularly England, were threatening to cease to recognize the
blockade unless the United States should make it more effective.

The capture of this fort does not form part of Sherman's
military campaign in his " Great March," but one of the numerous auxiliary movements directed by Gen. Grant in support
of the two leading campaigns,—" The Siege of Richmond and
Petersburg " and " Sherman's March."   In addition to reasons
already named, the possession of Fort Fisher would compel the
abandonment of Wilmington, open a new line of base of supplies

for Sherman, and afford a place of retreat to the protection of the Union fleet in case a sufficient Confederate force could be collected to destroy Sherman's supremacy in his march through the Carolinas.

The army and navy coöperated in the attempt to reduce Fort Fisher. The navy was in command of Commodore Porter; the military (6,500) was commanded by Gen. B. F. Butler, of whom we last heard in New Orleans. He procured an old gun-boat, fitted it up so as to look like a blockade-runner, loaded it with 250 tons of gunpowder, and, running it up close to the fort, exploded it. Butler expected the shock to demolish the seaward face of the fort, but it did not deface it. The navy then poured a rapid and well-aimed fire upon the works. A division of Butler's troops under Weitzel was landed under cover of gunboats. They captured a small garrison, and learned that Gen. Hoke had arrived with 6,000 troops from Richmond Believing the capture of the fort impossible, Weitzel so reported to Gen. Butler, who decided to abandon all demonstrations against it, and accordingly withdrew his troops from the penin-sula, greatly to the disgust of the navy.

The chagrin in the North was great over this failure, and Butler's action was so unsatisfactory to Grant that he at once sent the same troops back under a different commander, with 1,500 reinforcements to offset those which the enemy had re-ceived. Gen. A. H. Terry was selected to command the second attempt. The works were very extensive, and the enemy made a desperate effort to defend them. The land and naval forces

—11

made a combined attack. Terry's men pushed from traverse to traverse until the works were finally taken, Jan. 15th, including 169 guns, 2,083 prisoners, with ammunition and small arms.

SURRENDER OF WILMINGTON, FEBRUARY 22, 1865.—Gen. Schofield was at Clifton, on the Tennessee, preparing to go to Eastport, Miss., when he received the order summoning him to the East. He was directed to take Wilmington, and then coöperate with Gen. Sherman in his campaign against the Confederate forces being assembled under Gen. Johnston. He found Gen. Terry with 8,000 men about two miles above the fort, but too weak to advance against the Confederates, who were strongly intrenched at Fort Anderson. Schofield brought about 12,000 men, and at once commenced active operation against the enemy, who were defeated in several engagements. Wilmington was taken on the 22d of February. The Confederate forces, commanded by Bragg and Hoke, withdrew to unite with Johnston's army, while Schofield and Terry moved to Goldsboro to reinforce Sherman.

SHERMAN'S FINAL CAMPAIGN, 1865.—At Averysboro, thirty-five miles south of Raleigh, the left wing of Sherman's army suddenly came upon Hardee's forces, intrenched across his path. They were however driven back, and the march continued toward Goldsboro. At Bentonville, March 19th, Slocum was assailed by the entire Confederate army under Johnston, who expected to crush the left wing before the remaining forces could come to their aid. Slocum withstood six assaults from

Johnston's army, inflicting heavy loss upon it with his artillery. Night fell without giving Johnston any ground. During the night reinforcements arrived, and both armies fortified themselves for the morrow. Gen. Slocum awaited the arrival of Gen. Howard with the entire right of Sherman's army, while Gen. Schofield was improving this delay to get possession of Goldsboro in the enemy's rear, and Gen. Terry was advancing to the Neuse, at Cox's bridge, some ten miles higher up. But Johnston had taken the alarm, and during the night retreated so precipitately toward Raleigh as to leave his pickets behind, as well as his severely wounded. This was the last battle fought by the army confronting Sherman's. The Union loss was about 1,600 killed, wounded, and missing. The Confederate loss was about 2,300.

No further resistance being made, Sherman's army moved on to Goldsboro, where it rested and was re-clad; while Sherman, after a brief visit with Gens. Scofield and Terry, made a hasty trip to City Point (March 27th), where he met in council President Lincoln, Generals Grant, Meade, etc., and returned to Goldsboro on the 30th.

JOHNSTON'S SURRENDER, APRIL 26, 1865.—While Sherman was quiescent at Goldsboro, he was electrified to hear of the fall of Richmond and Petersburg. He immediately began a movement against Johnston, who still lay at Smithfield, but who now retreated to Raleigh, thence to Greensboro. Sherman pursued the Confederates to Raleigh.

The opposing armies were in these places—one at Greensboro, the other at Raleigh—when the news of Lee's surrender reached them. The decline of the Confederate cause brought overtures of peace from Johnston, which led to his surrender, April 26th, 1865, on the same terms as had been granted to Lee. The surrender of all the Confederate armies soon followed, the last being the command of Gen. E. Kirby Smith, at Shreveport, La., on the 26th of May. Under Johnston's command, 36,817 men were paroled, and 52,453 in Georgia and Florida.

ANNIVERSARY OF FORT SUMTER.—The 14th day of April, 1865, was the anniversary of the surrender of Fort Sumter by Major Anderson to Gen. Beauregard. It was celebrated by a large number of loyal citizens, who went down to Charleston and Port Royal to witness the raising, over the ruins of the historic fortress, of the identical flag that had been hauled down four years before when Beauregard first opened fire upon Fort Sumter. The flag had been thoughtfully preserved for the purpose. Henry Ward Beecher delivered the principal address on this occasion. The whole country was aglow with loyal rejoicing and congratulations over the surrender of Lee, which occurred April 9th, and the establishment of National authority over the site which fired the first gun of the Rebellion.

CHAPTER XII.

McCLELLAN'S PENINSULAR CAMPAIGN.

ORGANIZATION OF THE ARMY, 1861.- Immediately after the battle of Bull Run, the new military department of Washington and Northeastern Virginia was formed. The army became known as the Army of the Potomac. Gen. George B. McClellan was summoned by telegraph from West Virginia to take command of it. The change was officially announced July 25, 1861. The army around Washington was reduced by desertions, defeat, and by the expiration of the time of the three-months men, to about 50,000 men. Gen. Winfield Scott nominally remained General-in-chief until November 1st, when, by his own request, he was placed on the retired list, and McClellan was named to supersede him. Gen. McClellan at once commenced the organization of the great army authorized by Congress. Regiment after regiment flocked into Washington. The troops were armed and drilled, with a full knowledge of the perils and hardships and privations to be encountered. By the beginning of December, when Congress assembled, the Army of the Potomac had reached 185,000 men.

DIFFERENT ROUTES TOWARD RICHMOND.—In the spring of 1862, when the Army of the Potomac was to be put in motion for the capture of Richmond, Lincoln and McClellan did not agree as to what route should be taken. There were several

different ways by which the Union army could be furnished
with food and supplies while moving against Richmond. One,
by railroad through Gordonville: this was the longest route, and
most difficult to guard. The supplies could be taken down the
Potomac to Aquia Creek via Fredericksburg, then by rail to
Richmond. This route possessed the advantage of placing the
Union army in a position to defend the National capital.
Another route was that down the Chesapeake bay, ascending
either the York or the James river, and establishing a base on
one or the other at some convenient point. This plan necessi-
tated a division of the army in order to protect Washington
against a sudden attack upon it. The President wished the
army to move directly against the enemy overland. McClellan
wished to move down the bay on transports. Lincoln finally
yielded to McClellan's plan, on condition that a sufficient force
should be left for the protection of Washington.

DOWN THE RIVER TO YORKTOWN, APRIL, 1862.—The great
Army of the Potomac, numbering 155,000, in command of
Gen. McClellan, embarked at Alexandria in April, and was
taken down the Potomac in transports to Fortress Monroe.
The ultimate objects were, the destruction of the Confederate
army and the capture of Richmond, the capital of the Confederacy.

The Confederates had erected numerous breastworks extending across the peninsula which separates the York and James
rivers, defended by 20,000 men under Gen. J. B. Magruder.
The main body was centered at Yorktown, a place already cele-

brated in the annals of history by the decisive victory of Washington over Cornwallis. Yorktown was defended by a system of extensive fortifications. McClellan, after some preliminary skirmishing, began erecting a system of opposing works. Reinforcements arrived to swell the number of Confederate troops already assembled at Yorktown to 60,000. Generals Johnston and Lee arrived. Every preparation was made to defend the place to the utmost extremity. McClellan in the meantime was making coëxtensive preparations for its assault. He ordered big guns to be brought from Washington, and perfected his plans for a protracted siege upon the place. When everything was in readiness, after a delay of a month, to the great surprise of McClellan and the Nation the Confederates abandoned Yorktown and retreated toward Richmond.

The evacuation of Yorktown is one of the singular events of the war. It was evidently the original intention of the Southern army to meet the Federals in battle at this fortified town. It is probable that the most potent factor in inducing the Confederates to change their plans was that they might encounter the Federals at a safe distance from the Federal gunboats on the York river. The painful lesson taught them at Pittsburg Landing had not yet been forgotten.

THE BATTLE OF WILLIAMSBURG, MAY 5, 1862.—The Federals began a vigorous pursuit, without stopping in the deserted camp. On the afternoon of May 4th the Federal advance encountered the Confederate rear guard near Williamsburg. The next day the engagement took place all along the lines. The contest continued during the day. Gen. Hancock began a brilliant and spirited attack upon the enemy's left. Their resistance gradually weakened, until finally they broke and retreated, leaving nearly 700 dead upon the field. The loss to the Union forces was 300 killed and over 800 wounded.

In the afternoon of the 6th of May, 20,000 men commanded by Gen. William B. Franklin arrived in transports at West Point, on the York river, for the purpose of uniting with Gen. McClellan. They were attacked next morning by a division of the Confederate forces, who were repulsed. After the conclusion of this engagement Franklin speedily united his forces with Gen. McClellan's, and the Army of the Potomac continued its advance upon Richmond.

As McClellan approached Richmond, several skirmishes of little consequence took place along the banks of the Chicka-hominy. It appeared as though an immediate attack would be made upon Richmond. Great panic prevailed in the city. The Confederate Congress hastily adjourned. But at this juncture McClellan discovered a large body of Confederates at Hanover Court House, who threatened his communication by rail with White House Landing, and intercepted the approach of Gen. Irvin McDowell, who was to come with 40,000 troops to join McClellan. It also maintained communication between the Confederate authorities at Richmond and Fredericksburg. McClellan discerned the necessity of driving the Confederates from this place. The task was intrusted to Gen. Fitz John Porter. After a spirited assault the Confederates were driven from the field, and Hanover Court House was taken by the Federals, with a loss of 53 killed and 326 wounded. The enemy's loss was somewhat greater.

The chief military strength of the Confederacy was concentrated in the vicinity of Richmond. Their ablest generals were summoned to command. Preparations for a conflict more colossal than any that had hitherto taken place were made. Gen. McDowell was to coöperate with McClellan against Richmond, by marching due south by way of Fredericksburg. Gen. Nathaniel P. Banks was to proceed to Winchester, through the Shenandoah Valley, by Strasburg, toward Staunton.

STONEWALL JACKSON'S CAMPAIGN IN THE SHENANDOAH, 1862.—Gen. McClellan was anxiously awaiting the arrival of McDowell's 40,000 troops. His last orders at night were that McDowell's signals should be reported to him without delay. The wisdom of Gen. Johnston foresaw disaster for him in the probable union of these Federal forces. To prevent it became his object. Gen. T. J. ("Stonewall") Jackson was directed to move against the Union forces in the Shenandoah Valley, threaten Washington, and thus prevent McDowell from joining McClellan in his campaign against Richmond.

A portion of Banks's army under Gen. Shields had encountered Jackson's command at Winchester, March 23, and put them to flight. Banks pursued the retreating forces with steady and unvarying success as far as Strasburg. Here a sudden reverse overtook him. His army had been reduced one-half of the original number by demands made upon it for troops for other fields. Gen. Jackson had been reinforced by Ewell's division, which reached him May 1st. Discerning the advantage he thus had, he descended like an avalanche with his 15,000 men upon Banks, driving him down the valley. At Front Royal, Jackson captured a garrison of 700 men. He then hurried down the valley after Banks, to within a few miles of Harper's Ferry. Banks succeeded in making his escape across the Potomac. In this memorable retreat of fifty-three miles in forty-eight hours, several conflicts took place, the most spirited of which was at Winchester, where for five hours the Union army, numbering 5,000, withstood the attack of threefold their number. General consternation prevailed at Washington. The President called upon the governors of the Northern States to send militia for the defense of the National capital. He took military possession of the railroads. McDowell's advance from Fredericksburg to unite with McClellan was at once countermanded. He was ordered up the Shenandoah Valley with 20,000 men, in face of protests from himself and McClellan. Banks at Harper's Ferry and Frémont at Franklin were also directed to move on Jackson, who by this time had become alarmed for his own safety, and commenced a precipitous retreat, burning bridges behind him as he went. Several engagements took place between the retreating forces of Jackson and his pursuers under Frémont and Shields. By a skillful and masterly retreat Jackson succeeded in reaching Richmond. While there was no great battle fought in the campaign, it bore an important part in the McClellan peninsular campaign, for by means of 15,000 men

Jackson succeeded in neutralizing a force of 60,000, and prevented heavy reinforcements from joining McClellan when they were most needed.

FAIR OAKS, MAY 31, AND SEVEN PINES, JUNE 1, 1862.— While these stirring events were going on in the Shenandoah Valley, Gen. McClellan sent a corps comprising two divisions of about 20,000 to the south side of the Chickahominy, at a place called Fair Oaks, located about eight miles east of Richmond. General Johnston planned to attack and defeat these troops with a superiority of numbers, before reinforcements could be brought to them. Heavy rains converted the Chickahominy creek into a raging current, flooded the swamps, made the roads impassable, so that a relief expedition was well-nigh impossible.

The Confederates suddenly and unexpectedly made an impetuous charge upon the Federal ranks on Saturday morning, May 31. The regiment sent to support the pickets were completely demoralized, and carried exaggerated reports of the vast numbers of their assailants. The advancing forces were impeded in their progress by a determined stand of Federals at a rail fence; but as the ranks of the Confederates became decimated, new troops from the rear came forward. For three and a half hours the 8,000 troops under Gen. Casey held three times their number in check, inflicting terrible destruction upon them. The Federal troops fought heroically, but after a desperate conflict were forced back toward the Chickahominy. Late in the afternoon the arrival of Sumner's troops aided in stemming the victorious march of the enemy, and in saving the Federal forces from total rout. The close of the day found the Confederates in possession of the Federal camp. During the night important reinforcements arrived. The spirit of the Federal forces was raised, as their ranks filled up. The next morning (Sunday, June 1st) the Confederate advance was met by a vigorous and resolute stand by the Federals. The Federals pushed forward upon the yielding lines of the foe, until they occupied a position a mile in advance of that held at the beginning of the day's engagement. Thus the misfortunes of the defeat of the first day's battle of Fair Oaks was retrieved by the victory on the second at Seven Pines. The guns and ammunition captured by the Confederates the day before were not recovered, as they had been taken into Richmond at the close of the first day. The Federal loss during the two-days battle was 890 killed, 3,627 wounded, and 1,222 missing. The official report of Gen. J. E. Johnston gives his total number in killed and wounded and missing as 6,697.

The people in the North expected that an immediate advance would be made upon Richmond by McClellan after the battle of Seven Pines. It is quite probable that if an immediate pursuit had been ordered and an advance made upon Richmond, the result would have been disastrous to the enemy. But the difficulty of such a movement is apparent. Only a small portion of McClellan's army had crossed the Chickahominy. A freshet the day after the battle of Fair Oaks swept away the two or three bridges that had been constructed over the stream. Richmond was protected by eight fortifications and defended by more than 50,000 men. Operations intended to overcome such formidable defenses, when combined with heroic conduct, had to be conducted on a plan whose magnitude was greater than the obstacles to be overcome.

In accordance with maxims controlling Gen. McClellan, he proceeded to select his camp and erect fortifications, intrenching from Mechanicsville on his right to White Oak Swamp on his left, embracing a front of about four miles, mostly parallel with the Confederates. Portions of the immense army were in view of the spires of Richmond. The heart of the Rebellion lay before them.

In the battle of Fair Oaks Gen. J. E. Johnston, the Confederate General-in-chief, was severely wounded, and Robert E. Lee was called by the master spirits of the Rebellion to lead their hosts to battle.

CONCENTRATION OF CONFEDERATE FORCES.—While McClellan was making extensive preparations for the siege of Richmond, Gen. Lee was exerting every energy for a massive concentration of a formidable army. A large portion of the troops so mysteriously withdrawn at Corinth by Beauregard, appeared before Richmond. Gen. Jackson's force was summoned from the Shenandoah. About 100,000 men were assembled in the vicinity of Richmond to aid in its defense.

Gen. J. E. B. Stuart made a circuitous cavalry raid around the Federal army. He gained much valuable information, captured many prisoners, and destroyed about $7,000,000 worth of supplies, returning in safety to the Confederate fold.

The sudden apparition of Jackson's forces, the dangerous condition of the Federal base of supplies at White House, and the failure of McDowell to come to the aid of McClellan, induced him to recede from Richmond, and change his base from White House on the York river to Harrison's Landing on the James.

McClellan's Retreat and Seven Days' Battle, June 26 to July 2, 1862.—Orders were received on the 24th of June for the movement of the troops toward Harrison's Landing. This afforded an opportunity for the enemy to change from the defensive to the offensive policy, in which was inaugurated that remarkable series of engagements lasting a whole week with such destructive fury, and known in history as the "Seven Days' Battle."

Battle of Mechanicsville, June 26, 1862.—On the 26th of June the Confederate forces issued in vast numbers from the camps before Richmond, and commenced a bold assault upon the Union army. The attack was directed against General Stoneman's cavalry in the vicinity of Hanover Court House, and soon extended to the troops posted in the vicinity of Mechanicsville. Reinforcements were brought several times during the day by both sides. Late in the day a furious cavalry charge was met by Federal horse, and driven back. The conflict continued till half-past nine o'clock, with little advantage to either party, but the field of battle remained in possession of

the Union forces. Gen. Fitz John Porter was in command of
the entire corps of Union troops engaged during the day. He
was ably assisted by Generals McCall, Morrell, and Griffin.
Thus at the close of the first day, the enemy had gained nothing,
but were not disheartened. They had merely made a beginning of the gigantic enterprise which they had undertaken, and
were resolute in the prosecution, as the days following demonstrated.

Battle of Gaines's Mill, June 27.—During the night Gen.
McClellan gave orders to Gen. Porter for the removal of the
camp equipage, stores and ammunition to the James river. The
troops were also ordered to move forward. While these movements were progressing, the Confederates were receiving reinforcements, and preparing for another assault. The early dawn
next day, June 27, beheld 60,000 Confederate troops ready for
battle. Gen. Porter had received orders to remove his troops
two miles beyond Gaines's Mill. The enemy supposing this
movement a retreat from battle, followed and overtook the Federals, who were prepared to receive them. Here resulted the
bloody battle of Gaines's Mill, June 27th. The battle began at
eleven o'clock, and raged during the rest of the day with the
usual vicissitudes which characterize engagements in which vast
numbers of brave men contend for the mastery, with equal degrees of valor and fortitude. The enemy had repeatedly attempted to force the Union men into the low, marshy ground
between the mill and bridge. They almost succeeded in doing
it. With desperate energy the Federal troops, numbering

27,000, succeeded in holding their ground and in defending the bridge across the Chickahominy till night. The losses on both sides were heavy: Lee's was 7,700, and McClellan's was 7,000. The shades of night settled over the field of carnage and death, and put an end to the desperate conflict on the north side of the Chickahominy.

Battle of Savage's Station, June 29.—During the night most of the Federal troops and baggage trains were removed to the south side of the Chickahominy, and thus they gained some advantage over the pursuing enemy. After all the troops had crossed the stream, bridges were destroyed to prevent pursuit. The Union army withdrew as far as Savage's Station. No engagement took place on this day, but during the night vast quantities of commissary stores, ammunition and hospital supplies for which there were no means of removal at hand, were destroyed by orders of Gen. McClellan. Four car-loads of ammunition were run into the Chickahominy to prevent its falling into the hands of the enemy. The hospital at Savage's Station, containing 2,500 sick and wounded, with surgeons and attendants, had to be abandoned. These men fell into the hands of the enemy, but were treated with humanity.

On the morning of the 29th, the troops continued their march. An engagement took place at Peach Orchard. The main conflict for the day occurred at Savage's Station. It commenced at 5 P. M. and lasted until 9 o'clock at night. At midnight McClellan gave orders to fall back rapidly from Savage's Station to White Oak Swamp, as the Confederates were endeavoring to intercept their retrograde movement. And now the hitherto voluntary march of the Federals degenerated into a flight, pursued by the enemy.

Battle of Glendale or Frazier's Farm, June 30.—At White Oak Swamp another desperate engagement took place, known as Glendale, White Oak Swamp (or Frazier's Farm, by the Confederates). McClellan directed the lines to be held until the trains could reach a place of safety on the James, where the army could be concentrated to enjoy a brief rest after the fatiguing battles and marches through which they were passing; after which, he expected to renew the advance on Richmond. The last of the trains reached Malvern Hill by 4 P. M. It then remained for the troops to hold their ground till night, when they could march to the stronger position on Malvern Hill.

The fighting began between 12 and 1 o'clock (June 30), was very severe, and extended along the whole line. The Confederate artillery inflicted serious loss upon Franklin's command, but he held his ground till night. Their attempts to cross White Oak Swamp Crossing were unsuccessful. Slocum withstood the enemy's attack at the Charles City road. McCall's division was forced back, but Hooker came up from the left and Sedgwick from the rear, and together drove the foe from the field. Ineffectual assaults were made upon Kearny, Porter, Sumner and Heintzelman. The firing continued until after dark. During the night all the remaining corps of the Union army were withdrawn to Malvern Hill.

—12

Battle of Malvern Hill, July 1.—The morning of July 1 found the Union army posted on Malvern Hill, rising like an amphitheater and overlooking the river, which was crowded with transports and vessels of all descriptions. The hill was arranged with tier after tier of Federal batteries, rising to the plateau above. Generals Keyes, Slocum, Franklin, Sumner, Porter, Kearny and Heintzelman were there with their broken corps of the once splendid Army of the Potomac. The enemy was commanded by Generals Lee, Hill, Longstreet, Magruder, and Jackson. They opened a spirited engagement at four o'clock, Tuesday, July 1st. The fight was continued until ten o'clock at night. Three times the determined foe tried to capture the hill and drive the Federals down, but each time they were driven back with frightful carnage by the combined fire of artillery and musketry.

Thus ended the battle of Malvern Hill, the last of the Seven Days' Battle. Thus ended the last assault by the Confederates upon the troops of the Union in the " Peninsular Campaign." Thus terminated one of the most extraordinary campaigns which has ever occurred in the blood-stained annals of ancient or modern warfare. The loss on both sides was appalling. During the seven days' operation, the enemy lost over 20,000 men; McClellan's loss was about 16,000.

McClellan moved his troops to Harrison Landing, a strip of land along the north bank of the James river, five miles long, with several good wharves for the discharge of cargoes, situated eight miles from Malvern Hill. Being naturally well adapted for defense, the vigorous use of the spade soon made it impregnable against all attacks. The enemy had inflicted terrible punishment upon the Union forces, but had themselves received such calamitous reception that they withdrew from the conflict.

In effect, the Peninsular Campaign was a complete failure. It had not only failed in the capture of Richmond, but McClellan was compelled to change his base of operations, was forced to take the defensive, and retreat, in the series of battles. Immense quantities of stores had been captured or destroyed by the Confederates, and the Union army was cooped up on Harrison Landing.

Richmond being relieved from immediate peril of attack, Lee headed his army toward the North, to crush the Federals under Pope and threaten Washington.

CHAPTER XIII.

POPE'S CAMPAIGN.

THE ORGANIZATION OF THE ARMY OF VIRGINIA.—The recent reverses around Richmond induced the President to put forth more strenuous efforts to strengthen the Union, and to resume an offensive campaign against the Confederates. He called for a levy of 300,000 troops, and preparations were immediately made by the various States to comply with the requisition. Gen. Henry W. Halleck was summoned to Washington, and invited to assume the duties and discharge the functions of General-in-chief of the land forces of the United States. The order was dated July 11, 1862, but he did not take command until the 23d. A new army, called the Army of Virginia, was organized, comprising the three corps of Frémont, Banks, and McDowell. The troops under Generals Sumner, Burnside and Porter were sent in the latter part of August to reinforce this newly organized army. Gen. John Pope was summoned from his Western successes, June 26th, 1862, to assume the chief command of the new department. Frémont, regarding Gen. Pope as his junior, accordingly tendered his resignation, which was accepted, and Gen. Sigel was assigned to his corps. The Army of Virginia now numbered more than 40,000. Its duty was to cover Washington, defend Maryland and the lower Shenandoah Valley, and finally to threaten Richmond from the north, and there unite in the operations of McClellan against that city. The failure of McClellan before Richmond and Lee's subsequent invasion of the North compelled a revision of these designs.

CEDAR MOUNTAIN, AUGUST 9, 1862.—Gen. Pope was ordered to cross the Rappahannock and threaten Gordonsville. From the base of the Blue Ridge mountains he expected to be able to defend the approaches to Washington, to flank the columns which might be sent to the Shenandoah Valley, while he was preparing for an aggressive movement toward Richmond. Gen. Lee ordered Jackson with his veteran troops and Ewell with his division to Gordonsville to oppose Gen. Pope's advance. A. P. Hill's division soon followed, increasing the Confederate forces to 25,000 men in the vicinity of Gordonsville. Pope's forces had already advanced to Culpeper Court House. On the 9th of August a Union division met the Confederates near Cedar Mountain. A furious engagement occurred. The enemy was strongly posted, and was assailed by a force less than one-half of its own. The Confederates had the advantage in position, in numbers, and in the result. Pope then began a concentration of his forces, and expected the next day to operate upon Jackson's base, and compel him to fight on equal terms. During the night, however, Jackson withdrew from his position, and recrossed the Rapidan. The Union losses were about 2,400 against 1,300 for the enemy. While Pope's cavalry was in pursuit of the fugitives, it was discovered that Lee's whole army was moving in that direction, and near at hand. The pursuit was discontinued, and a retreat to the Rappahannock commenced.

Lee began his northward movement August 13th, as he believed that Richmond was in no great danger, and that by threatening Washington the Army of the Potomac would be recalled from the capital city of the Confederacy.

McClellan was ordered to transfer his army to Acquia creek and Alexandria, and both the Army of Virginia and the Army of the Potomac were placed under the command of Pope. McClellan evacuated the peninsula on the 17th of August. Lee was determined to strike the army under Pope before it should be reinforced by McClellan's hosts. Gen. Pope, who had expected to renew the battle against Jackson in the vicinity of Cedar Mountain, now realized that his only hope of success lay in fighting a series of retreating battles against Lee until the arrival of the Army of the Potomac. He took position to the rear of the Rappahannock, August 17, to be better able to receive aid and to oppose the invading army.

All efforts of Gen. Pope and his army to prevent the Confederate forces from crossing the Rappahannock at Waterloo bridge and elsewhere were of no avail. The main purpose of the resistance by the Union troops at the stream was to gain time and enable Gen. McClellan to reach the scene of action with the Army of the Potomac.

During the night of the 21st the Confederates threw pontoon bridges over the stream, and crossed in great numbers. The following day the batteries of both armies along the river continued to exchange shots. These skirmishes, of greater or less importance, were preliminary to the more decisive engagements soon to take place. While they progressed, many were slain, bridges burned, much property destroyed, and desolation spread over the face of the country.

SECOND BATTLE OF BULL RUN, AUG. 29 AND 30, 1862.—A mysterious delay characterized the movements of the Army of the Potomac, and Gen. Pope was ultimately compelled to meet the whole military strength of the Confederacy in Virginia, without the aid of the main Union army.

The operations of the Confederate generals were skillful and complicated. While Lee was engaging the attention of Pope, Gen. Jackson was reaching for a position in his rear. When Pope discovered the intention of the Confederate generals, he hastened toward Manassas Junction, and directed McDowell and Sigel to proceed with their troops to Gainesville, and Heintzelman and Reno to proceed to Greenwich.

Gen. Lee sent Jackson toward Pope's right wing to flank him. Passing through Thoroughfare Gap, he occupied a position to the rear of Pope's army. Gen. Pope, seeing the isolated position of Jackson's army, determined to " bag " and capture him. But the Army of the Potomac not promptly reinforcing him, his plans failed. An engagement took place in which the Federals had the advantage. Pope took possession of Manassas, and effected a consolidation of his troops, about 60,000 in number, Thursday night, August 28. It was thought that the decisive battle of the war was about to be fought. This great bat-

tle was commenced at daylight on Friday, August 29th, 1862.
The Confederate forces numbered not far from 100,000 men.
The first day's battle was favorable to the Federals. During
the engagement an opportunity was afforded to surround Jackson's forces, who were seeking to break through the Union center, and to form a junction with Lee. Gen. Pope had planned
to crush or capture Jackson's division, but Gen. Porter failed
to execute the orders sent to him, and the plan failed.

The second day was disastrous to the Union army. The overwhelming host of the enemy bore down upon the Union troops
with irresistible power. When night came Gen. Pope ordered
a retreat to Centerville. The order was promptly executed.
At Centerville reinforcements under Franklin and Sumner arrived from McClellan's Army of the Potomac. Had these been
sent a day earlier, the result of the conflict might have been
different. It was expected that Lee would follow up his victory
by an attack of the Union forces next day. But the heavy losses
suffered by both, and the great exertion which both had put
forth, made a short interval of delay and repose necessary. The
Federal army bivouacked at Centerville, awaiting further movements of the enemy.

On the first of September the Confederates were massing
forces for the purpose of attacking the Federal wagon-trains.
Gen. Pope sent a division of troops to attack them. A fierce
conflict took place near Chantilly, three miles distant from Centerville. The enemy was repulsed, after which the Federal
troops returned to camp.

The retreat of the whole Federal army was resumed on the night of September 1st, toward Washington, and on the 3d the grand armies of Virginia and the Potomac had arrived in their old quarters, protected by thirty forts, which sheltered the Federal capital.

Thus ended the campaign of Gen. Pope in Virginia, one of the most disastrous to the Federal cause that had yet taken place. The Union loss was about 14,000 and the Confederate loss about 9,000.

The battle of Chantilly cost the Union army two able officers —Generals Philip Kearny and Isaac Ingalls Stevens. The former was devotedly loved by his soldiers, and feared by the enemy. He was a stranger to fear, and in every engagement he was seen moving majestically in the fiercest and thickest of the combat. On the battle-field, taking his sword in his only hand, the reins in his teeth, he had often led his troops in the most desperate and irresistible charges. In this engagement he rode forward, unattended by any of his staff, into a gap that threatened the safety of the Federal lines, and fell mortally wounded, into the hands of the enemy. The next morning a flag of truce was sent into the Union lines, bearing with it the remains of the deceased hero.

He had served with distinction in the Mexican War, fought as a volunteer in the French army in Algeria and the Crimea, and led the patriotic troops of New Jersey in the memorable " Peninsular Campaign."

The failure of Gen. Pope to successfully check the advance of the Confederate army north is due to the fact that his numbers, without the Army of the Potomac, were much less than those of Lee, and the union of the two armies was not perfected in time to meet the advance of Lee's army. Pope was completely outgeneraled by the sagacity of Lee and the splendid marching capacity of Jackson; but he was brave, and loyal, and when he fought it was with a will beyond his discretion. He failed to divine the movements of his foe, and in consequence was not able to fight to the best purpose.

Pope attributed his defeat to the failure of Fitz John Porter to obey his orders to attack Longstreet on August 29th.

After the return of the troops to the works around Washington, Gen. Pope tendered his resignation of the command of the Army of Virginia and the Army of the Potomac, and requested to be transferred to some other post of duty. He was immediately appointed to the command of the department of the Northwest, in which lay the territory of the revolted Indian tribes.

Before leaving Washington, Gen. Pope preferred charges against several officers, chief of whom was Gen. Porter, for disobeying orders. The charges were investigated at a later period by a court-martial convened in Washington. It was proven in the trial that Porter entertained a personal hostility to Pope, and had sent telegrams ridiculing the order and management. Gen. Porter was found guilty of the charges preferred against him. The finding was approved by the President, Jan. 21,

1863. Porter was cashiered, and dismissed from service, and "forever disqualified from holding any office of profit or trust under the Government of the United States." In 1878 a board of officers retried him, and an entirely new light was thrown upon the case. It was shown that Porter's act "saved the Union Army from disaster on the 29th of August." By an act of Congress, Porter once again received a commission to the United States Army, and in 1886 he was placed on the retired list.

LEE'S INVASION OF MARYLAND, SEPTEMBER, 1862.—The remarkable successes which the Confederates had achieved in Virginia inspired them with confidence, and made them more aggressive. Lee, accordingly, began the invasion of Maryland. He passed through Leesburg, crossing the Potomac about forty miles above Washington. On the 6th the advance army commanded by Gen. Jackson reached Frederick, and took possession of that town. Such Federal property as fell into their hands they retained or destroyed. The property of individuals was not to be molested, in accordance with a proclamation issued by Gen. Jackson when he entered the State.

Lee imagined a strong disunion sentiment was slumbering in the breasts of the people of Maryland, and that the presence of his army in their midst would start active and open resistance to the Government. In his proclamation Lee endeavored to convince the people of that State that they had suffered innumerable wrongs at the hands of the National Government. and tendered his services and those of his army to assist in

recovering their "inalienable rights" as freemen. But the
Confederate army received little sympathy and coöperation
from the citizens of Maryland. The army marched through
Middletown, Boonsboro, Williamsport, and reached Hagerstown
September 9th.

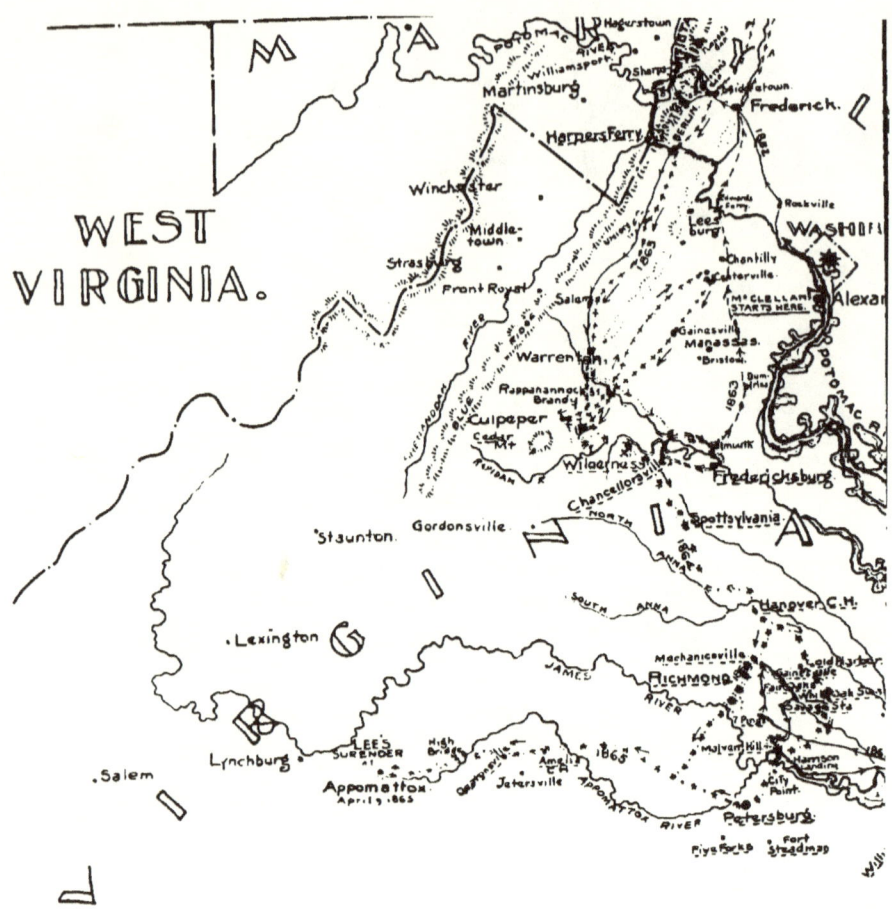

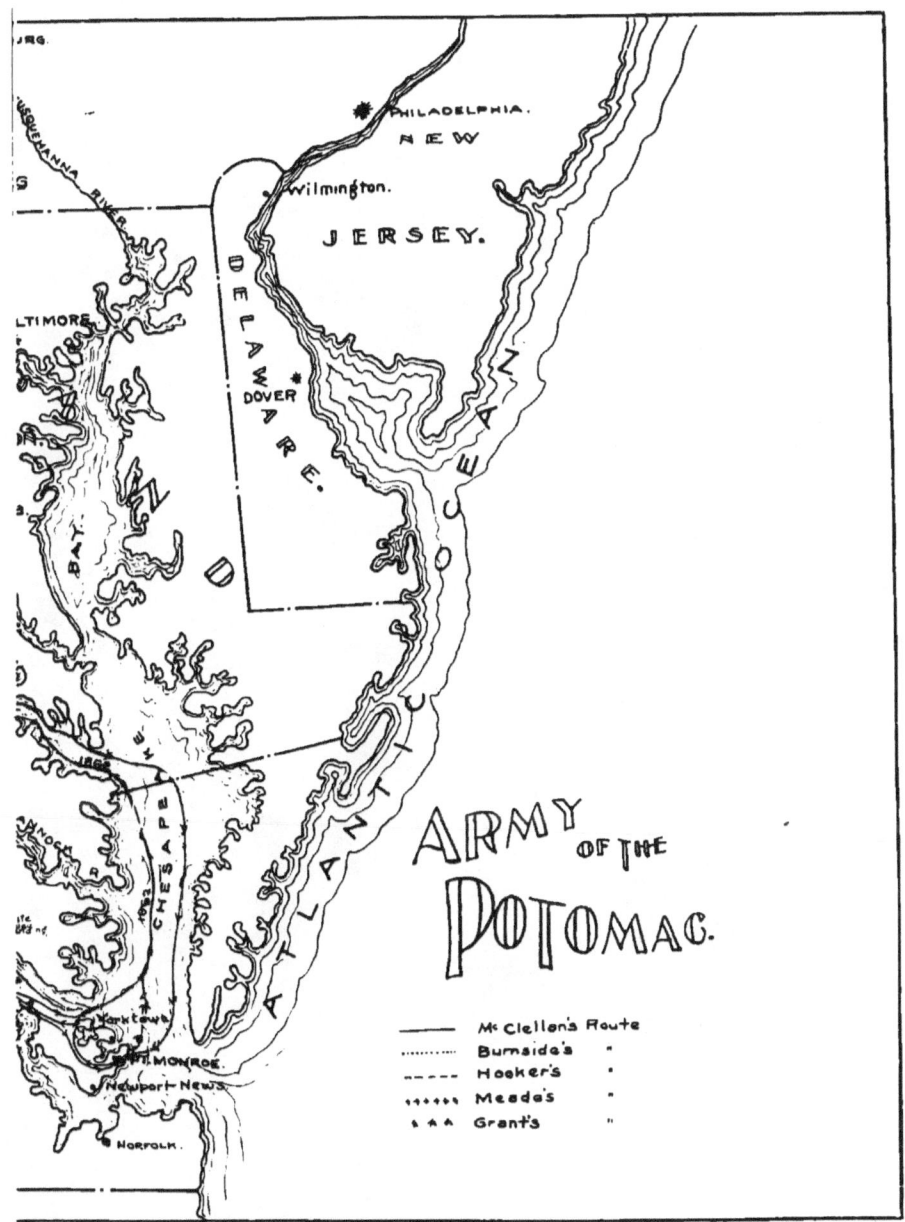

ARMY OF THE POTOMAC.

—————— McClellan's Route
.... Burnside's   "
— — — — Hooker's   "
+ + + + + Meade's   "
▲ ▲ ▲ Grant's   "

CHAPTER XIV.

FROM ANTIETAM TO FREDERICKSBURG.

SOUTH MOUNTAIN, SEPT. 14, 1862.—Gen. McClellan was reinstated to the command of the Army of the Potomac after the resignation of Gen. Pope. Leaving troops for the defense of Washington, he put his army in motion in pursuit of Lee. The loyalty of the people of Maryland and the approach of McClellan's army induced Lee to move south with the intention of crossing the Potomac at Williamsport and Harper's Ferry. Gen. McClellan placed his army in such a position that it was impossible for Lee to retreat without giving battle.

The left wing of the Federal army pursued the enemy to South Mountain. Here was a stubborn and bloody contest. The Union forces succeeded in dislodging the enemy from Turner's and Crampton's Gaps, and took possession of the field as it was abandoned under the friendly covering of the night. This engagement was called the battle of South Mountain by the Federals, and the battle of Boonsboro by the Confederates.

The Union loss was about two thousand, and the Confederate loss as many in killed and wounded, besides 1,500 prisoners.

The Union army had forced a passage through the mountains, but Lee had gained time to concentrate his scattered forces.

THE FALL OF HARPER'S FERRY, SEPT. 15, 1862.—Scarcely
had the exultant news of the victory of South Mountain been
fully realized, when all joy was dispelled by the sad tidings of
the disastrous defeat of the Union forces at Harper's Ferry.
This famous place, so often the scene of conflict and disaster in
the progress of the war, had been intrusted to Col. Dixon H.
Miles. When McClellan was reinstated to the command of the
Army of the Potomac, he recommended the withdrawal of the
11,000 troops at Harper's Ferry, but Halleck unwisely overruled him,—and soon they were withdrawn as Confederate
prisoners of war!

Lee sent Stonewall Jackson with 20,000 men against Harper's Ferry. Skirmishing commenced on the afternoon of the
12th of September, and continued until Monday, September
15th. During the progress of the conflict, the enemy had been
reinforced. In vain had Col. Miles, on Sunday, implored for
reinforcements. The place had been threatened for a week,
but adequate precaution had not been exercised to save it to the
Nation. At 8 o'clock on Monday morning the Federal ammunition was exhausted. Col. Miles immediately called a council of
war, which determined to capitulate, as further resistance would
lead to a needless loss of life. Previous to the surrender, all the
cavalry, about two thousand in number, succeeded in cutting
their way through the Confederate works, and in making their
escape. After capitulation had been proposed, but before its
terms had been agreed upon, Col. Miles was mortally wounded

by one of the bursting shells which continued to fall from the enemy's cannon.

BATTLE OF ANTIETAM, SEPT. 17, 1862.—After the defeat of the enemy at South Mountain, they continued their retreat toward the Potomac. Lee halted when he reached the heights between the village of Sharpsburg and Antietam creek; here he concentrated his scattered corps. Jackson returned with his wearied troops flushed with the victory at Harper's Ferry, and all prepared for the impending conflict.

McClellan reconnoitered the Confederate position on the 15th of September, and the next day he developed his plan of attack. Hooker occupied the right of the Union army, Burnside the left, and Meade the center. Hooker crossed Antietam creek late in the afternoon. Scarcely more than a skirmish ensued before darkness came.

Early on the morning of the 17th of September the conflict began. General Hooker's division opened the engagement. The assault became furious. Hooker was seriously wounded, and compelled to leave the field. Gen. Sumner took his command. Four times the ground he contended for was lost, and four times retaken. The operations of Burnside on the left wing were as vigorous as those of Hooker on the right. At four o'clock Gen. McClellan sent word to Burnside to advance and get possession of the enemy's batteries in front of him, at all hazards. After a spirited engagement the hill was taken, but as no reinforcements were sent to him by McClellan, who had 15,000 reserves in the rear, he was unable to hold what he had gained against the augmented forces of the foe. He was driven back to a position in front of the bridge. The Union advance was impetuous, the Confederate defense was as obstinate. The artillery in the center did effective work. The protracted struggle had nearly exhausted both sides. At length darkness descended upon the horrible scene, and closed the conflict of the day. On the one hand, the enemy had not been driven from the field; on the other, the Union troops retained the position of original assault, expecting to renew the conflict. Both armies rested on the 18th. But on the morning of the 19th, when McClellan's cavalry moved toward the river, they discovered that Lee had quietly moved off across the Potomac during the night, leaving his dead and desperately wounded on the field.

The Union loss was 12,469 as reported by McClellan. Lee reported his loss at 10,000, while his division commanders placed the aggregate in killed, wounded and missing at 13,533.

The effect of this battle was a victory for the Union army. The North was saved from further invasion, and Washington relieved from imminent danger.

Gen. Lee dispatched Stuart, the noted cavalry leader, on a raid into Pennsylvania with 1,500 horse. He made a circuit of McClellan's army October 9th to 12th. Crossing the Potomac at Williamsport, he proceeded as far as Chambersburg. He foraged the country, plundered stores, destroyed property, and took away as much booty as his troopers could carry. The Union cavalry went in pursuit of them, but they succeeded in making their escape, and again joined the ranks of Lee's army.

The Confederate army under Lee passed down the Shenandoah Valley. His own headquarters were at Berrysville, and his army in the vicinity of Winchester. He had been reinforced by the troops from West Virginia. McClellan, after a delay at Antietam, moved southeast of the mountains, and located his headquarters at Salem.

It was evident that the future plans of the commanding generals of the two armies were incomplete and undeveloped at this time. Reconnoitering expeditions were sent out to ascertain the plans of the opposing armies. Several skirmishes occurred, productive of no decisive results. Winter was fast approaching; almost two months had elapsed since the battle of Antietam, and nothing of importance had taken place. General dissatisfaction existed with the tardy manner in which McClellan had pursued the enemy. On the 5th of November, while at Warrenton, an order was conveyed to him by Gen. Buckingham that he had been relieved of the duties as commander of the Army of the Potomac, and had been superseded by Gen. Ambrose E. Burnside. He was ordered to report at Trenton, N. J.

McClellan held the devotion of his officers, and the whole body of the army were enthusiastic in their affection for him. Burnside himself would gladly have served under McClellan, but he had no alternative except to disobey orders; so he reluctantly assumed command of the Army of the Potomac and McClellan took his departure on Nov. 10th.

BATTLE OF FREDERICKSBURG, DEC. 13, 1862.—The movement of the army toward Fredericksburg was commenced on a

—13

direct line for conducting operations against Richmond, which was now contemplated. As Burnside moved from Warrenton along the north bank of the Rappahanock, Lee made a parallel movement along the south bank. By forced marches the Confederate army succeeded in occupying Fredericksburg in advance of the Union army, and at once proceeded to fortify their front. By Nov. 20th the Federal army was concentrated at Falmouth, which is on the north side of the stream, across from Fredericksburg. The next day Burnside demanded the surrender of the city, which was refused. Lee had assembled an army of about 90,000 men,—opposed by a force of 120,000.

Finally, preparations for the crossing of the river were commenced on the 11th of December. Those constructing the pontoon bridges, being exposed to a deadly fire from the Confederate sharpshooters, were three times driven back. Volunteers charged upon the sharpshooters, and drove them away, after which the bridges were completed, and the army passed over the river without any obstruction.

On the 13th of December began the obstinate and bloody battle of Fredericksburg. The enemy had exerted every energy to fortify themselves with impregnable defenses. A large portion of the army was posted behind a stone wall four feet high. The Federal troops made a valiant and determined effort to drive the foe from their defenses. Again and again they charged upon the enemy's works, but each time they were driven back with frightful slaughter. Of all the Federal troops engaged, those under Franklin alone had gained an advantage.

At length it became evident that any further attempt to take the heights would be futile, and result in a continuation of the reckless destruction of life. The troops were compelled to retire from the scene of their heroism, and took a position beyond the range of the batteries of the unconquerable foe.

No fighting of any importance took place on Sunday, the 14th. Some skirmishing occurred on the next day. During the following night, Burnside withdrew his forces across the Rappahannock to their former position.

The Federal loss in this battle was 1,128 killed, 9,105 wounded, 3,234 missing. The Confederate loss was about 5,000. The great disparity of Federal loss was due to the superior advantages of position and protection enjoyed by the Confederates, and to their vast number of guns brought into action.

Burnside wished to repeat the assault on the 14th, but the firm protests of his officers against such suicidal madness induced him to give way in his desires.

Lee was blamed for not leaving his defenses to complete the demoralization of the Army of the Potomac. For Lee to have left his works before the defeat of Burnside, would have been to invite defeat; and for him to have assailed the Union army in their defenses at Falmouth, would have been a repetition of Burnside's blunders.

The usefulness of Burnside as commander of the Army of the Potomac was at an end. Officers and soldiers alike felt that he had misjudged in ordering an assault upon the strong defenses of Fredericksburg. At his own request he was relieved of this command by the President, and Joseph Hooker was appointed to succeed him. Hooker arrived at Falmouth on the 26th of January to assume the responsibilities of his new duties. A period of several months elapsed before the Army of the Potomac again met the enemy in battle.

CHAPTER XV.

CHANCELLORSVILLE.

THE BATTLE OF CHANCELLORSVILLE, MAY 1–3, 1863.—
When Gen. Hooker took command of the Army of the Potomac,
its spirit and efficiency were at a low ebb. Desertions occurred
at the rate of 200 a day. The number absent from their regiments as shown by the rolls was 2,922 officers and 81,964
soldiers and non-commissioned officers—in hospitals, on leave,
or detached on duty; but many had deserted. The frequent
audacious Confederate cavalry raids during the winter indicated the confidence and elation of the enemy, and the apathy
born of despair, of the Federals. The Union army, though still
greater in numbers, was probably at this time no match on equal
terms for its better disciplined, self-confident and more determined foe. Hooker very properly devoted two months to organizing his army, disciplining his troops, and exalting the spirits
of his men. His energy and resources were such, that in a short
time he had at his command an army equal in numbers and
efficiency to any ever seen on this continent, save that which
McClellan commanded in the first three months of 1861. The
infantry numbered 100,000; artillery, 10,000; and cavalry,
13,000. As horses and feed were both scarce in the South,
there was not and never had been a Confederate cavalry force
that could stand against the one at Hooker's command.

Stoneman was dispatched up the north side of the Rappahannock April 27th, 1863, with orders to cross above the Orange & Alexandria Railroad; to strike Fitz Hugh Lee's cavalry, near Culpeper Court House, capture Gordonsville, and cut off Lee's communication with Richmond by destroying the Fredericksburg & Richmond Railroad, telegraph lines and bridges.

The next day, April 28th, Hooker set his infantry and artillery in motion from Falmouth for a campaign against Lee. Howard's and Slocum's corps crossed the Rappahannock at Kelly's Ford, and the Rapidan at Germania Mills, next day, and then moved toward Chancellorsville. Meade's corps crossed the Rapidan at Ely's Ford, lower down. Couch crossed with his corps at the United States Ford, on pontoons. These movements had been masked by a feint of crossing below Fredericksburg. Reynolds's, Sickles's and Sedgwick's corps, however, did cross some distance below Fredericksburg, after the river had been forded above. Thus far, Gen. Hooker had signal success in seizing the fords and crossing the streams. Never did a general feel more sanguine of administering a great and crushing defeat to his opponent. " I have Lee's army in one hand and Richmond in the other," was his exultant remark as he rode up to the single but capacious (at once mansion and tavern) house that then, with its appendages, constituted Chancellorsville.

Leaving a small force for the defense of Fredericksburg, Lee pushed his main army, at least 50,000 strong, down the Gordonsville road to a point half-way to Chancellorsville.

Hooker had left Gen. Gibbons in command of Falmouth, to guard the stores; and Sedgwick had his own corps of 22,000 men below Fredericksburg, leaving the Union forces about 70,000 in the vicinity of Chancellorsville. And here was fought, on the 1st, 2d and 3d of May, one of the bloodiest battles of the war. Hooker had planned to move from above Fredericksburg, while Sedgwick, in command of the other wing, was to move from below; and thus, by a simultaneous movement, crush the foe between them.

Gen. Hooker had been obliged to leave behind him most of his heavier guns. He was enveloped in a labyrinth of woods and thickets, which were traversed by narrow roads, every inch of which was familiar to the Confederates, and unknown to Hooker and his men. His ignorance of the region of woods prevented Hooker from bringing most of his troops into action at any one time.

While Pleasonton's artillery was supporting Sickles's infantry to arrest the impetuous charge of 25,000 troops under Stonewall Jackson, night descended upon the scene, but did not end the contest. In front of these batteries fell Stonewall Jackson.*

Mortally wounded in a dense wood, shrouded by the gloom of night, while men were falling all around him from the grape

---

* "Gen. Jackson rode ahead of his skirmishers, and exposed himself to a close and dangerous fire of the Confederate sharpshooters, posted in the timber. It was now between 9 and 10 o'clock at night; the little body of horsemen was taken for Federal cavalry, and the regiments on the right and left fired a volley into them, with the most lamentable results. Several of his staff were killed. Gen. Jackson received one ball

and canister of the Union guns, it may seem difficult to determine whether Jackson was shot by his own or by Union men. The best authority substantiates the theory that his wounds were inflicted by his own men.

His loss was the greatest the Confederates had yet sustained in the fall of a single man, though Albert Sidney Johnston had military talent of a high order. Jackson's power over his men was unexcelled by any officer. It was justified by his soundness of judgment, as well as by his intrepidity of spirit. His attacks were soundly planned, and the opposing forces well calculated. He refused to sacrifice the lives of his men in vain endeavors, with the same spirit that led him in his most brilliant charges.

While Gen. Hooker was leaning against a pillar of the Chancellorsville house watching the battle, a cannon-ball struck the pillar, hurling him to the floor insensible. At this very moment Gen. Sickles was committing great havoc upon the Confederate lines, but as his cartridges were running low, he sent twice to

---

in his left arm, shattering the bone and severing an artery; a second passed through the same arm below the elbow; a third passed through the palm of his hand. He fell from his horse, and was caught by Captain Wormly, to whom he said, 'All my wounds are by my own men.'

"The firing was responded to by the Federals, who made a sudden advance; and actually charged over Jackson's body. He was not discovered, however; and after the Federals were driven back he was rescued. One of the litter-bearers was shot down, and Jackson fell from the shoulders of the men, receiving a severe contusion, and injuring his side. He was taken to the hospital, and died eight days after. His remains were taken to Lexington, Va., his own home."—[From the Life of Stonewall Jackson: By a Virginian.]

Hooker for assistance. But as Hooker was lying unconscious, and Couch, who was next in rank, had not assumed the responsibility of command, no aid was sent to Sickles, and he was compelled to fall back. Had a corps been sent to Sickles, he believes victory would have been his. By noon, Hooker regained consciousness and assumed command. But the precious hour had passed while the army was without a head.

After Lee had dealt a telling blow to Hooker's forces at Chancellorsville, he learned that Sedgwick had carried the heights of Fredericksburg. Leaving Hooker inactive from the blow already inflicted upon him, he turned upon his new foe, crowding him back to the river, and next day across it.

Hooker's plan of having Sedgwick fall upon the rear of Lee's army simultaneously with his own attack in front, and between them crush the enemy, had failed. How hazardous an attempt at concerted action of a great army from distant points, was not now learned for the first time.

After Sickles was out of the way, Lee turned his whole force toward Hooker, who was quietly sitting behind his hastily constructed defenses at Chancellorsville. But the enemy had been marching and fighting until they were exhausted, and were slaughtered in their reckless assault on our batteries on Sunday, May 3d; and Lee was not willing to repeat the attack. The day passed with but little skirmishing, and during the night Hooker recrossed the river to his old camping-grounds at Falmouth.

This defeat cost the Union army in killed and wounded, 17,197 men, and two generals,—Berry and Whipple. The

Confederate loss is variously estimated at from 12,000 to 18,000 men, and Generals Paxton and Jackson—"Stonewall" Jackson, whose presence was like magic to his troops.

The operations of the cavalry under Stoneman had been ill-advised, feeble, and inefficient. If his forces had been kept together he could have severed all communications between Lee and Richmond, isolating him from supplies, and rendered his position precarious and dangerous. Dissipating his forces as he did, he was too weak to meet the enemy, and kept running from them instead of running after them, and gave his expedition the appearance of a furtive raid on smokehouses and hen-roosts, rather than that of a great military movement of a stupendous war.

Thus ended the campaign at Chancellorsville,—the second serious disaster that the Army of the Potomac had sustained within a period of six months. The hearts of the people of the South beat in exultation as they beheld the ascendency of the Southern arms. Gloom and depression pervaded the homes of the loyal people in the North, while the Southern sympathizers became clamorous for a termination of hostilities upon the basis of independence of the South.

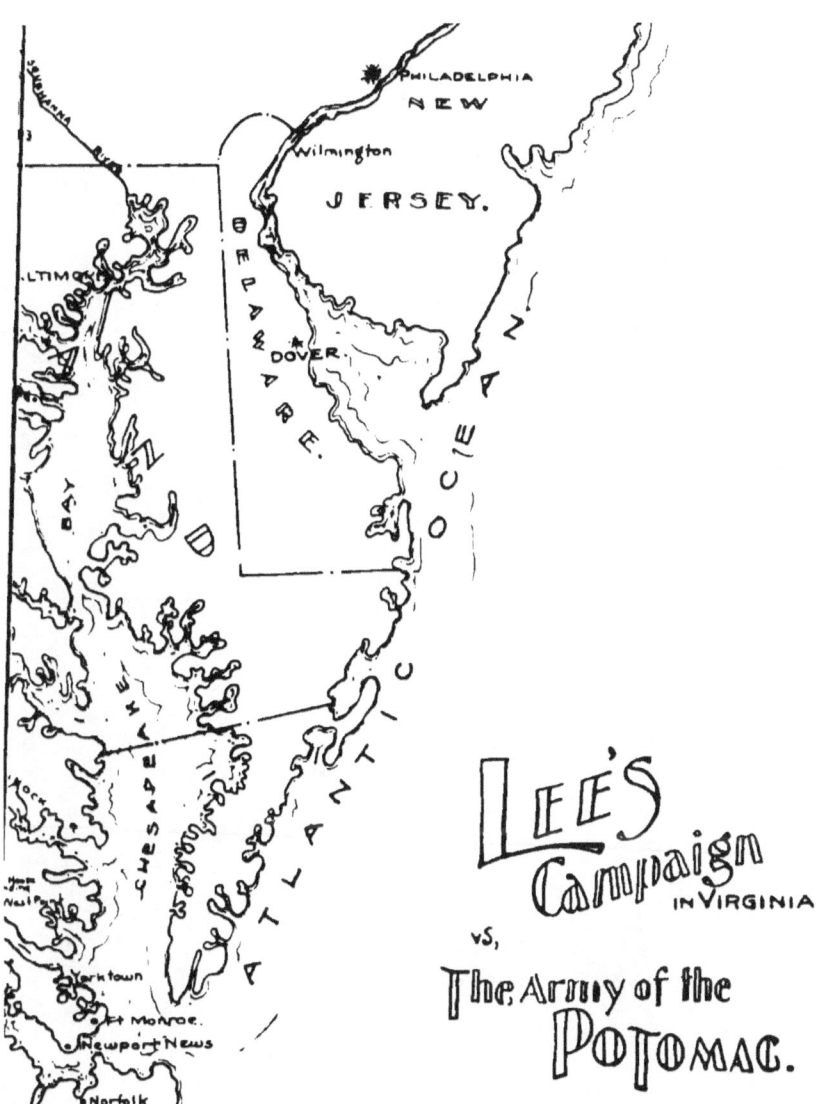

LEE'S Campaign IN VIRGINIA vs, The Army of the POTOMAC.

LIBRA

CHAPTER XVI.

GETTYSBURG.

Lee's Second Invasion of the North, June and July, 1863.—After the battle of Chancellorsville the two opposing armies occupied exactly the same positions which they did some days after the battle of Antietam,—Hooker at Falmouth and Lee across the river at Fredericksburg. Hooker lost some 20,000 men by expiration of their term of service. His army had been depleted after the sanguinary battle of Chancellorsville. Gen. Lee's forces had been reinforced by the hasty return of Longstreet from his sterile demonstration before Suffolk, and by drafts upon every quarter from which a regiment could be secured.

Gen. Lee, with probably a superiority of numbers, for a temporary period, after a month of rest and waiting set his army in motion up along the south bank of the Rappahannock, concentrating forces at Culpeper Court House. And then began his second invasion of the North. Passing down the Shenandoah Valley, on June 14 he defeated R. H. Milroy at Winchester, and took about 4,000 prisoners. The Government had taken the alarm, organized two new military departments in Pennsylvania, and called on the nearest States for a large number of militia.

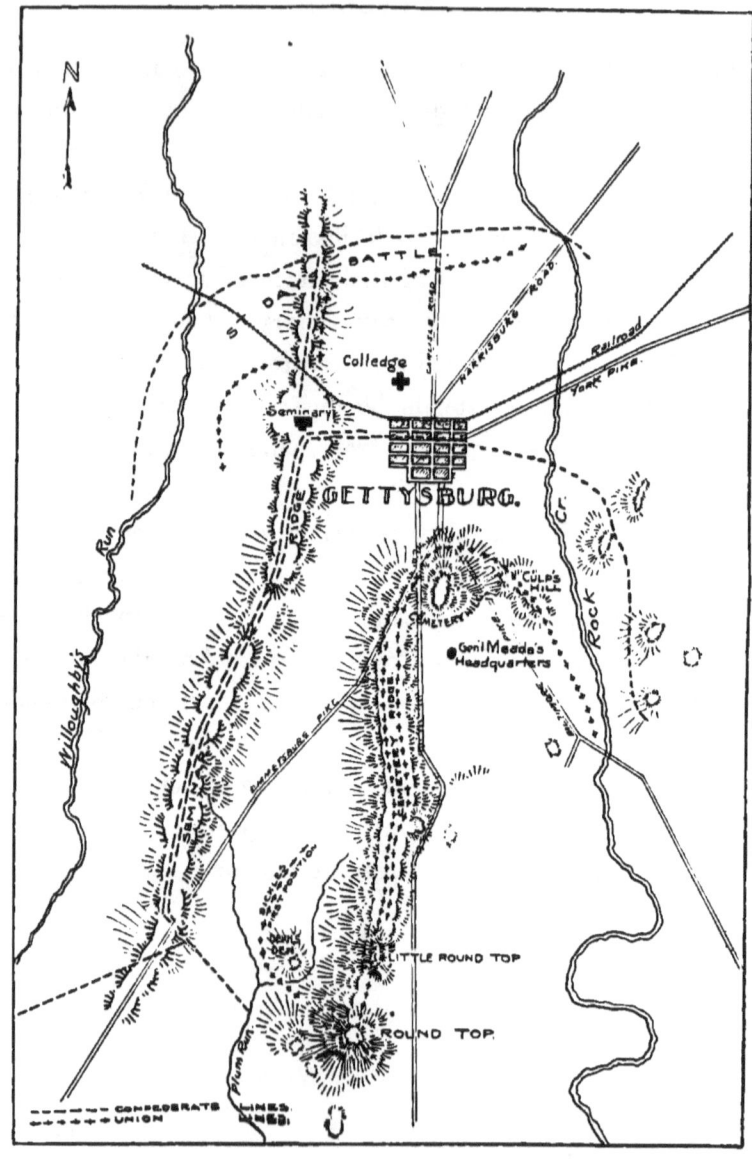

Gen. Hooker began to march north along the Blue Ridge, watching its passes, through Dumfries to Centerville, covering Washington on the right. Meantime our cavalry under Pleasonton was constantly confronted by that of Lee under Stuart, and nearly every day witnessed some skirmishing along the passes of the mountains.

The Confederates crossed the Potomac, taking possession of Chambersburg, Carlisle, and York. Gen. Hooker crossed the Potomac at Edwards Ferry, and advanced to Frederick. His army, being strengthened by 15,000 men from the defenses of Washington, numbered about 100,000, while Lee's army was about equal in size.

It was very imperative that a force sufficiently strong should be concentrated to repel the invaders. With this purpose in view, Gen. Hooker desired the troops stationed at Maryland Heights opposite Harper's Ferry to be withdrawn from that point. Gen. Halleck, General-in-chief at Washington, objected to the withdrawal of the troops, and instructed Hooker to defend the place on the left and Washington on the right, and meet the invading army. After communicating with Halleck, and receiving his instruction, Hooker sent the following resignation:

SANDY HOOK, June 27, 1863.

Maj. Gen. H. W. Halleck, General-in-Chief: Your original instruction required me to cover Harper's Ferry and Washington. I have now imposed upon me, in addition, an enemy in front, of more than my numbers. I beg to be understood, respectfully but firmly, that I am unable to comply with this condition, with the means at my disposal, and earnestly request that I may at once be relieved from the position I occupy.

JOSEPH HOOKER, *Maj. Gen.*

Halleck never had been favorable to Hooker as commander of this army. He had prevented his selection as the successor of McClellan, and had opposed his selection after the defeat of Burnside, and now very naturally improved the opportunity afforded. The next day Hooker was relieved of the command at Frederick, and the army was placed under the command of Gen. G. G. Meade, who was advised that he might do what he pleased with the Maryland Heights men; while Couch and his militia at Harrisburg, estimated at 20,000, were also placed under his orders.

Such a change of commanders on the eve of a great battle for no more urgent reasons has but few parallels in history. Whatever his faults, Hooker was loved and trusted by his soldiers, who knew less of Meade. If they had been consulted, they would have cast an overwhelming majority vote in favor of Hooker.

BATTLE OF GETTYSBURG, JULY 1–3, 1863.—Gen. Ewell of the Confederate army occupied York June 28th, and levied upon the town for $100,000 in cash, and a vast quantity of food and clothing. Lee had hastened to concentrate his whole army at Gettysburg when he heard that the Union army had crossed the Potomac. Meade had fixed a line along Pipe creek, some fifteen miles southeast of Gettysburg, as advantageous ground whereon to meet the foe; but an unexpected encounter precipitated the grand collision, and brought on the great battle of Gettysburg.

On July 1st Gen. Buford marched upon Gettysburg, where

he encountered the van of the Confederate army, under Gen. Heth, of Hill's corps, and drove them back upon their division, by whom our troops were in turn repelled. While Gen. John F. Reynolds, in command of two corps, was rapidly coming up, and while he went forward to reconnoiter, he fell mortally wounded by a Confederate sharpshooter.

And now began a rapid concentration of forces. The Union troops had been greatly outnumbered in the engagement north west of the village July 1st, and were driven into and through Gettysburg. They were rallied on Cemetery Hill, just south of the village. The Confederates did not press the advantage, fearing reinforcements had come,—as indeed they had.

During the afternoon and night the entire Confederate army and the entire Union army, save one corps which arrived on the forenoon of the 2d, had been concentrated along the ridges at Gettysburg, facing each other at distances of from one to two miles.

The next day, July 2d, was spent in skirmishes and preparation for battle, until about three o'clock, when a fierce general assault was made upon the front and flank of Sickles's corps, who had advanced from one-half to three-fourths of a mile nearer the Confederate line than Meade had instructed him to do. A desperate struggle ensued, but he was forced back with heavy loss to Round Top, which the enemy assailed with great vehemence and determination. They at one time had nearly carried it, but when reinforcements were thrown upon their front, they in turn were driven to the ridge from which Sickles had been expelled, and to which he should not have advanced. When night closed on the 2d day of July, the Confederates felt encouraged and confident. Their loss, though great, was not so heavy as Meade's.

After several sharp conflicts on Friday, July 3d, there was a pause while the enemy was making its disposition of troops and posting its batteries for one supreme effort, which was to decide the terrible contest. At length, at one o'clock, 115 heavy guns from Hill's and Longstreet's front concentered a terrific fire upon Cemetery Hill, the center and key of the position of the Federal army. A little behind the crest of the hill had been Meade's headquarters. About 100 Union guns made fit reply to the enemy. For two hours the artillery duel waged. Finding our guns had become heated, Meade gave orders to cease firing, to cool them; and believing that the Union guns had been silenced, the enemy's infantry emerged from behind the batteries, and, moving swiftly forward, supported by the reserves, confident of victory, made one determined, desperate and consummate effort to drive the valiant defenders of the Union from their stronghold. On they came—Pickett's splendid division, the flower and pride of their army, in the lead, in that famous but fatal charge. Grape and canister and musket-ball were concentrated upon the advancing foe. Their lines melted away like snow before a summer's sun. It was a fruitless sacrifice. They gathered up their broken fragments and retreated in defeat.

Gen. Meade, though not brilliant and daring in his exploits, was wise and able. The Confederate batteries were strongly posted on Seminary Ridge; his on Cemetery Ridge. He had fought a defensive battle and won a decisive victory. Had he assailed Lee's batteries, the result might have been different. Had Lee assailed Burnside on the heights of Falmouth, he no doubt would have met a similar defeat. Burnside chose rather to assail Lee's army intrenched in a stronger position than Meade's at Gettysburg.

Meade did not follow the retreating Confederate army immediately. His ammunition had become scarce. He did not know that Lee's was more completely exhausted. Nearly one-fourth of his army lay dead or wounded on the field of battle. The rest of the army were worn out with the desperate struggle during the two-days battle. Only one brigade, standing at ease, constituted the reserve, not brought into use. If he had pressed his victory by an immediate attack upon Seminary Ridge, his forces might have met a repulse. These are the reasons Meade did not immediately pursue the retreating foe.

The evolution of events after Meade took command of the Army of the Potomac showed that he had made a mistake in not bringing the Maryland Heights and Couch's troops from Harrisburg, within aiding distance as a general engagement became imminent. They were placed at his disposal. With French's 11,000 from Maryland Heights and Couch's 15,000 or 20,000 at Harrisburg, his force would have been sufficient to intercept the retreat of Lee, and administer a much more crushing punishment upon the Confederate army.

—14

The Union army lost 2,834 killed, 13,709 wounded, 6,643 missing (mainly taken prisoners); total, 23,186.

The Confederates lost 22,500 killed and wounded, besides about 6,000 prisoners.

During the 2d and 3d the cavalry of both armies kept hovering around the flank of the adversary, with occasional collisions. At the close of the battle, Gen. Pleasonton, in command of the cavalry, being satisfied of the demoralization of the enemy and of the depletion of his ammunition, urged Meade to order a general advance. He chose, however, not to do this. On the 4th an advance division of Gen. Couch's militia, about four thousand strong, arrived as reinforcements to the Union army.

When Meade became convinced that the enemy was in full retreat, on the 5th he ordered Gen. Sedgwick's Sixth Corps to follow on the track of the fugitives. Reinforcements were soon sent to the aid of Sedgwick, but he chose rather to hover around their rear, watching them, than to bring about a general engagement.

Gen. Lee recrossed the Potomac at Falling Water and Williamsport. Owing to the fact that the weak guard left by Lee at these places had been taken by Gen. French, a delay occurred in the retreat of Lee's army, which enabled the pursuing forces of Meade to overtake them while they were collecting material for the reconstruction of the bridge which had been destroyed.

A council of the corps commanders called by Meade to consider the expediency of an attack upon Lee's army, next morning, decided against it by a vote of three in favor and five against it. While Meade agreed with the minority, he did not wish to take the responsibility of overruling the majority. The night of the 13th, Lee's army crossed the Potomac, and continued its march south, with occasional skirmishes between the opposing forces.

CHAPTER XVII.

GRANT'S OVERLAND CAMPAIGN.

Lieut. Gen. U. S. Grant in Command of all the Armies of the North, March 12, 1864.—On the 29th of February, 1864, Congress revived the grade of Lieutenant-General, a rank hitherto accorded only to George Washington (Gen. Scott being such only by brevet), and authorizing the President to assign the officer of that rank to command of all the armies of the United States. Major-General Ulysses S. Grant, who had achieved a series of brilliant victories in the West, was chosen to this command, receiving his commission of Lieutenant-General on the 9th of March following.* On the 10th he visited the Army of the Potomac, with headquarters at Brandy Station, and after making a flying visit to Sherman in the West to perfect plans for a simultaneous movement of the armies in the West toward Atlanta, and the Army of the Potomac toward Richmond, he returned to Brandy Station, and established his headquarters in the field, instead of at Washington as Halleck had done. Gen. Meade retained immediate command of the Army of the Potomac, which had been reorganized and consolidated from five corps into three, commanded respectively by

---

*He was nominated to the rank, March 1, 1864, and assumed command of all the armies on the 12th of March.

Generals Winfield S. Hancock (2d), George S. Warren (5th), and John Sedgwick (6th). It was stationed in the vicinity of Culpeper Court House; while Lee's Army of Northern Virginia was posted along the Rapidan from Barnett's Ford to Morton's Ford, a distance of eighteen or twenty miles. Gen. Burnside, commanding the Ninth Corps in Maryland, crossed the Potomac and joined Meade's army, though his corps was not formally incorporated into the Army of the Potomac until after the crossing of the Rapidan. Gen. Halleck was announced as relieved from his command at his own request, and assigned to duty in Washington as "Chief of Staff to the Army."

On the very day that Sherman set out on his "Great March" south, General Grant with an army of more than 100,000 men commenced the "Great Overland Campaign" against General Lee and Richmond. The order for the movement of the army was issued May 2d, and the army set in motion at midnight following, crossing the Rapidan on Lee's right at Germania and Ely's Fords.

The advantage of this movement was found in the fact that it established an easy avenue of communications for supplies, keeping the army near navigable waters, connected with Washington and other depots of supplies. No protecting force would be necessary to cover these short land routes from rivers to the army. The objection consisted in the character of the country to the south of the Rapidan, through which the army had to march a distance of fifteen or twenty miles, and in which it would be obliged to fight the first battle.

The Battle of the Wilderness, May 5–6, 1864.—The
" Wilderness," which is now historic, is a tract of broken table-
land, seamed with ravines, and covered with forest, and over
a very large part of its extent was an almost impenetrable under-
growth. Several good roads crossed the Wilderness. Besides
these there were numerous wood roads, connecting mines, farms,
main roads, etc. In this labyrinth, numbers, artillery and cavalry were of little account; but local knowledge of the ground,
a command of the roads, and advantage of position, were of
prime importance.

Gen. Grant had expected, by moving his army at midnight,
to be able to pass through this wilderness to the open country
unmolested. But Lee, alert and vigilant, discovered Grant's
movement. Moving his army eastward to meet the Union advance, he formed his lines of battle in the Wilderness some six
miles east of his strong defenses on Mine Run, which proffered
a safe refuge in case of disaster. The battle opened unexpectedly to the Union Generals on the morning of May 5th, and continued for two days with persistent and desperate fighting. Gen.
Lee had intrenched the whole front of his army, behind which
he was willing to receive an attack but from which he was not
desirous of advancing. As the battle in the Wilderness was not
of Grant's choosing, but wholly Lee's, Grant resolved to resume
his march, and accordingly moved southward, aiming to concentrate his army on the high ground around Spottsylvania
Court House.

The Union losses in this terrible conflict in the Wilderness were 2,265 killed, 10,220 wounded, and 2,902 missing.

On the Union side Gen. James S. Wadsworth was killed, and Gens. Hancock (slightly), Getty, Gregg, Owen, Bartlett, Webb and Carroll wounded.

Lee's loss was no doubt considerably less than Grant's, as he was fighting on the defensive most of the time, and, in the case of Ewell and Hill, well intrenched. Nevertheless, their loss was severe, as their own estimate, which is the lowest made, places it at 8,000. Gens. Sam Jones and Albert G. Jenkins were killed. Among the wounded were Gens. Longstreet (disabled for months), Pickett, Pegram, and Hunter.

SPOTTSYLVANIA COURT HOUSE, MAY 8–12, 1864.—On the evening of May 7th, Grant commenced a night movement to the left of Lee, toward Richmond. This brought Lee's army forward. Several spirited conflicts resulted in the march southward between the opposing forces.

On the 9th the Union troops were concentrated around Spottsylvania Court House, confronted by the Army of North Virginia under Lee. While placing his guns, and bantering some of his men who winced at flying bullets, Gen. Sedgwick was instantly killed by a Confederate sharpshooter in a time of comparative quiet. Gen. H. G. Wright succeeded to his command next day, when a general engagement took place with no decisive results.

Gen. Grant next morning dispatched to the War Department the following pithy bulletin:

HEADQUARTERS IN THE FIELD, May 11, 1864—8 A. M.

We have now ended the sixth day of heavy fighting. The result to this time is much in our favor.

Our losses have been heavy, as well as those of the enemy. I think the loss of the enemy must be greater.

We have taken 5,000 prisoner by battle, whilst he has taken few from us but stragglers.

I propose to fight it out on this line if it takes all summer.

U. S. GRANT,

Lieutenant-General Commanding the Armies of the U. S.

The next day was spent in reconnoitering, skirmishing, and getting ready for battle. The afternoon and night were rainy. When morning came, the rain gave place to a fog of intense density. Under cover of this fog, Gen. Hancock advanced toward the Confederates in two lines. Before him was a salient angle of earthworks protecting the foe, behind which Gen. Edward Johnson's division of Ewell's corps rested. Swiftly and noiselessly sweeping over the rugged and wooded space intervening between the two lines, the Union troops pressed up to the very earthworks unobserved. Dashing with a thundering cheer over the front and flank of the enemy's works, and surprising the foe in his trenches, they captured Gen. Edward Johnson, Brig. Gen. Geo. H. Stewart,* and about 3,000 prisoners, who were sent to the rear. After the Confederates' surprise was over, and their rally to this point was complete, one of

---

* Stewart and Hancock were old army friends before the opening of the war. When Stewart was brought before Hancock as a prisoner, the latter extended his hand and very cordially inquired, "How are you, Stewart?" Stewart haughtily replied, "I am General Stewart, of the Confederate Army, and, under the circumstances, I decline to take your hand." "And under any other circumstances, General, I should not have offered it," was the prompt and fit response of the victor.

the most remarkable conflicts ever recorded in the annals of history ensued. Charge followed charge in rapid succession. Five desperate assaults by Lee upon the captured works followed, but without success. The men fought hand-to-hand, with their banners planted on opposite sides of the same breastworks. Five dreadful assaults by the enemy were all repelled with frightful carnage, but Hancock was unable to advance any farther. Rain set in about noon, but the fighting continued until midnight, when Lee's army was withdrawn from the conflict, and fortified a line immediately in front of Hancock's.

The Union army resumed its march next day toward Richmond. As it moved southward, new bases were established at Port Royal, and later at White House, on the York river. The base on the north of the Rapidan was abandoned for a new one at Fredericksburg, and that at Fredericksburg for the one at Port Royal, and this one for the one at White House, as the army made successive marches toward Richmond.

SHERIDAN'S RAID TOWARD RICHMOND, MAY, 1864.—Gen. Sheridan, with the better part of his cavalry led by Merritt, Wilson, and Gregg, was on May 9th dispatched on a raid toward Richmond. Moving southward, and destroying railroads, stores, and supplies, he met the Confederate cavalry under Gen. J. E. B. Stuart at Yellow Tavern, a few miles north of Richmond. Gen. Stuart and Brig. Gen. J. B. Gordon were mortally wounded, and their force driven toward Ashland, leaving the road to Richmond open. The outer works of the Confederate capital were taken, but the inner works could not be taken with the force at hand; and Sheridan moved north, and again joined the Army of the Potomac, after an absence of little more than two weeks, in season to take part in the bloody battle of Cold Harbor.

GENERAL BUTLER'S MOVEMENT AGAINST RICHMOND IN MAY AND JUNE, 1864.—Gen. Butler, commanding at Fortress Monroe, was sent to menace Richmond from that direction, at the same time Grant began his Overland Campaign. Embarking his infantry and artillery, 25,000 strong, Gen. Butler proceeded up the James river, and then passed southward by land to within three miles of Petersburg. Gen. Beauregard was summoned from Charleston with all the available forces from that section, to oppose Gen. Butler's demonstration. News from Washington to the effect that Lee could not long withstand the advance of Grant's vicorious army, led Butler north to participate in the expected speedy capture of Richmond. Gen. Beauregard was not long in following the Union army toward Richmond, and suddenly made a desperate attack upon it, which resulted in a loss of about four thousand men to Gen. Butler's army, and almost an equal number to the Confederates. There was some fighting along the front of the lines from the 17th to the 21st, with considerable loss on each side, but with no decisive results.

NORTH ANNA, MAY 23-26, 1864.—On the 22d of May, while Grant was moving his army from Spottsylvania Court House south, he ordered Gen. Smith of Butler's command to bring all the available troops, some 10,000 in number, to join the Army of the Potomac. Gen. Beauregard received from Gen. Lee a like order for troops, which was complied with. After Butler's army had been diminished he settled down to a policy of inaction behind intrenchments.

Gen. Grant's flanking advance from Spottsylvania Court House to North Anna was admirably executed, without any loss. But this movement was readily detected from the high ground held by Lee, who possessed the best and most direct route to Richmond. Gen. Grant was compelled to make a considerable detour eastward, over inferior roads. When the Union army reached North Anna river, it found its old antagonist planted across the stream in an admirable position, and prepared to dispute any further advance. Hancock, Warren and Wright effected a passage of the river with little difficulty, but Burnside was driven back when he attempted to push his corps across the river between the right and left wings of the Union army. Realizing that Lee's position, with his left resting on Little river and his right protected by a swamp and his front strongly fortified, was almost impregnable, Grant,* after deliberate and careful

---

*An incident in Grant's march, told by him: "I was seated on the porch of a fine plantation house, waiting for Burnside's corps to pass. Meade and his staff, besides my own staff, were with me. The lady of the house, a Mrs. Tyler, and an elderly lady were present. Burnside, seeing me, came up on the porch, his big spurs and saber rattling as he walked. He touched his hat politely to the ladies, and said he supposed they had never seen so many live Yankees before. The elderly lady spoke up promptly, saying, 'Oh, yes, I have. Many more.' 'Where?' said Burnside. 'In Richmond.' Prisoners, of course, was understood."

reconnoissance, cautiously withdrew his army, May 26, from the front of the enemy's lines, recrossed the river, and, pushing eastward for a distance, again set south for Richmond. Passing down to the Pamunkey, which he crossed at Hanovertown, he pushed on for the Chickahominy.

COLD HARBOR, JUNE 1–12, 1864.—Gen. Lee, marching by the shorter route, again intrenched his army so as to intercept the movement southward of the Army of the Potomac. Grant had shown his aversion to sacrificing the lives of his men at North Anna, while another avenue toward Richmond was open. Now he believed that the great object of the campaign required him to disregard the advantages of position possessed by the fortified enemy. Gen. W. F. Smith, with 10,000 men detached from Butler's command, arrived in the latter part of May, and took post on the Union right. Gen. Meade gave orders for an advance with a view to forcing a passage of the Chickahominy. On the afternoon of the 2d of June an assault was made upon the advance lines of the Confederates, who were driven to their second line, which was much stronger than the first. Grant and Meade resolved that the Confederate lines should be broken on the morrow.

Before sunrise on June 3d the whole Union front moved forward bravely, firmly and swiftly to a valiant assault of the foe. They were repulsed, however, with terrible slaughter. Greeley says:

"Twenty minutes after the first shot was fired, 10,000 of our men were stretched writhing on the sod, or still and calm in death; while the enemy's loss was little more than 1,000. And when, some hours later, orders were sent by Gen. Meade to each corps commander to renew the assault at once, without regard to any other, the men simply and unanimously refused to obey."

The total loss at and around Cold Harbor was about 13,000, of whom 1,700 were killed, 9,000 wounded, and about 2,300 missing. There is no record of the Confederate loss from the 27th of May to 12th of June, but it is estimated at about three or four thousand killed, wounded, and missing.

Gen. Lee, overestimating the effect of the repulse upon the morale of our men, hazarded a night attack upon the hastily constructed defenses of the Federal front, but he was repulsed at every point. On the 6th an armistice of two hours, from four to six o'clock, was agreed upon for the removal of the wounded lying between the armies, and for the burial of the dead.

Grant now decided to cross the Chickahominy far to Lee's right, move across the James, and attack Richmond from the south. This exposure of the Federal capital to a possible attack from Lee met with little favor among authorities at Washington, who had a settled and reasonable repugnance to any movement that would open the way to Washington.

The Army of the Potomac was put in motion for the passage of the James river on June 12th.

Gen. Grant's movement from Rapidan to Cold Harbor is called "The Overland Campaign" in contrast to McClellan's movement down the Potomac and Chesapeake two years before.

MARCH UPON PETERSBURG, JUNE, 1864.—While Gen. Grant was crossing the James, he ordered Butler to attempt speedily to take Petersburg with the corps of Gen. Smith, which had been returned to him from the Army of the Potomac. It became known that the van of Lee's army under A. P. Hill was already south of Richmond.

Petersburg, the head of sloop navigation on the Appomattox river, twenty-two miles south of Richmond, is the focus of all railroads excepting one connecting the Confederate capital with the south and southwest. It was poorly defended at this time, and could have been taken if Gen. Smith had conducted a vigorous movement against it. But inaction and hesitancy permitted the opportunity to capture the place to pass by. During the night of June 15th many of Lee's veterans found rest and shelter behind the works. The next day the Confederate Army of Virginia had taken refuge in and around Richmond and Petersburg, while most of the Army of the Potomac had arrived in the vicinity of the same places.

The desperate struggle for Petersburg had drawn the enemy mainly to that city. Gen. Grant, believing that a large part of the enemy had not yet arrived, ordered a general assault upon Petersburg on the 18th.

The assault was not a success. The Federal troops were repulsed with heavy losses and a few prisoners. The enemy, sheltered behind their works, bore but light loss.

It had now been established that Petersburg could not be carried by direct assault, no matter what force might be hurled against it. From that day the siege of Petersburg and Richmond was resolved upon, and the regular work of conducting the siege was begun. Grant kept Lee constantly occupied in warding off his attacks. His cavalry was sent on various expeditions; one point of line would be threatened, and then another attacked. The Confederate chieftain repelled all attempts to gain the southern capital. But he witnessed his army wearing away from day to day faster than it could be reinforced, while the heavy drains upon the Union ranks could be replenished by frequent reinforcements. In vain did Lee try to break through the lines of his antagonist, or to divert his attention by raids threatening Washington. He only beheld the Union lines press closer and firmer around his dwindling and weakening army, as it lay intrenched and besieged in the Confederate capital.

THE MINE EXPLOSION, JULY 30, 1864.—Gen. Burnside's corps held a position directly in front of Petersburg, where a fort projected in advance of the Confederate lines, and extended within 150 yards of the Union lines. Under this fort a mine had been run from a convenient ravine within our lines, which was entirely screened from the enemy's observation. On the 30th of July the mine was fired, annihilating the fort and destroying the garrison of 300 men, leaving a gigantic hollow of loose earth, 150 by 60 feet, and twenty-five or thirty feet deep. The Union guns opened all along the front upon the astonished enemy, and a strong storming party was ordered to press through the gap thus formed.

Gen. Grant speaks of the mine affair as follows:

"There had been some delay on the left and right in advancing, but some of the troops did get in and turn to the right and left, carrying the rifle-pits as I expected they would do.

"There had been great consternation in Petersburg, as we were well aware, about the rumored mine that we were going to explode. . . . We had learned through a deserter who had come in that the people had very wild rumors about what was going on. They said we had undermined the whole of Petersburg; that they were resting upon a slumbering volcano. I somewhat based my calculations upon this state of feeling, and expected that when the mine was exploded the troops to the right and left would flee in all directions, and that our troops, if they moved promptly, could get in and strengthen themselves before the enemy had come to realize the true situation. It was just as I expected it would be. We could see the men running without any apparent object except to get away. It was half an hour before musketry-firing, to any amount, was opened upon our men in the crater. It was an hour before the enemy got artillery to play upon them, and it was nine o'clock before Lee got up reinforcements to help in expelling our troops.

"The effort was a stupendous failure. It cost us 4,000 men, mostly, however, captured,—and all due to the inefficiency on the part of the corps commander, and the incompetency of the division commander who was sent to lead the assault."

EMBARRASSMENTS.—Gen. Sherman, who was at Atlanta, wanted reinforcements. He was willing to take the raw troops being raised in the Northwest. Grant kept watch that Confederate reinforcements should not be sent from Virginia, to move against Sherman from his north or east. It was feared that Gen. Kirby Smith, in command of the trans-Mississippi river forces, might also go against Sherman; but a force was held ready to hold him in check. In the midst of these embarrassments, Halleck informed Grant that there was an organized scheme on foot in the North to resist the draft; he suggested that troops might be required to put the rising down, and advised him, at the same time, "to take in his sail and not go too fast."

WELDON RAILROAD TAKEN, AUGUST 18, 1864. — While Sheridan was conducting a telling campaign against Early in the Shenandoah Valley, Grant was active before Richmond and Petersburg. He ordered a demonstration against Richmond on the south side of the James, August 14th, to prevent more reinforcements from being sent to Early. The threatening position was maintained for a number of days, with more or less skirmishing, and some tolerably hard fighting. Instructions had been given to prevent anything like a general battle unless there should be opportunities for a decided success.

This demonstration against Richmond caused Lee to withdraw many of his troops from Petersburg. Grant then ordered Gen. Warren to capture Weldon Railroad, a road of great importance to the enemy, as the avenues for bringing Confederate supplies to the army were already being much contracted. It was evident that the capture and maintenance of this road would

—15

bring about some desperate fighting. The movement was made on the morning of August 18th. After some heavy fighting the road was carried, the new position fortified, and reinforcements sent to hold it. Lee made repeated attempts to dislodge Warren's corps, but without success, and with heavy losses. The cost to the Union army in the entire movement for the possession of the Weldon Railroad was about 4,550 men killed, wounded, and missing, most of them prisoners; while Lee's loss was some less than half that number.

REAM'S STATION, AUGUST 21, 1864.—Hancock, who had been recalled from the north of the James in the demonstration against Richmond, moved rapidly toward the Weldon road in the rear of Warren. Striking it near Ream's Station, August 21, he commenced tearing up the road. After having destroyed a considerable portion of it, he was vigorously attacked by Hill. When night came, Hancock withdrew from Ream's Station. His loss was 2,400 (1,700 prisoners) out of 8,000, and Hill's was but little less.

This disaster did not loosen Warren's hold upon the Weldon Railroad. He had made his position impregnable, and Lee was compelled to see one of his important lines of communication pass from him.

This closed the active operations around Richmond for the winter. There were frequent skirmishes among the pickets, but no serious battle took place between the contending forces until the following spring.

CHAPTER XVIII.

SHERIDAN AND EARLY IN THE SHENANDOAH VALLEY, 1864.

SIGEL'S DEFEAT AT NEWMARKET, MAY 15, 1864.—Grant's comprehensive plan of campaign embraced not only the Overland Campaign, Sherman's March to the Sea, and Butler's movement toward Richmond, but the coöperative movements directed up the Shenandoah and Kanawha valleys. The former was under Gen. Sigel, and the latter under Gen. Crook.

Sigel accordingly moved up the valley on May 1, 1864, with 10,000 men, and was met near Newmarket by a Confederate army of equal force under Breckinridge. Sigel's army was defeated with a loss of 700 men, and driven back to Cedar creek, near Strasburg.

Gen. Crook moved from Charlestown, with a force of about eight thousand men, at the same time Sigel left Winchester; but by dividing his forces he was compelled to retreat from the enemy, and missed an opportunity to strike a telling blow against him.

Gen. Grant relieved Sigel of command, and named Gen. Hunter in his place. The pressure upon Gen. Lee's forces led to the withdrawal of Breckinridge, with the better part of his forces, for the defense of Richmond, while W. E. Jones was left in command of the remaining forces.

MARCH ON LYNCHBURG, JUNE 18, 1864.—The two armies met at Piedmont. Jones was killed, his army routed, and about fifteen hundred prisoners taken, and 3,000 small arms. Hunter advanced to Staunton, where he was reinforced by Crook and Averill, bringing his numbers up to 20,000 men.

Hunter was ordered to cross the Blue Ridge and take Lynchburg, the chief city in the western part of Virginia, situated in a rich and populous region. It was of great importance to the Confederates, as it had at that time extensive manufactories, was located on the James river and canal, and in unbroken railroad communication with Richmond and Petersburg on the one hand and the farther South on the other. Gen. Lee dispatched a considerable force from Richmond under Gen. Early to the relief of the city. Early arrived at Lynchburg the day before the attack was commenced, June 18th. Hunter's ammunition ran low, while great numbers were rallying to overwhelm him; he had no choice but to retreat, closely pursued as far as Salem. Hunter marched north into West Virginia, over an exhausted and desolated region, living on the country as he went. The loss of horses and the suffering of his men were great. He was compelled to make a circuitous and harassing movement, to escape severe punishment, by way of the Kanawha and Ohio rivers, and by Parkersburg and Grafton. This took a long time, and rendered his army of no service until its return.

EARLY'S MOVEMENT ON WASHINGTON, JULY, 1864.—Hunter's failure before Lynchburg, followed by his circuitous march to return to the contested soil of Virginia, left the Shenandoah

Valley in possession of Early, and Washington open to a possible raid. Early took advantage of this weakness. Summoning all the forces he could muster, he marched toward the National Capital.

Gen. Lew Wallace, in command of a small force at Baltimore, moved forward in the face of overwhelming numbers, and met the enemy at Monocacy. While he did not expect to gain a victory, he succeeded in delaying the advance upon Washington.

Grant, learning of the gravity of the situation, directed Meade to dispatch Wright's corps to the relief of Washington. The Nineteenth Corps, arriving at Fortress Monroe, on its way from Louisiana to reinforce the Army of the Potomac, was directed to Washington. Both these corps arrived at Washington on the 11th, the day on which Early arrived before the city. The troops in defense of Washington now numbered 40,000, while those of Early, reduced to about 15,000 men, beat a retreat. Gen. Wright pursued feebly through Leesburg and Snicker's Gap to the Shenandoah, where his advance was attacked and driven back with a loss of 500. Wright retreated to Leesburg, turned his command over to Crook, and returned to Washington.

Grant, deceived by advices that Early was returning to Lynchburg and Richmond, ordered the Sixth and Nineteenth Corps to be returned by water to Petersburg, so as to strike a telling blow against Lee before Early's return. Crook, who was left in command of the depleted forces on the Potomac, moved through Harper's Ferry to Winchester, supposing there was nothing there to stop him. Early had not gone south, but was close at hand, and, falling upon Crook's force, drove his command pell-mell to Martinsburg, with a loss of 1,200 men, his own loss being much less.

Early was undisputed master of that region. As he moved north, the people of Maryland and southern Pennsylvania were thrown into consternation.

McClausland was sent on a sweeping raid northward. Passing through Carlisle, and entering Chambersburg, he demanded $100,000 in gold or $500,000 in currency, under penalty of conflagration. The money not being instantly produced, the town was fired, and two-thirds of it destroyed.

The Sixth and Nineteenth Corps, which had proceeded no farther south than Georgetown, were recalled from their southern destination and sent to Harper's Ferry, where they joined Crook with part of Hunter's long-expected infantry on the very day Chambersburg was burned. The whole force started in a delusive pursuit of Early's army.

SHERIDAN IN COMMAND IN THE SHENANDOAH, AUGUST 7, 1864.—News of the disaster to the Union cause lead to the appointment of Maj. Gen. Philip H. Sheridan to operate against the invading forces. He was placed in command of the newly organized " Middle Department," composed of the late departments of West Virginia, Washington, and Susquehanna, and two divisions of cavalry which were sent to him by Grant.

Sheridan's whole force now numbered about 30,000 men, and Early confronted him with about 20,000.

Grant informs us that when Sheridan was appointed (August 7, 1864) to the new command, but two words of instruction were necessary. They were, " Go in " and Sheridan went in.

Sheridan met Early Sept. 13, at the crossing of Opequan creek. The enemy was strongly posted behind his fortifications, but his forces were separated, having sent two divisions to Martinsburg for the destruction of the Baltimore & Ohio Railroad. A well-planned and vigorous assault upon the Confederates drove them in utter rout through Winchester. The Union loss in this battle was fully 3,000, while the foe lost 3,000 in prisoners alone.

Early fell back to Fisher's Hill, eight miles south of Winchester, taking post in what was regarded as the very strongest position in the valley. Pursuing closely, Sheridan attacked him two days later, and gained a more decisive victory than at Opequan. His loss was light, while that of the enemy was more severe,—1,100 prisoners and 16 guns were taken. The pursuit was so sharp that Early was compelled to leave the valley and take to the mountains. Sheridan pursued him as far as Staunton, and swept the valley on his return pursuant to the instructions addressed by Gen. Grant to Gen. Hunter on August 5th.

SWEEPING THE SHENANDOAH VALLEY, SEPTEMBER AND OCTOBER, 1864.—All the grain and forage not already appropriated to the needs of one or the other of the armies which frequently chased up and down the fertile valley, were gathered up, or, with the barns and mills which held them, consigned to the torch.

The following is an extract from the report sent by Gen. Sheridan to Gen. Grant:

"WOODSTOCK, VA., Oct. 7, 1864 — 9 P. M.

"*Lt. Gen. U. S. Grant:* . . . I have destroyed over 2,000 barns filled with wheat and hay and farming implements, over 70 mills filled with flour and wheat; have driven in front of the army over 4,000 head of stock, and have killed and issued to the troops not less than 3,000 sheep.

"This destruction embraces the Luray valley and Little Fort valley, as well as the main valley.

"A large number of horses have been obtained, a proper estimate of which I cannot now make.

"Lt. John R. Meigs, my engineering officer, was murdered beyond Harrisonburg, near Dayton. For this atrocious act, all the houses within an area of five miles were burned.

"Since I came into the valley from Harper's Ferry, every train, every small party and every straggler has been bushwhacked by the people; many of whom have protection papers from commanders who have been hitherto in that valley.

"The people here are getting sick of the war. Heretofore, they have been living in great abundance. . . ."

The excuse for the devastation of the valley was the certainty that whatever was left there would be used to feed the enemy's armies and facilitate raids and incursions on the Union posts. The Confederates had established a precedent in the burning of Chambersburg. They threatened to burn New York city after Sheridan's raid through the Shenandoah Valley. In fact, the atrocity was actually attempted a few weeks later. Emissaries were stationed throughout the city, who simultaneously set fire to the large hotels wherein they had taken lodgings. Each fire was quickly extinguished, after but little damage had been done.

BATTLE OF CEDAR CREEK, OCTOBER 19, 1864.—Reinforcements were sent to Early. He advanced down the valley, and thoroughly organized his forces in the forest-screened camp near Fisher's Hill. Sheridan had been summoned to Washington. When Early became aware of his adversary's absence, he decided to attempt to retrieve his shattered fortunes. Issuing from his camp at night, his army moved over rugged paths, climbing up and down steep hills, over almost impassable ground, with canteens left in camp lest they should clatter against their muskets and make a noise. Early suddenly and unexpectedly fell upon the Union forces in camp at Cedar Creek at the dawn of October 19th. All was amazement and confusion in the Union ranks. The attack was furious. The enemy swept over the defenses, and after a brief but ineffectual resistance Sheridan's troops were put to flight. Gen. Wright, who was in temporary command, made great effort to stem the ebbing tide, and eventually succeeded in arresting the retreat of most of his men.

Sheridan, having left Washington on the 18th, reached Winchester that night. The next morning, as he started to join his command, ominous sounds of battle were wafted to his ears, and men came running from the front in panic, telling the story of disaster. Sending the cavalry at Winchester across the valley to stop the stragglers, he at once hastened to the scene of action, and addressed the fugitives as he met them: " Face the other way, boys! We are going back to our camps! We are going to lick them out of their boots!" Confidence was restored. The flight was ended. Intrenchments were erected, and the army placed in position. A furious assault was made by the Confederates, but they were repulsed by one o'clock. At three o'clock the order was given to the Union troops, " The entire line advance." On they went in a determined charge upon the hitherto exultant foe, driving them back over the ground they had gained, in great disorder and utter rout. The famished infantry sank down in their recovered quarters to shiver through the night, as the rations and cooks that were there in the morning had long since paid tribute to the enemy, or found shelter in Winchester.

The Union loss was about three thousand in the double battle. The Confederate loss was heavier, including 1,500 prisoners, 23 guns (not counting 23 guns lost by the Federals in the morning, and recovered at night), besides small arms, wagons, etc.

This battle practically closed the campaign in the Shenandoah Valley. Several small cavalry skirmishes occurred after this. Early's army was practically destroyed. He had lost, as Sheridan says, more men killed, wounded and captured, than he (Sheridan) had commanded from first to last. What remained of Early's forces, with the exception of one division of infantry and a little cavalry, was sent to Richmond. After the withdrawal of the Confederate forces most of the Union troops were sent to reinforce the army of the Potomac.

This victory, snatched from the jaws of defeat, affords one of the rare instances in which an army thoroughly defeated in the morning is more thoroughly victorious in the evening, being reinforced in the meantime by a single man.

The battle of Cedar Creek has been dedicated to all lovers of poetry, in the popular poem, " Sheridan's Ride," by Thomas Buchanan Read.

CHAPTER XIX.

PEACE COMMISSIONS, AND SURRENDER OF LEE.

PEACE COMMISSIONS OF JULY, 1864. Two unsuccessful efforts were made during July, 1864, to open the door to the termination of hostilities between the North and the South. One of these originated with certain Confederates, then in Canada, viz.: Messrs. Clement C. Clay, of Alabama; James P. Holcombe, of Virginia; and Geo. N. Sanders. They agreed to proceed to Washington in the interests of peace, if full protection were guaranteed them. Horace Greeley was appointed a commissioner to go to Niagara to meet the gentlemen, and inaugurate proceedings which might lead to the restoration of peace, the abandonment of slavery, and the preservation of the whole Union. Nothing, however, came of the interview.

Another irregular and wholly clandestine negotiation had been at the same time in progress at Richmond, with similar results. Rev. Col. James F. Jaques, Seventy-third Illinois, with Mr. J. R. Gilmore, of New York, had, with President Lincoln's knowledge but not with his formal permission, paid a visit to Richmond on a peace errand. A long, familiar and earnest discussion occurred between these men and President Davis. The Confederate chief presented his ultimatum, which, after stating that he had tried to avert war, read as follows: " War came; and now it must go on until the last man of this generation falls in his tracks and his children seize his musket and fight our battle, *unless you acknowledge our right to self-government. We are not fighting for slavery. We are fighting for independence; and that or extermination we will have.*"

The knowledge of the fact that the South was fighting not only against the abolition of slavery but against the Union, was worth a great deal to the Union cause in the North. Factions hitherto opposed to the continuation of the war were by this proclamation rallied to the support of a vigorous prosecution of war measures.

HAMPTON ROADS PEACE COMMISSION, FEBRUARY, 1865.—Negotiations for the termination of hostilities were again set on foot, in February, 1865. Alexander H. Stephens, Vice-President of the Confederate States; John A. Campbell, Assistant Secretary of War; and Robert M. T. Hunter, a Confederate Senator from Virginia, were permitted to pass Grant's lines before Petersburg, and proceeded to Fortress Monroe. They were met by Secretary Seward and President Lincoln. But as the commissioners were not authorized to concede the reunion of the States, and as the President would not treat on any other basis, the meeting was of short duration, and the parties separated without accomplishing anything.

THE CONFEDERATE GLOOM AND DESPAIR.—The winter after the departure of the Peace Commission was spent in comparative quiet. It was one of gloom and despair to the Confederates as they beheld their own numbers diminish in spite of every effort to increase them, and witnessed their adversaries tighten-

ing their hold, which would inevitably crush them. Their desertions were numerous, not only among those who were with Lee
around Richmond, but throughout the whole Confederacy. At
the eleventh hour they attempted to recruit their depleted ranks
by freeing and arming such slaves *only* as were deemed fit for
military service. They had already conscripted all able-bodied
men between the ages of eighteen and forty-five. Now they
passed a law conscripting the boys from fourteen to eighteen,
calling them junior reserves, and the men from forty-five to
sixty, calling them senior reserves.*

South of Lee was Sherman, moving with unimpeded progress.
West of him was Stoneman's cavalry division, and Thomas with
his victorious army which had overwhelmed Hood. North of
him was Sheridan with 10,000 cavalry at Winchester, ready
to destroy the remnant of Early's force. And in his front stood
Gen. Grant with a force outnumbering his two to one, and
ready to lock him in the embrace of death. The number of
Confederate desertions indicated that they had lost hope and
had become despondent. Many in the South were making ap-
plication to be sent North, where they might find employment
until the war was over, when they would return to their
Southern homes.

SHERIDAN OPENS THE CAMPAIGN, MARCH, 1865.—Setting
out from Winchester on the 27th of February, Sheridan began

---

*Gen. Butler, in alluding to their conscription, remarked that they
were thus " robbing the cradle and the grave."

a magnificent cavalry raid, aimed at Lynchburg and the enemy's communications generally. His instructions from Grant left him the liberty of joining Sherman to the south, or uniting with the Army of the Potomac, as conditions might arise. Passing down through Staunton with a force of 10,000 mounted men, on March 2d he fell upon Early at the head of some 2,500 men intrenched at Waynesboro. His force was almost instantly routed, and 1,600 prisoners taken. In fact, there was little left of Early's force excepting himself, who, perceiving the drift of the battle, absented himself, and found refuge in some of the neighboring houses or in the woods. This was Early's last appearance in public life.

Lynchburg had taken the warning, and received reinforcements. While the continuous spring rains flooded the streams so as to make them unfordable with pontoon trains, Sheridan destroyed the James river canal, and tore up the Lynchburg Railroad as far west as Amherst Court House. Some 2,000 negroes had joined his command, assisting considerably in the tearing-up of the railroad and in the work of destroying the canal. Passing through Columbia, he reached White House on March 19; and after resting here, he passed down to the James, and reported to Gen. Grant for orders before Petersburg on the 27th, in time to take part in the reduction of the Confederate capital.

LEE'S ATTACK UPON FORT STEDMAN, MARCH 25, 1865.— Foreseeing the speedy downfall of the Confederate cause, unless a telling blow should be struck against some part of the encircling armies, and an avenue of escape opened, Lee resolved to anticipate Grant's initiative movement by an attack upon the Union lines. This attack was made upon Fort Stedman, nearly east of Petersburg, where its success would have probably cut Grant's army in two, and opened a door for a successful withdrawal of the Confederate army southward by the most direct route, to unite with Johnston, in an endeavor to overpower Sherman.

The assault was made by Gen. John B. Gordon, early on the morning of March 25th, and Fort Stedman with three contiguous batteries was taken by surprise. The 20,000 men whom Lee had massed in the rear as support had failed to respond promptly, for some cause, and the forts were promptly retaken, and all the Confederate troops who entered them, about 4,000 in number, were taken prisoners. In short, it was the "Mine Explosion" repeated, with points of disaster reversed. Aside from prisoners, the loss to each side was about 2,500. Gen. Meade, perceiving the depleted ranks of the enemy in his front, in a spirited attack captured the strongly intrenched picket line. Lee thus, instead of freeing himself from Grant's grip, had only tightened it by his assault.

FIVE FORKS, APRIL 1, 1865.—Grant prepared arrangements for a final campaign, which resulted in the capture of Lee's army. The determined advance was commenced by the Union left on the 29th of March. To the flanking of the enemy's right was now imposed the additional task of intercepting and precluding Lee's withdrawal to North Carolina. Hence, the strategy of making a simultaneous attack upon the right and left flanks of the enemy was abandoned, and three divisions of the Army of the James were withdrawn from the bank of the James river, where they had so long menaced Richmond, and were brought over to join the troops facing Petersburg.

Gen. Lee, alive to his peril, left some eight thousand men under Longstreet to protect the works at Richmond, and hastily withdrew the rest of his infantry through rain and mire, to the support of his endangered right.

Gen. Sheridan, in command of the cavalry, held the extreme Union left, near Five Forks. Gen. Warren was ordered to support the cavalry, and placed under Sheridan's command. Sheridan succeeded in advancing up to a point from which he planned to make an assault upon Five Forks by the middle of the afternoon of April 1st. Warren was slow in moving his troops. Sheridan sent messenger after messenger, directing that officer to report to him. Finally he went himself in search of him, but could not find him. Sheridan then issued an order relieving Warren of the command and placing Gen. Griffin in charge of his corps. The troops were then brought up, and the assault was made in brilliant order, completely demolishing the enemy's right, and forcing him in great disorder from the field. About four thousand prisoners, many small arms and some artillery fell into Sheridan's hands, while he lost during the day about one thousand men.

Grant says: "Here a desperate hand-to-hand conflict took place. The men of the two sides were too close to fire, but used their guns as clubs. . . . Lee's losses must have been fear-ful. In one place a tree eighteen inches in diameter was cut down by musket-balls. All the trees between the lines were very much cut to pieces by the artillery and musketry. It was three o'clock in the morning before the fighting ceased. Some of our troops had been under fire twenty hours."

BATTLE OF PETERSBURG, AND ABANDONMENT OF RICHMOND. Grant ordered the guns opened upon the works of Petersburg from right to left, even though darkness had already fallen upon the scene. The lurid light and the roaring sound pro-claimed the signal victory just achieved, and predicted more decisive triumphs near at hand. The next morning (Sunday, April 2d) the outer works of Petersburg were carried. Lee made frantic efforts to recover his lost ground, but was repulsed with heavy loss. Gen. A. P. Hill, the hero of many a Confed-erate battle, was mortally wounded while reconnoitering during the day. Though Petersburg was still in his possession, Lee saw he could not hold it much longer. His losses had exceeded 10,000 men. To hold out any longer was to insure the capture or destruction of his entire army.

At 10:30 A. M. he telegraphed to Jefferson Davis in Rich-mond these words:

"My lines are broken in three places. Richmond must be evacuated this evening."

The message found Mr. Davis, at 11 A. M., in church. It was handed him amid awful silence. He read it, and immedi-ately went quietly and soberly out—never, never to return as

—16

President of the Confederacy. Not a word was spoken; but the whole assemblage felt that the missive contained words of loom.

The news of the impending crisis soon passed from lip to lip. The calm and peaceful Sabbath day was soon changed into one of clamor and excitement. " Suddenly, as if by magic, the streets became filled by men, walking as though for a wager, and behind them excited negroes with trunks and luggage of every description." Hundreds of thousands of dollars of Confed erate money were destroyed. Hundreds of barrels of liquor were rolled into the street, and the ends knocked in, flooding the streets with the fiery liquid. Gen. Ewell ordered the four principal tobacco warehouses to be fired. The flames spread to other parts of the city. Pollard vividly depicts the scene that followed, thus:

" Morning broke upon a scene such as those who witnessed it can never forget. The roar of an immense conflagration sounded in their ears; tongues of flame leaped from street to street; and in this baleful glare were to be seen, as of demons, the figures of busy plunderers, moving, pushing, rioting, through the black smoke, and into the open street, bearing away every conceivable sort of plunder.

"The scene at the Commissary depot, at the head of the dock, beggared description. Hundreds of government wagons were loaded with bacon, flour, and whisky, and driven off in hot haste to join the retreating army. Thronging about the depot were hundreds of men, women and children, black and white, provided with capacious bags, baskets, tubs, buckets, tin pans, and aprons; cursing, pushing, and crowding; awaiting the throwing open of the doors and the order for each to help himself.

"About sunrise the doors were opened to the populace, and a rush that almost seemed to carry the building off of its foundations was made, and hundreds of thousands of pounds of bacon, flour, etc., were soon swept away by the clamorous crowd."

On Monday morning the Union troops occupied the city, un-resisted by any force. The fire was extinguished as soon as possible, but not until it had burned the very heart of Richmond. The loss must have been millions, as fully one-third of the city was consumed. Libby Prison and Castle Thunder remained unharmed.

About one thousand prisoners were taken, besides 5,000 sick and wounded who were left in the hospitals.

Petersburg was of course abandoned simultaneously with Richmond. No explosions nor conflagrations attended the abandonment of this city. So noiselessly was it done, that the Union pickets within a stone's-throw knew not that the enemy was making the move.

The Retreat of Lee.—Lee hoped to be able to escape, form a junction with Gen. Johnston, and crush Sherman's army before reinforcements could arrive.

The once formidable Army of Virginia, now reduced by desertions and heavy losses, mainly in prisoners, to 35,000 men, was concentrated at Chesterfield Court House, and then moved rapidly westward to Amelia Court House, where Lee expected supplies which he had previously ordered to that place for his famishing army. They were destined to meet with disappointment here, as an order from Richmond summoned the train to that city to aid in bringing away the fugitives; and it was taken without unloading the supplies intended for the army. Gen. Grant was soon in pursuit of the retreating Confederate army. Sheridan's cavalry, striving to head off the flight of the fugitives, formed the van of the pursuing forces. **The rest of Grant's army** followed in close pursuit, moving in parallel lines with Lee's army to the south of it, attacking vigorously whenever any portion of the hostile forces came within fighting distance. Some of these engagements were sharply contested, and, as the men fought without breastworks, the losses were heavy. The seventy miles from Richmond to Appomattox was a long trail of blood. There were collisions at Jetersville, Deatonsville, Deep creek, Sailor's creek, Paine's Crossroads, and Farmville. The most important of these was at Sailor's creek, a small tributary of the Appomattox running northward into it, where Custer, supported by Crook, broke through the Confederate lines, capturing 400 wagons, 16 guns, and many prisoners.

Ewell's corps, following the train, were thus cut off from the rest of Lee's army, and were held in check until the arrival of the Union Sixth Corps, when a deadly fire was opened upon them. Ewell's veterans, thus inclosed between the cavalry and the Sixth Corps, without a chance of escape, threw down their arms and surrendered. Seven thousand men were made prisoners, among whom were Ewell himself and four other generals.

SURRENDER OF LEE, AT APPOMATTOX COURT HOUSE, APRIL 9, 1865. — The remainder of the army continued its retreat during the night of the 6th, and reached Farmville early on the morning of the 7th, where they obtained two days' rations, and stopped to rest and prepare their food. The approach of the Federal troops, near noon, again set the Confederates in motion in a vain endeavor to escape the inevitable fate awaiting them.

Arriving at Appomattox Court House, April 9th, a week from the day they had set out from Richmond, they found Sheridan's dismounted cavalry across their paths, and the four trains of supplies which they had expected had been captured.

The Army of Virginia, unaware of the presence of the Federal infantry, expecting to break through the column of cavalry which blocked its way, made its last charge. The removal of Sherman's cavalry by his orders, after a sharp engagement, disclosed to the astonished Confederates a solid line of blue-coated infantry and glittering steel as Sheridan and his troops passed hurriedly around the enemy's left, prepared to charge the confused, reeling masses. Hope was changed into despair, and the Confederate general, yielding to the fiat of fate, sent a white flag waving to Gen. Custer. Hostilities were suspended, with the assurance that negotiations for the surrender of the Confederate army were then pending between Generals Grant and Lee.

Grant had first demanded Lee's surrender on the afternoon of the 7th, but Lee refused to consider any terms of surrender then. Several notes had been interchanged by them, and on the 9th the two commanders met in the house of Mr. McLean, where the surrender of the Confederate army took place.

MORALE OF THE ARMIES.—Of the proud army which defeated McDowell at Bull Run, and drove McClellan from before Richmond, suffered a backset at Antietam, shattered Burnside's hosts at Fredericksburg, triumphed over Hooker at Chancellorsville, valiantly though unsuccessfully met Meade at Gettysburg, and baffled Grant's bounteous resources for a time in the " Over-land Campaign " in the Wilderness, at Spottsylvania, on the North Anna, at Cold Harbor, and before Petersburg and Rich-mond, but a mere wreck remained on the day of the final sur-render. After the fall of Richmond the morale of the National troops had greatly improved, while that of the Confederate was more than correspondingly depressed. Each day witnessed the depletion of the Confederate ranks on this memorable re-treat. When Lee finally surrendered at Appomattox, there were only 28,356 men left to be paroled. Of this number not more than 10,000 were able to carry their arms on this hopeless and almost foodless flight. Nineteen thousand one hundred and thirty-two Confederates were captured from March 29th up to the date of the surrender at Appomattox, which does not include the great number of killed, wounded and missing during the series of conflicts which marked the headlong and disastrous flight of the foe. The number of cannon taken between these two dates, including those at Appomattox, was recorded at 689.

GRANT'S GENEROUS TERMS.—In accordance with the terms of surrender, the officers were required to give their individual paroles not again to take up arms against the Government of the United States until properly exchanged; and each company and regimental commander signed a like parole for the men of their commands. The arms, artillery and public property were to be packed, stacked, and turned over to the proper officers. Officers were permitted to retain their side-arms. Each soldier claiming a horse was permitted to " take it home, to be used for plowing." The starving Confederates were immediately fed by their captors. Each officer and man was permitted to return to his home, not to be disturbed by the United States authority so long as he observed the parole and the laws in force where he might reside.

The exceeding generosity of these terms to an army which had fought so stubbornly against its adversary, was a surprise to many who remembered the " unconditional surrender " at Fort Donelson and at Vicksburg. Grant's behavior was marked by a desire to spare the feelings of his great opponent. There was no theatrical display. His troops were not paraded with banners flying and bands playing. The humiliated and defeated troops were not marched before the lines of their captors to stack arms. He did not demand Lee's sword, as was customary on such occasions. Cheering, the firing of salutes, and other demonstrations of exultation over the victory, were promptly stopped.

Even Pollard, the Southern historian, in " The Lost Cause," pays a high tribute of respect to Grant on this occasion, in these words:

"Indeed, this Federal commander, in the closing scenes of the contest, behaved with a magnanimity and decorum that must ever be remembered to his credit, even by those who disputed his reputation in other respects, and denied his claims to great generalship. He had with remarkable facility accorded honorable and liberal terms to a vanquished army. He did nothing to dramatize the surrender ; he made no triumphal entry into Richmond ; he avoided all those displays so dear to the Northern heart ; he spared everything that might wound the feelings or imply the humiliation of a vanquished foe. There were no indecent exultations ; no ' sensations ' ; no shows: he received the surrender of his adversary with every courteous recognition due an honorable enemy, and conducted the closing scenes with as much simplicity as possible."

President Lincoln arrived at City Point, March 24th, and was in constant communication with Grant from that date until the surrender of the Confederate army. He was mainly at City Point, but, accompanied by Admiral Porter, he went to Gen. Weitzel's headquarters, in the house so recently and suddenly abandoned by Jefferson Davis. He was recognized, and the crowd of blacks became so great to welcome and bless their emancipator, that a military force had to be called to clear a way for him through the streets. He repeated his visit to Richmond two days later, attended by Mrs. Lincoln, Vice-President Johnson, and several United States Senators. He returned to Washington on the day of Lee's surrender, which was considered the close of the war.

As soon as Lee's surrender became known, Secretary Stanton telegraphed an order to the headquarters of every army and department, and to every fort and arsenal in the United States, to fire a salute of 200 guns in celebration of the event. To Grant he dispatched: "Thanks be to Almighty God for the great victory with which He has this day crowned you and the gallant armies under your command. The thanks of this department, and of the Government, and of the people of the United States— their reverence and honor have been deserved—will be rendered to you and the brave and gallant officers and soldiers of your army for all time."

CHAPTER XX.

OUTSKIRT MOVEMENTS.

THE CIVIL WAR lasted four years. During this time 2,265 engagements took place between the Union and Confederate troops. These conflicts ranged in importance from the insignificant raid, skirmish, or fight, to the decisive battle of Gettysburg, in which the loss of life was appalling. The average number of engagements for each week from the beginning to the close of hostilities was eleven. The total number of battles in which the Union loss was 100 or more in killed, wounded or missing, was 330.

In the preceding chapters the more important movements, battles, and operations of the main armies, have been described. Many outskirt movements were conducted. Only the more important can receive even a passing notice, to bring them within the compass of this volume.

Gen. Banks, while in command of New Orleans, conceived the plan of directing an expedition up the Red river, 1864. His objects were, the capture of Shreveport and the dispersion of Kirby Smith's army. To this end, Admiral Porter, with a strong fleet of ironclads, was to embark 10,000 men from Sherman's old army at Vicksburg, under Gen. A. J. Smith, and move up the river. Banks was to march overland with 15,000 men, and meet Smith's force at Alexandria. Gen. Steele was to march from Little Rock to Shreveport with the bulk of his Arkansas troops.

Fort DeRussy was captured March 14th; Alexandria fell on the 16th without a struggle. The Union forces pushed their way to Sabine Crossroads, with occasional skirmishes, when their advance was suddenly attacked and precipitately routed by Confederate forces numbering not less than 20,000 men, under Kirby Smith and Dick Taylor. The Federal loss was 2,000. The Union troops retreated to Pleasant Hill, where they were reinforced. Here the enemy fiercely attacked them next day, April 9th, but he was defeated and driven from the field. In the whole campaign the Union loss in killed, wounded and missing was 5,000; the Confederate loss was less.

Gen. Banks decided to give up the expedition, and began to conduct a retreat. The Shreveport movement or Red river expedition was a failure. It had all the promise of success, and with its resources and available forces would have succeeded if properly managed. On his way back after the victory of Pleasant Hill, a sharp attack on Banks's rear at Cane river resulted in the repulse of the enemy.

The fleet had proceeded up the river, but the reverse of Sabine Crossroads compelled its return. The river, when low, would not float the larger vessels. The high water of spring was fast falling. The vessels ran aground. The fleet was much annoyed by the Confederate sharpshooters and batteries along the shores. The attacking foe was driven away from the river-banks with some loss. The grounded vessels were set afloat with considerable difficulty. The river had become so low that vessels could not pass over the falls below Alexandria. It seemed as if the entire fleet would be destroyed. Col. Bailey, an engineer of fertile brain, planned the construction of dams, by means of which the passage over the falls was made in safety.

Alexandria was burned by accident on the retreat, but the enemy naturally claimed that the city was willfully destroyed with a desire for revenge.

About the time of Banks's advance to Alexandria, Gen. Steele left Little Rock, Arkansas, with an army to coöperate in the Red river expedition. Banks's disaster had greatly emboldened the enemy, and endangered Steele's army. A large number of his supply-wagons were taken. When he learned of Banks's retreat, Steele began his backward movement. At Marks Mills the enemy took a number of his men prisoners. When at Jenkins's Ferry, on the Saline river, a large force under Kirby Smith attacked the Union forces, April 30, but met a repulse. Steele, after having suffered severely, finally reached Little Rock.

A Union expedition, fitted out at South Carolina by Gen. Gillmore, was sent to reclaim Florida. It was under the immediate command of Gen. Truman Seymore. He advanced to Jacksonville, Fla., with 600 men, and then to Olustee, where he met a disastrous defeat by an enemy much inferior in numbers to his own. This was February 20, 1864. In a short time both opposing forces were called to participate in the absorbing events around Richmond.

An attempt was made in the early part of March, 1864, by Gen. Judson Kilpatrick at the head of a cavalry force, to penetrate the defenses at Richmond and liberate the Union prisoners confined in Libby prison. Col. Ulrich Dahlgren was killed. Much damage was inflicted upon the enemy's railroads and bridges, but the attempt to enter Richmond failed.

An expedition of 4,000 men against Sabine Pass, La., in September, 1863, under Gen. Wm. B. Franklin, aided by gunboats from Farragut's fleet, failed. Two gunboats were disabled and captured by the enemy. The rest of the expedition returned to New Orleans.

An effort on the part of the Confederates to recover Fort Donelson, early in February, 1863, was unsuccessful.

In April, 1863, Col. Streight with about 1,600 men set out on a raid into northern Georgia. At Cedar Bluff he was forced to surrender to Gen. Forrest in command of a body of cavalry.

Many of the outskirt movements have been enumerated under the chapters on " War in Missouri," " Coast Operations," or in connection with the main campaigns. Many others might be alluded to here, but the students of history in search of details of the minor events are referred to the numerous works prepared on a more comprehensive plan than this one.

CHAPTER XXI.

FINANCIAL MEASURES TO PROVIDE REVENUE FOR THE CIVIL WAR.

EMPTY TREASURY AT THE OPENING OF THE CIVIL WAR.—
During President Buchanan's administration, in time of peace,
the resources of the Government were not sufficient to meet the
expenditures. The National debt increased more than $36,000,-
000 from July 1st, 1857, to July 1st, 1860. Congress had authorized the issue of Treasury notes to meet the deficit in
receipts, and on February 5th it authorized the issue of
$25,000,000 of bonds, bearing interest at 6 per cent., payable
within not less than ten nor more than twenty years. The Secretary of the Treasury was able to place only $18,415,000 of
bonds, and this at an average discount of 10.97 per cent.

When Lincoln became President he found an empty treasury,
the credit of the Nation gone, and a public debt amounting to
about $80,000,000, with daily revenues insufficient to meet the
expenditures. Among the final acts of the Congress which
closed its session on the 4th of March, 1861, was one which provided for a loan of $10,000,000 in bonds, or the issue of a like
sum in Treasury notes. The President was empowered to issue
Treasury notes for any part of loans previously authorized but
not obtained. Under this statute, notes were issued to the
amount of $12,896,350, payable in sixty days after date, and

$22,468,100, payable in two years. This was the initial step to obtain revenue, aside from regular incomes, to meet the expenditures of the Government, which soon became enormous.

POWER TO RAISE MONEY.—The Constitution gives Congress the power: (1) " To levy and collect taxes, duties, imposts, and excises "; (2) " To borrow money on the credit of the United States "; (3) " To apportion taxes among the several States according to their population."

The chief dependence of the United States for revenue had always been upon customs. The expenses of the Government during the years 1863 and 1864 amounted to more than the entire expenditures of the Government from its foundation up to the time of the opening of the Civil War. This enormous financial drain taxed the resources of the nation, and called for a more varied and comprehensive system of revenue than had yet been inaugurated in our financial system. This system was not the product of a single act of legislation, but of a series of acts which grew out of pressing needs of the hour, to meet the expenditures of the Government and for the preservation of National credit. It included six sources of revenue, namely: Customs duties, internal revenue, non-interest-bearing Treasury notes, interest-bearing Treasury notes, bond issues, and the National banking system.

CUSTOMS DUTIES.—THE MORRILL TARIFF.—The Morrill tariff went into effect April 1st, 1861. It was a high tariff, and was a radical change in policy from the tariff laws of 1846 and

1857, which were the lowest ever in force. Under the Morrill tariff, imposts which had averaged about 19 per cent. on dutiable articles and 15 per cent. on the total imports, were changed to 36 per cent. on dutiable articles and to 28 per cent. on total imports. At the special session of Congress, called by President Lincoln July 4, 1861, the schedule of dutiable articles was extended, and the rates increased. It became a law August 5th, 1861. On December 24, as a war measure, the duties on tea, coffee and sugar were increased, and the duties were again increased by the tariff act of July 14, 1862.

Non-Interest-Bearing Treasury Notes.—These notes include the "old demand notes," the "legal tenders" or "greenbacks," the "fractional currency," and the "National bank notes."

"Legal Tenders" or "Greenbacks."—The law authorizing the issue of "legal-tender" Treasury notes passed February 25, 1862. It provided for the issue of $150,000,000 in these notes, to be "lawful money and legal tender in payment of all debts, public and private, except duties on imports and interest on bonds and notes of the United States." There was much opposition to the legal-tender feature of the bill, but it was finally agreed upon on the ground of extreme necessity. The bill provided for the exchange of these notes for six-per-cent. bonds, redeemable at the pleasure of the United States after five years. This provision was repealed the next year. The smallest note issued under this act was five dollars, but in a later act the limit was reduced to one-dollar notes. The total amount authorized to be issued was $450,000,000.

These notes depreciated in value until July, 1864, when they were worth only 35 cents on the dollar. They again rose in value, but fluctuated from time to time until the passage of the specie-resumption act of January, 1875, which provided that the legal-tender notes should be redeemed in coin after January 1, 1879. After the passage of this act they rose to face value, because they were interchangeable for gold. The act of 1878 required that these notes, when redeemed, should be reissued. There were $346,681,016 of the legal tenders or greenbacks (a name given them from the green color on their backs) in use, Oct. 1, 1897. Some discussion has been going on relative to the retirement of these notes. President McKinley, in his message to Congress in December, 1897, recommended that these notes when once redeemed should not be reissued without the receipt of gold for them.

FRACTIONAL CURRENCY.—The issue of demand notes in 1861, the evident fact that Congress must continue to issue paper money, and the vast expenditures of the Government with but a small amount of coin in the country (estimated then at $210,000,000), led the State banks to suspend specie payment, Dec. 30, 1861. The Government was soon forced to a similar financial policy. All gold and silver disappeared from circulation. The 3, 5, 10, 25 and 50 cents silver-pieces, which had been employed as change, were no longer to be found in use. When these passed out of circulation, the people were left without any denominations less than the dollar bill. No change could be found anywhere. Some kinds of business were almost paralyzed. Newspapers, car fare, etc., were paid in postage stamps and " token " pieces of copper and brass that passed as cent-pieces.

Fractional notes were issued by private firms, and various expedients were resorted to for the payment of small debts. An act was passed July 1, 1862, for the use of postage and other stamps in payment of fractional parts of a dollar. The Assistant Treasurer made these stamps exchangeable for United States notes, in sums of not less than five dollars. In March, 1863, $50,000,000 of fractional currency was issued, in denominations of 5, 10, 25, and 50-cent bills. These notes were reissued by the Government as old and worn notes were returned to the Treasury.

Since the restoration of fractional silver to the channels of commerce, the 5, 10, 25, and 50-cent paper note is as great a novelty as the silver change was during the war.

DEMAND NOTES.—One of the provisions of the act of July 17, 1861, authorized the issue of $50,000,000 in notes of not less than ten dollars nor of more than fifty, bearing interest at a rate of 3.36 per cent., payable in one year; or they were PAYABLE ON DEMAND WITHOUT INTEREST. They were to be exchanged for coin, or to be used by the Government in the payment of salaries or other dues, and were called demand notes because they were redeemable in gold on the demand of the person holding them.

—17

INTERNAL REVENUE.—On the first of July, 1862, the bill " to provide internal revenue to support the Government and to pay interest on the public debt " was signed by the President. It was one of the most complete systems of taxation ever devised by any government. Spirituous and malt liquors and tobacco were heavily taxed. Manufactures of various kinds were taxed 3 per cent. Banks, insurance, railroads and telegraph companies, and in fact all other corporations had to pay tribute. The butcher paid 30 cents for every beef, 10 cents for every hog, and 5 cents for every sheep slaughtered. Carriages, billiard tables, yachts, gold and silver ware, and all other articles of luxury were taxed. Every profession and calling, except the ministry of religion, was included. Almost everything a person ate, drank, wore, bought, sold, or owned, was taxed. So comprehensive was the law that thirty printed pages of royal octavo and more than 20,000 words were used to express the provisions.

In 1861 a bill passed, levying a direct tax of $20,000,000 to be apportioned among the States, of which sum $12,000,000 was assigned to the States which did not secede from the Union. Each State was allowed 15 per cent. for the expense of collecting her quota. All the loyal States and Territories except Delaware and Colorado assumed the payment of the tax.

The bill of 1861, levying a direct tax, provided also for an *income* tax,—the first ever levied by our general Government. The tax was 3 per cent. for residents and 5 per cent. for foreigners on the excess of income over $800. Before this act went into effect it was repealed by the act of July 1, 1862, which placed a tax of 3 per cent. on the excess of $600 up to $10,000, and a tax of 5 per cent. on the excess of $10,000. The law went into effect in 1863. March 3d, 1865, the law was amended so as to place a five-per-cent. tax on incomes up to $5,000 (exemption being left at $600),and a ten-per-cent. tax on the excess of $5,000 income.

In March, 1867, the exemption was raised to $1,000, and a uniform rate of 5 per cent. was substituted for the 5 per cent. and 10 per cent. rates. Three years later the exemption of $1,000 was increased to $2,000, and the rate was reduced to 2½ per cent. This law was passed to continue in effect for one year. The last levy under the law was in 1871, and the last tax was collected in 1874.

The income tax collected in the year 1864 was $20,294,733, and the total amount collected from 1863 to 1874 inclusive was $346,908,740.

ISSUING BONDS.—Bonds are written promises by the Government to pay a specified sum of money to the holder, at the end of a certain period of time, with interest at a given rate, payable semi-annually or quarterly. Government bonds are prepared and then sold under certain regulations, at the best rates the Government can command.

Bonds have been issued from time to time by the Government since its formation, but the Civil War made it necessary to issue them in vast sums. They were in denominations of $50, $100, $500, $1,000, etc. One billion one hundred and nine million dollars' worth of bonds were issued between July 1st,

1861, and August 31, 1865 (when our debt was greatest), and the money was used for war purposes. Most of the bonds issued were known as "5-20s." An act was passed authorizing the issue of 10-40s, and other denominations; but these were not popular, and comparatively few were taken.

INTEREST-BEARING TREASURY NOTES.—These notes passed under various names, depending upon the rate of interest and the time for which they were issued. Secretary Chase, making a summary of the Treasury operations in 1861, says: "There were paid to creditors, or exchanged for coin at par, at different dates, in July and August, six-per-cent. two-years notes, to the amount of $14,019,036. There was borrowed at par in the same months, upon sixty-days six-per-cent. notes, the sum of $12,877,750; there was borrowed at par, on the 19th of August, under three-years seven-thirty bonds, $50,000,000." This last issue is popularly known as "seven-thirties." By it certain banks furnished $50,000,000 in coin, and received in payment three-year notes bearing interest at 7.30 per cent., convertible in six-per-cent. twenty-year bonds. By 1866, the whole amount of interest-bearing notes was $577,000,000.

NATIONAL BANKING SYSTEM.—Another important feature of our financial system during the Civil War was the inauguration of the National Banking system, which, with little modification, has continued in use to the present. The bill passed in February, 1863. Arguments in support of the bill were given as follows: The banks would furnish a market for bonds; they would absorb the circulation of State banks, and that without harsh measures; they would create a community of interest between the stockholders of the banks, the people, and the Government, where there now existed a great contrariety of opinions and diversity of interests: adequate safeguards would be established against counterfeiting; the currency would be uniform, and take the place of the notes of 1,600 banks, differing in style, and whose notes were easily imitated and altered; that while the notes of one-sixth of the existing banks had been counterfeited, 1,861 kinds of imitations were afloat, 3,039 alterations extant, in addition to 1,685 spurious notes, in which hardly any care had been taken to show any resemblance to the genuine.

The act of June 3d, 1864, was a substitute for the act of February 25, 1863, and provides for a Bureau of Currency in the Treasury Department, at the head of which is a Comptroller.

In the United States Bank, the Government was a large stockholder, and the officers of the Treasury practically directed the operations of the bank, and sometimes accommodated political friends on easy terms, rendering legitimate banking impossible. Under the National Banking system the Government is not a shareholder, and takes no part in the management of the banks, except to see that the laws controlling them are complied with. Under the system of multiform State banks, the notes were of varying value at different times and in different places. In the disastrous financial influences of the War of 1812, a large majority of these banks were wrecked, their notes never redeemed, **and a great financial loss entailed by the people. Under the** present system the bank notes are of uniform value throughout the Nation, and no bill-holder can suffer loss.

The circulation of the banks was at first limited to $354,000,000, and was distributed among the States and Territories according to wealth and population conjointly. The repeal of this provision has made banking free. Any company numbering not less than five, with a capital of not less than $50,000, may form a banking association. The company must purchase United States bonds, and deposit them with the Treasurer of the United States. On receipt of these the Treasurer causes to be printed for the bank an amount of national bank notes in such denominations as the authorities of the bank may name, but the amount of notes shall not exceed nine-tenths of the bonds purchased. The amount varies from 60 per cent. when the capital stock is $3,000,000 or more, to 90 per cent. when not over half a million. The bank receives interest on the bonds it has purchased, and loans the money printed by the Government as well as the deposits of its patrons. It is required to maintain a reserve fund in gold and silver coin equal to about 20 per cent. of its capital. By this provision the holders of the national bank notes may convert them into coin, by presenting them to the bank that issued them. It is also required to set apart 10 per cent. of its profits each year as a surplus fund, until such fund is equal to 20 per cent. of the capital stock of the bank. This surplus provides a means to make good any losses that may occur.

CHAPTER XXII.

COST OF THE WAR.—NATIONAL DEBT.— CLOSING EVENTS.

COST OF THE WAR.—THE NATIONAL DEBT.—At the close of the war the National debt was $2,800,000,000 (round numbers). Hundreds of millions of dollars were expended out of the revenues of the Government as the war progressed. Besides this, the incidental losses were innumerable in kind and incalculable in amount. There were heavy expenditures by the States, cities, and towns, amounting to about $458,000,000.

Other nations have made costly sacrifices in the struggle for their existence, or in pursuit of their ambitions; but none has expended, in the same length of time, an amount equal to that expended during the Civil War by our National Government.

The amount of the Confederate debt is unknown. It is estimated that if all the expenditures during the war and debts at the close of it, including the destruction of property, could be added, North and South, it would be equivalent to the sum representing all values in the United States as they were estimated at the beginning of the war.

The total expenditures of Great Britain during the French Revolution and the career of Napoleon, covering a period of twenty-three years, was $4,850,000,000, but the combined expenditures of any four years did not equal the amount spent by the United States in the same length of time. The one grand

(263)

feature of this lavish expenditure of wealth by our Government is, that it was directed and enforced by the people themselves.

The fourteenth amendment to the Constitution provides that the validity of the public debt shall not be questioned, and on the other hand that neither the United States nor any State shall pay any debt or obligation that has been incurred in aid of insurrection against the United States. The Confederate debt was void by the interpretation of this clause, and was so recognized North and South under the terms of the reconstruction of the Southern States.

Loss of Life.—Willing as were the people to contribute of their money to the suppression of the Rebellion, still more readily did they respond to the call to arms. Twelve calls were made for men during the war; the first, April 15, 1861, the last in December, 1864. The term of service varied in different calls, from three months in some to three years in others. In the loyal States the Government called for more than 2,750,000 men. Of this number, about 103,000 had not responded when the war closed, but about 120,000 " emergency men " were furnished by the States at the time of Morgan's raid and during the summer of 1863, which would make the actual number of men in the service greater than the number of men called for. This number does not represent the number of different individuals engaged, as many men enlisted more than once, and were counted each time they enlisted. The greatest number of men in service at any one time was in April, 1865, when 1,000,516 were on the muster-rolls, of whom 650,000 were in actual service.

Of those who gave their lives to preserve the Union, 67,000 were killed in battle, 43,000 died of wounds, 230,000 of disease and other causes; making a total of about 340,000.

The number of men enlisting in the Confederate service is not known, but it is certain that every available man was drafted into service who did not voluntarily go. The number killed in battle, including those who died of wounds and disease, was probably as great as that of the North.

CAPTURE OF JEFFERSON DAVIS.—Jefferson Davis took a hasty departure from Richmond on Sunday, April 2, as the Confederate army began its hasty flight from the doomed city. Journeying by rail from Richmond to Danville, he halted at this place, set up his government, and issued a stirring proclamation designed to revive the failing spirits of his confederates. Astounded at the news of Lee's surrender, his government took wheels and retreated to Greensboro, South Carolina, where another halt was made. The imminent danger of Johnston's army again set the tottering government of a failing cause in motion, —this time in wagons and on horseback, as the railroad south had been destroyed. Passing through Salisbury and Charlotte, N. C., Yorkville and Abbeyville, S. C., to Washington, Ga., the officers gradually abandoned the sinking craft, until Mr. Davis was attended only by Mr. John H. Reagan (late Confederate Postmaster-General), his military staff, and his family. While encamped near Irwinsville, Ga., he was surprised on the early dawn of May 11th by the Union cavalry, and himself, his wife, her sister, and his children, and a small body of escort, were taken prisoners. His family were taken by water to Savannah, and there set at liberty. He was taken to Fortress Monroe, and kept in confinement for two years. Mr. Davis was indicted for treason by a grand jury in the United States court for the district of Virginia, on the 13th of May, 1867. He was liberated on bail in the amount of $100,000. His bondsmen were Cornelius Vanderbilt, Horace Greeley, and Gerrit Smith—a lifelong abolitionist. His trial never occurred, and he was included in the general amnesty proclamation in 1868. After his discharge, he became president of a life insurance company in Memphis, Tenn. He died in New Orleans, Dec. 6, 1889.

DEATH OF LINCOLN.—The 14th day of April was the fourth anniversary of the surrender of Fort Sumter to the Confederates by Major Anderson. The whole country was aglow with rejoicings and congratulations at the overthrow of the Rebellion and the return of peace. A large crowd of prominent persons had assembled at Fort Sumter to witness the raising of the tattered flag over the historic site from which it had been lowered at the time of the first bombardment of the fort. In the midst of these rejoicings a terrible calamity befell the Nation, which cast a gloom over the triumphant scenes of a closing contest.

President Lincoln, while seeking relaxation from the many weighty cares which he had borne, attended Ford's Theater, in Washington. Here he was stealthily approached from the rear, and, without word or warning, an assassin placed his pistol behind the left ear of the President as he was intent upon the play, and fired a mortal shot. President Lincoln had held a cabinet meeting during the day, and listened to an account of the surrender of Lee as it was given by Gen. Grant, who had just arrived from Appomattox, and by his own son, Capt. Robt. Lincoln, who was on Grant's staff and an eye-witness to the surrender. President Lincoln had invited Gen. Grant and wife to accompany himself and wife to the theater, but Gen. Grant took his departure from the city during the day to visit his children, who were attending school at Burlington, New Jersey. The assassination occurred on the evening of Good Friday, April 14. The play was " Our American Cousin."

The name of the assassin was John Wilkes Booth, an actor, of Baltimore birth. Being intercepted by Major Rathbone, the only other man in the box besides the President, the assassin inflicted a serious wound in his arm with a dagger. Rushing to the front of the box, Booth exclaimed, " Sic semper tyrannis ! " (So be it always to tyrants.) He placed his hand on the railing in the front of the box, and leaped over it on to the corner of the stage; but as he jumped, the spur on one of his heels caught in an American flag draped across the front of the railing, and he fell, spraining his ankle, which greatly impeded his flight, and afforded a clue to his pursuers. He was finally hunted down by soldiers and shot in a barn in Virginia.

The dying President was carried to a house across the street, where he expired the next morning, and Vice-President Andrew Johnson became chief executive. Ford's Theater, in which the shocking event occurred, has been remodeled in the interior, and is now (1899) used by the Government for claim offices of the

Pension Department. The house in which Lincoln died has recently been purchased by the National Government, and both buildings are numbered among the places of interest which attract the attention of tourists in Washington.

The funeral train passed over the same route which Lincoln had taken from his home in Springfield, Illinois, to Washington, four years before. To the sorrowful crowds that gathered at every station, and even along the track in the country, it seemed as if the light of the Nation had gone out. He was buried amid the mourning of the whole Nation, at Oak Ridge, near Springfield, May 4th, where an imposing monument was dedicated to his memory in 1874.

His gentlemanly manner, magnanimity of spirit and purity of private life, are an inspiration to the youth of the land. His powerful grasp of details, his unerring logic, his perception of human nature, and his comprehension of weighty problems made him a specially fitted agent of Providence to reign as supreme executive during the tumultuous scenes of the Civil War.

MUSTERING OUT.—The armies of Sherman and Meade, returning from the field, were brought to Washington for a " Grand Review " by the President and his cabinet. The review commenced on the 23d of May, and lasted two days. The procession passed a grand stand in front of the White House. It was an impressive sight, and a fitting close to the turbulent scenes of the four years of bloody conflict. The city was elaborately decorated. The streets were crowded with throngs of visitors, who had come to witness the scenes of the occasion. The Stars and Stripes were waving from every house and store.

The men in the march were well-drilled, well-disciplined and orderly soldiers, inured to hardships, and fit for any duty. They were well dressed and well fed for army life, but their bronzed faces and tattered and smoky battle-flags told the story of their past experience.

Thoughts of the abolition of slavery, the suppression of the Rebellion, the preservation of the Union, the "welcome home" of friends and relatives, and the return to peaceful pursuits of life, all mingled with the shouts and rejoicing of the spectators to fill the hearts of the soldiers with ecstatic joy. Grant was there, the commander who had never taken a step backward; Farragut, the hero of New Orleans, was there; the aggressive and unfailing Sherman, the patient and adamantine Thomas, the intrepid and genial Hancock, the fiery Sheridan, the brave and impulsive Meade, the brilliant Custer, and hosts of others of lesser rank but of equal merit, were there.

Yet amid all of the festivities and rejoicings there was much sorrow. Three hundred and forty thousand of those who had taken up arms had long since laid them down to join the muster-roll of the Eternal One. Nearly every participant had left some one forever silent on the field of battle. Many well-known faces were missing. John F. Reynolds, Pennsylvania's valiant and patriotic son, who fell in the battle of Gettysburg; the gallant, dashing and inimitable Philip H. Kearny, who lost his life while penetrating the Confederate lines at Chantilly; the courageous and sagacious James B. McPherson, who was killed as Hood was driven from Atlanta; the zealous and venerable James S. Wadsworth, who gave his life to stem an adverse tide in the battle of the Wilderness; the simple, inflexible and intrepid John Sedgwick, who fell a victim to Confederate sharpshooters while he was directing the placing of artillery in front of Spottsylvania Court House;—these, and many other officers of high rank who were left silent on the field of battle, were not permitted to witness the exultant close of the war, or participate in the final grand review.

Words fail to express the homage due the patriotic leaders who gave their services, and some their lives, for the preservation of the Union of the States. No tribute of respect in honor of these men can be too highly colored. They deserve the affection of the people and the admiration of posterity for all generations. Their names should be reverently held in memory, and their deeds should be cherished as a rich legacy to a great nation. No monuments too costly or too grand can be erected in commemoration of their services to their country. Their works will shine forth with lustre after shafts of marble and granite shall crumble to dust.

As we pay our highest respects to the distinguished and gallant men who directed the affairs of the Nation and conducted the stupendous campaigns of the great Civil War, we must not forget the man who stood behind the gun, and the services he rendered. He it is that forever deserves the gratitude of the Nation he helped to save. He had to endure the severest hardships and face the greatest dangers. He had to bear the heat and burden of the day, endure long, fatiguing marches, and to be exposed to the inclemency of an uncertain and ever-varying climate. His first duty was obedience. His place was to the front, while the general's was to the rear. He had to do, and to dare. He had to face perilous emergencies and impending dangers. The private soldier looked into the cannon's mouth and faced musket and bayonet, while his general heard them only as they sounded their reverberations from the distance as the tide of battle swayed back and forth. The private soldier stood amid the desolating scenes of rapacious carnage as his comrades were falling thick and fast around him, while his commander generally stood away from immediate danger to view and direct the contending forces arrayed in deadly conflict. The private soldier endured all without the expectation of reward or the hope of immortalizing a name. His spirit was suffused with patriotism as fervid as any that ever graced the pages of history, poetry, fiction, or song. His name is legion, and though no towering monument marks the place where he rests, his valor and devotion to country will consecrate the spot as hallowed ground.

All honor to the gallant and patriotic heroes, both privates and officers! Green be the graves where they sleep. Calm be the resting-place of the brave and true. Forgotten be the animosities and heartaches of the long and bitter strife. Unsullied be the banner they fought to protect, and sacred be the trust committed to our hands.

INDEX.

—18   (273)